Dedication

To Mardell and Clyde Wilson with love
and to the one in whom there was no guile.

Other Books by Ted Andrews

Simplified Magick

Imagick

The Sacred Power in Your Name

How to See and Read the Aura

How to Uncover Your Past Lives

Dream Alchemy: Shaping Our Dream to Transform Our Lives

The Magical Name

Sacred Sounds: Transformation Through Music and Word

How to Meet and Work with Spirit Guides

How to Heal with Color

Magical Dance

Enchantment of the Faerie Realm

Forthcoming Books by Ted Andrews

The Healer's Manual

Animal Speak

TABLE OF CONTENTS

Introduction

THE HIDDEN SIDE OF CHRISTIANITY

Occultism is the search for the hidden. It is the search for the concealed deity within humanity, within the planet, within the solar system and within the cosmos itself. It is the seeking out of causes, meanings, and significances of all aspects of life. It is not limited to any particular field of study or endeavor.

"Occult" is a six-lettered word derived from the Greek, meaning "hidden." It refers in metaphysics to the hidden knowledge of the truths of God and life. It is hidden knowledge—knowledge that is obscured to most people for some time.

There are those who would argue that it is "obscure" because God did not want humanity to discover it. If that were so, electricity, mathematics, and even the alphabet would be considered "sinful," as they were once obscure and hidden. Electricity is understood entirely by very few, but even those few would never deny its existence or its usefulness. We need to approach the metaphysical and mystical study of our selves and our lives in the same manner.

Many people fear exploring or opening to what is different or does not conform. Even more refuse to consider the possibility of hidden teachings within their own belief systems—teachings other than what is normally accepted. It is unfortunate that the term has acquired such a negative connotation, for what is truly occult is obscured only because humanity refuses to exercise the discipline and dedication necessary to seek it out. Things are only "occult" until someone applies them for the benefit of humanity—until they become familiar.

This is especially true when it comes to the hidden teachings of one's belief system—to one's personal religion. All religions, all mystery systems, all metaphysical philosophies, are nothing more nor less than systems of props which serve to steady and support the mind and consciousness of the individual until it has prepared itself for higher evolution—for stepping out and exploring the more intense and hidden aspects of divine life.

In all persons, the qualities essential for accelerating growth and spiritual evolution are innate, and yet even if recognized, most people need a system of releasing them. This system should be one that allows increasing comprehension. It should be a system that adapts itself to the individual and one that enables the awakening and experiencing of divine forces without overwhelming the individual in the process. This was the task of the ancient mystery schools and this was to be the task of Christianity. As we will see, Christianity was meant to be a modern mystery school.

"In all ages and among all races there existed a tradition concerning certain esoteric schools or fraternities, wherein a secret wisdom unknown to the general public might be learned and to which admission was obtained by means of an initiation in which tests and rituals played their part. Today, in the centers of the civilized world, this belief is still alive, and although it may be ridiculed by the orthodox-minded, an unprejudiced observer cannot fail to note that some of the noblest men have been among its advocates, and that the greatest creative intelligences have, almost without exception, borne witness to a source of inspiration in the unseen . . ."[1]

True Christianity has an occult origin with which few are familiar. Occult Christianity refers to the hidden wisdom and knowledge—the hidden spiritual knowledge—of the Christ, the

---

[1] Fortune, Dion. *The Esoteric Orders and Their Work.* (Northamptonshire, Aquarian Press, 1982), p. ix.

highest and greatest of the Solar Archangelic beings. It is the knowledge referred to in Biblical scripture: "And the disciples came up and said to him, 'Why dost thou speak to them in parables?' And he answered, 'To you it is given to know the mysteries of Heaven, but to them it is not.'" (Matthew 13:10–13).

The ancient teachings in all societies were couched in allegory and symbology so that each individual could receive from it that which he or she was capable of understanding. Each individual had the opportunity and the responsibility to uncover the significance of the teaching as it related individually to him or her—and build upon it from that point forward.

These teaching ciphers were employed in most of the ancient mystery systems. It is why most of the masters and initiates were schooled in myths and tales, and the power of words. They learned to construct and use tales that veiled the deeper mysteries, preventing them from being profaned and at the same time revealing them to those who were qualified to understand them. Parables and allegories were common teaching devices. They concealed deep truths of ancient universal mysticism, often in the guise of presenting moral truths in an understandable manner. The most subtle of the parable ciphers contained seven possible interpretations, with the seventh or highest being the most complete. The other six only revealed part of the hidden mystery.

Much of the information concerning cipher teaching comes down to us through the ancient bardic traditions, common to most major societies. The Greek initiates learned a great body of work, and they had to learn to play them upon musical instruments. The Irish poets and bards studied their work for fifteen years (along with other occult sciences such as philosophy, astronomy, magic . . .) and they had to be conversant with 250 prime tales and parables and up to one hundred subsidiary ones. The Irish Shanachies concealed their mysteries through historical tales. The Navajo singers recited creation stories that would take two to three days to complete.[2]

Every major ceremony had its corresponding tale which simultaneously veiled and revealed the mysteries of the people. Whether they were the Irish Ollahms and Shanachies, the African Griots, the Norse Skalds, the German Meistersingers, the French Troubadours,

---

[2] Yolen, Jane. *Favorite Folktales from Around the World.* (New York, Pantheon Books, 1986), pp. 11–12.

the Anglo-Saxon Gleemen, the Norman Minstrels, or any other initiates of the mysteries, the use of tale, myth, and allegory as a means of teaching and touching each individual in the degree most beneficial to that individual was a commonality of all the ancient mystery systems. Christianity was no exception, as evidenced by the parables that have come down to us within its scriptures.

Modern Christianity is inconsistent in many ways with its original teachings. Much of this inconsistency is due to the numerous interpretations and reformations it has encountered in the past 20 centuries. We must begin to recognize that every popular tradition has elements of truth, but that truth is usually distorted. The generalities may be accurate, but the details may be in error. We must also remember that we each must individually respond to the the teachings. When these teachings are in story form, we must not only look at the historical aspects, but we must remember that every myth, story, and parable has its own meaning and integrity to which only the individual human soul is capable of responding.

Occult Christianity is the effort to restore the mystical coherence and cosmology of our lives and the universe. It provides the opportunity for experiencing an internal mysticism, power, and responsibility that connects us to all times and all space. Modern Christian theology has become too rationalistic and insensitive to touch the human soul. We are approaching a time where it is necessary to bring the occult teachings of Christianity into the daylight of new understanding and wisdom—into a new experience of Christian Gnosticism.

What follows is not an attempt to examine all aspects of the occult teachings of Christianity. Nor is it an attempt to interpret Christianity from strictly a historical or orthodox religious perspective. That could not be done within the scope of any single work. Neither is it an attempt to confuse and shatter the faith of the orthodox Christian communities. Rather, it is an attempt to show the scope of Christian occultism as it affects each person upon the planet. It is an attempt to restore coherence between the individual experience of spirituality and the divine life of the universe. It is an attempt to demonstrate how the individual can use the times at the changes of the seasons, periods when the veils between the physical and the spiritual are thinnest, to begin a process of individual initiation that will restore the true gnosis or knowledge of the import of the Christ Mysteries within all lives on this planet.

Theologians may scoff. Strict traditionalists may take offense, but true gnosis is a special quality of knowing—a knowing that has at its core personal transformation through personal experience. Christian Gnosis is the quality of knowing that which is hidden within its teachings. It is a knowing that is not found through the traditions of science or religion. It demands and requires an original experience—a "source experience," as defined by Carl Jung. It requires an awakening to the world of shadows and an awakening of the transcendent energies of the heart. It requires the individual to learn to walk the road of shadows where secret knowledge of the soul dwells.

This is the quest of Occult Christian Gnosticism. It may mean going contrary to the world and to the world's notions of reasonableness. It means discovering that the improbable is not beyond one's reach. It means opening to the divine wisdom and then experiencing it directly, without becoming lost within it.

Occult Christianity places the responsibility for humanity's spiritual growth back where it belongs. Not in the hands of the priest, the minister, or the preacher—but in the hands of the *individual*. Therein lies the excitement, and the joy, and the adventure of human living. The power and pleasure of evolving demands new knowledge, new perceptions, new honesty, and new sacrifice that will test our maturity. "The training given in Occult schools is designed to produce the adept, a human being, who, by intensified training, has raised himself or herself beyond the average development of humanity and is dedicated to the service of God."[3]

Occultism places religion upon the basis of experience—not upon blind faith or vicarious atonement. It is the search for truth and enlightenment, and these are reflected in many things. They can be found in many places. Truth is always truth, whether reflected in the tarot or found within the Bible. The discovery of truth can be inspired by the Koran or revealed within the Upanishads. Occultism removes the cataracts of superstition that blind humanity. It returns to us the opportunity to grow. It returns to us the Christianity that we deserve. There is nothing wrong with being an Occult Christian. It is in fact more than Christian. It is the Human-Christ evolving!

---

[3] Fortune, p. xii.

"Is a lamp acquired to be put under a bushel basket or hidden under a bed? Is it not meant to be put on a stand? Things are hidden only to be revealed at a later time; they are covered so as to be brought out into the open. Let him who has ears to hear me, hear!"

(Mark 4: 21–23)

PART ONE

THE OCCULT CHRIST

"Yonder is the Sun and Truth is His fire!"

Vedic Hymn

"Real esoteric Christianity has not yet been taught pub-
licly, nor will it so be taught until humanity has passed
the present materialistic stage and becomes fitted to
receive it."

Max Heindel
The Rosicrucian Cosmo-Conception

"The Light was in the world and the world was made by
it and the world knew it not."

John 1:10

Chapter One

THE GREAT WORK

"Before Abraham was, I Am."

John 8:58

"One can always search more and more deeply into the mystery of Palestine, for behind it lies . . . infinity!"

Rudolph Steiner

If metaphysics and occultism teaches humanity anything, it should be that everything is connected and related. It should teach us that there are processes in motion beyond what is ostensibly visible—processes which unite and link all life through time and space. Nothing is insignificant within our lives. Everything has import, and though the connecting threads may not always be apparent, they can be discovered by those willing to put forth the discipline and dedication.

Our connections to the life energies of others extends much further than our immediate biological family, and even though society separates according to race, sex, creed, politics, and so on, students of the occult work to break down these walls of separateness. They work to see that all are connected and that all actions affect everything upon the planet and all life within the universe.

1

These effects may seem minimal or even non-existent to many, but it is the task of the "New Age" disciple to extend the perceptions to the significance of everything and everyone at all times. This is what leads to true spiritual responsibility.

As we become aware of the correspondences and the connections of all aspects of our life—past and present, physical and spiritual—we can learn to use our many energies and potentials more consciously to re-create our lives. We learn to become a *cause*—a cause of beauty, goodness, and truth. We learn to align our energies with the laws and purposes of the divine. We adhere to the infinite.

All of the lessons, the teachings, and mysteries of life unfold within the natural course of our own existence. We do not achieve higher consciousness and spirituality through artificially contrived situations, but through the applications of our realizations within the day-to-day life circumstances that we encounter. Learning to look upon life from a universal rather than a personal perspective is what helps unfold the sleeping potential that lies within each of us. As students of the Mysteries, it is our task to recognize these relationships and then to begin the process of creating new ones—ones that are more in line with the divine.

The primary role of this text is to begin that process of revealing the cosmic processes in which we are all participating. Regardless of personal beliefs or religious persuasion, there is a common cosmic process operative within our lives, whether we are aware of it or not. This is most important to understand. There are laws of nature and of spirit, and they operate at all times within our lives. It was the teaching of these laws that formed the skeletal framework of the ancient mystery schools and most major religions. It was expressed best through an axiom which has come down to us through the Delphic Oracles: *Vocatus atque non vocatus Deus aderit* ("Calling or no calling God will be present").

Christianity was to be a modern mystery system. Part of its purpose was to take those hidden mysteries that were being held exclusively within select groups and to present them to all of humanity. "Bringing the gospel of the kingdom of Heaven" is the presenting of the mysteries within the reach of all of humanity. Unfortunately, many of those mystery teachings of early Christianity have been censored, edited, and deleted, but they are not lost. They can still be uncovered by anyone willing to put forth the appropriate effort and dedication.

The process of uncovering the hidden mysteries of Christianity begins with looking upon the events of that time from a universal rather than a historical perspective. Yes, it was a historical event, but it was only one facet of a magnificent cosmic process initiated ages prior. It is this cosmic process that we will explore throughout the rest of this chapter and which will be elaborated upon throughout the rest of the book. We will begin to see the correspondences—the occult significance—of events that have been influencing most of us upon the planet without our realization. To paraphrase the Delphic Oracle mentioned above: "Whether we are aware of it or not, this divine process is in operation."

Many today are disillusioned with modern Christianity. It does not fulfill the spiritual needs of the individual. It still holds to an idea of "acceptance on blind faith" of that which cannot be understood or won't be explained by its leaders. The Church-Head has become the focus rather than the spiritual essence behind it. The church has established itself as the life of the people, where the people are truly the life of any church. It was St. Augustine who pronounced that faith in the established church should take the place of everything else, and so the process of individual initiation into the esoteric mysteries of Christianity was suppressed. Thus, the modern Christian Church fails in many ways to link and reunite us personally with the divine and cosmic aspects of the universe. It limits our perspectives and our ability to experience the divine directly. Although it may initially appear contrary to traditional Christianity, the purpose of this work is to enhance the understanding and reverence of the more orthodox and historical Christian theology.

We will approach Christianity from the perspective of a mystery school, designed to assist the individual in the process of unfolding his or her highest potential and for the teaching of the Christ Mysteries. As such it will fulfill a variety of functions:

1. It will show how the Christ mysteries were designed to initiate a change of orientation and life impulse in all of humanity and how it is attached to the entire planetary evolution of our past, present, and future.

2. It will explore the processes set in motion to take the mysteries of the spiritual and natural laws out of the

hands of the privileged and select, and make them accessible to all.

3. It will show how the historical aspects of the Christ ministry were a dynamic analogy of the ancient mysteries, acted out on the stage of life, so that, as long as an individual was aware of the major events, he or she had a key to opening the mysteries. Historically, it is an enactment through the life of Jesus of what had only been enacted previously in the Mystery School Initiation Rituals.

4. It will show how the Christ Mysteries were to restore the balance of the masculine and feminine energies upon the planet, within the individual and within society.

5. It will reveal the hidden significances of the major events and people in the historical life of the master we call Jesus.

6. It will show the continuing cycle of the Christ energies as they play upon and affect all of humanity and life upon this planet in accordance with the changes of the seasons.

7. It will present seasonal rituals that can be used to access and manifest the Christ energies more powerfully and effectively, so as to open to higher states of consciousness.

8. It will reveal the Cosmic Christ as the Solar Archangel and the angelic hierarchy working with and through the Christ to assist all of humanity in the evolution process, along with dynamic ways of invoking and amplifying their assistance throughout the year.

9. It will reveal the preparations for the incarnation of the Christ through the one we know of as Jesus, and its import and effect upon all those who are to be part of the "Aquarian Age."

10. It will reveal many of the secret doctrines of true Christianity, as still found within modern scriptural texts, and their alignment with the ancient mystery teachings. It will reveal how the understanding of the occult significance of these doctrines are key to the achievement of the "Great Work" in the life of the individual.

THE GREAT WORK IN THE PAST
AND IN THE NEW AGE

The "Great Work" is often defined as the process of becoming more than human. It involves a concentrated and consciously directed effort to overcome imbalances, weaknesses, and limitations, while unfolding the inner potentials and opening to higher consciousness. It is the turning to one's personal growth and development, purification, and consecration. It involves the acquiring of self-knowledge, self-mastery, and self-realization.

In all of the ancient traditions, there are references to the procedures involved in this process. Within all of them there are threads of commonality. They all required the study of humanity in all aspects. They all involved the conscious effort toward improvement. They involved the development of a realization of humanity's ultimate perfection. They all involved a spiritual discipline aimed at altering, transforming, and expanding human consciousness. They involved a philosophy of life by which one could live according to that higher state of consciousness while within the physical world.

This great work was often divided into three categories. These are most often referred to as the lesser, greater, and supreme mysteries of the tradition. Much of the teaching of these mysteries was accomplished through allegory and parable, so that the individual could work with it at his or her own level and thus learn to extract continually deeper significance from such.

The lesser usually had to do with those lessons associated with ethics, behavior, and involved other people and our relationships with them. They involved the unfoldment and development of the personality. It is often called the level of the seeker, one who is searching for something more than what is found within the physical. It involves the test of good character, and the teachings necessary to maintain a sound mind and body, along with a control of instincts and passions.

The greater mysteries usually involve the development of our individuality, our own creatively distinct energies. It involves moving from the psychic sight to spiritual insight. The focus begins to move from the outer to the inner. It usually involves probationary periods in which the dedication to higher principles are tested. There occur encounters with higher teachings and greater development of dedication. This is a dedication that does not involve neglect of the physical, for it is only by our work in the physical that we learn to apply our teachings. It is the understanding that the responsibilities and duties in the physical have precedence over one's "personal work in the mysteries." We must first fulfill our responsibilities and obligations to the self and to others. This is what demonstrates our dedication to the higher.

This kind of dedication is referred to often within Christian scripture. "Render unto Caesar the things that are Caesar's, and unto God the things that are God's" is one of the strongest (Mark 12:17). Many references exist as to how best to achieve the "kingdom of heaven." Most have an outer, more obvious significance, but they also have underlying significance as well. No scriptural phrase epitomizes the esoteric significance of dedication as that of "no greater love hath man than he that gives his life for another." This does not refer to giving up and dying for another, but that rather it is sometimes necessary to give up focus upon one's self and one's own development so that another may get ahead or be helped. Often parents give up on things they may wish to do, so that their children can have an advantage in life. Many individuals want to be more actively involved within the metaphysical and spiritual fields, but they cannot do it because of obligations and duties to family, and so on. It is the greatest expression of love! It is often the test of dedication found within the greater mysteries as they reveal themselves within the individual's life circumstances.

The supreme mysteries are the teachings around the spiritual essence of life and its true effects within the physical. They involve understanding how everything is connected and works. They involve learning to set things in motion for the benefit of all and not just for the immediate. It is the aligning of one's own energies with the more Universal rhythms and energies of life.

All of these are found within the Christian mysteries for those who learn how to seek them out. They are still accessible to all who are willing to work for them. These are the mysteries as taught in ages past and are simply reexpressed and revealed to all through that avenue which we now call Christianity.

Part of the responsibility of the modern spiritual student is to understand the mysteries and teachings as they were presented in the past and learn to reexpress them in accordance with one's highest creativity in the present. This kind of responsibility requires that the ancient teachings and the modern be reexamined from a more universal perspective.

This is a powerful time in which to be living. It is powerful for individuals and for the planet. Astrologically we are moving into a "new age," what is called the "Aquarian Age." We can determine astronomically the shifts of planets and solar systems within the universe and their relationships to each other. When it comes to the spiritual validities of what is attributed to this oncoming "new age," we must initiate an exploration of the evolvement of spiritual and mystical teachings throughout the ages of humanity. It will require a new focus and perspective in the consciousness of humanity. The new age is not a new time or place but a new state of consciousness. This is the purpose of all mystery teachings throughout the ages.

Any new age, new consciousness, new perspective creates a time of greater energies and opportunities for change. It opens many new doors and closes those no longer beneficial. It creates lessons in change and the process of life and death. It opens opportunities for individual development and advancement. It requires greater ability to discriminate on all levels. It demands a reeducation and individual exploration of all that has gone before. It demands we turn to the sacred traditions of the past as embodied by the world's greatest religions and to the valid mystery schools of all esoteric traditions. It incorporates the best of modern science and synthesizes what can be learned from it with the ancient mysteries in a creative manner.

In this new consciousness that is unfolding, the hidden aspect of true Christianity is unveiling itself. Demonstrations of the spiritual side of the lessons which the Master Jesus gave will now be comprehended in their true form by greater and greater numbers. The spiritual energies and lessons of the Christ—as demonstrated and given to humanity through the vehicle of the one known as Jesus—will be available to the many who over the past twenty centuries have opened to higher consciousness themselves through the wider revelation of the ancient mysteries.

As the hidden side of Christianity unveils itself, there will occur greater opportunities for all to take higher initiations. There will occur a blending of the old with the new, and a linking with the supersensible realms in a fully conscious manner. There will be an increase of the blending of mysticism, physics, biology, engineering, and art. There will occur a dissolution of the negative glamour around the esoteric traditions, and there will unfold a higher manifestation of the ritual and ceremonial aspects of all religions. Each will have the opportunity to develop the Christed consciousness.

We are coming to the end of an age. At the end of any age there is difficulty and trial. Usually the predominant religion of the previous age reaches its final point of crystallization. Its true spirit is often lost. The form of the religion becomes supreme. Those aligned with the religion can feel the inadequacy of the old and yet they are often not ready to accept the new. With Occult Christianity, this can change. The old need not be discarded. New life can be breathed once again into it, but it will demand that the mysticism and spirit that has been lost be found. It demands that what is hidden be revealed. In this manner we keep the threads of the past intact with those of the present, so that a new tapestry of spirituality can be woven for the future.

COSMIC PREPARATIONS FOR THE BIRTH OF CHRISTIANITY

All life within the universe is hierarchical. The evolution of life has been described and defined in many ways by many societies. The hierarchies beyond humanity have been assigned many names—some more specific than others. In the Judeo-Christian traditions, the hierarchy of angelic life operates around and assists the growth of humanity in many functions. The Bible is one of the great books of angelology existing in the world, describing over and over the interplay of these beings within the life of humanity. Even the angelic kingdom has its hierarchy and divisions that have come down to us through the esoteric lore. The mythologies of almost all ancient societies speak of such beings.

From Genesis to Revelation, angels fill Biblical scripture. Although the sect of the Sadducees did not believe in them (Acts 23:8), Jesus makes reference to them throughout the scriptures, i.e. Matthew 26:53, Luke 15:10, John 1:51, etc. He spoke of them as real beings, and strongly hinted at their association with him. "Thinkest thou that I cannot pray to my Father, and he shall presently give me more than twelve legions of angels?" (Matthew 26:53).

In Old Testament scripture, they were referred to as the Sons of God (Genesis 6:2, Job 1:6, Job 2:1, Job 38:7, Psalms 29:1, etc.). A study of Biblical teachings on angelology reveals different grades and ranks, a hierarchy of evolution even within its kingdom. Angels have come to be associated with every aspect of the universe and all life within it. Every planet and star is a reflection of the light of an angelic being.

The greatest of the archangels was one known as Metatron. He has been called the Angel of Countenance, the Angel of the Covenant and many other titles, including Messiah. In Qabalistic lore, it was Metatron who gave to humanity the Qabala and the Tree of Life teachings, so that we could ascend beyond our normal state of life, to teach us that all we need is available to us if we know how to manifest it properly.

"In Talmud and Targum, Metatron is the link between the human and the divine."[4] Metatron has been associated with the liberating angel, the Shekinah or Love-Wisdom aspect of the Divine, which we will explore later in this text—both of which help to align him with the New Testament titles of Christ and Messiah. According to legends and scriptures, Metatron has been associated with Isaiah's suffering servant who would become the Messiah of Christian theology.[5]

Angel
Detail from engraving
by Albrecht Dürer.

The term Messiah was often equated with Metatron of the Old Testament and the Christ of the New. Paul has Messiah in mind when he refers to the angel above the various principalities. (Colos-

---

[4] Davidson, Gustaf. *A Dictionary of Angels* (New York: The Free Press, New York, 1967), p. 192.
[5] Ibid., p. 193.

sians 1:16, Ephesians 1:21). To the Jewish mystics of the time, the phrase "Son of Man," as well as "Son of God," had an angelic/messianic significance, with possible ties specifically to Metatron. This is further supported by Old Testament texts, i.e., Daniel 8:13–14. For the masses it simply referred to being just a man.

The Talmud and Midrash speak of Metatron and the link to the Divine Love-Wisdom (Shekinah). They refer to Metatron as the Messiah and as "One with God." When the authors of the scriptures write of the revelation of who and what Christ Jesus is, a world of possibilities opens. It lends great new significance to such scriptural phrases as "I and my Father are one," and "Before Abraham was, I am."

These connections are subtle, but the scriptures are often sketchy in many references to angelic identification. These, along with the association of the Shekinah with Metatron help to point toward the Christ as an archangelic being.

The Sons of God can also be likened to the Sun Gods—beings of great light and nurturance. They are one and the same. Keeping this in mind then, the highest and greatest of the archangelic beings in this solar system would be the Solar Archangel associated with humans, and thus our own sun. This being we know as Metatron in more ancient times, or as the Christ in modern times.

This great being has been defined in many ways, and embodies specific qualities. Predominant among these is the Love-Wisdom aspect. The great wisdom and love often referred to or held as a goal in the spiritual development of societies is the identification of, and alignment with, the one known as the Cosmic Christ. It is pure Wisdom embodied in the being and symbolized by the essence of the Christ. In the appendix of this book is a list of sources—Biblical and mystical—in which are found many of the references to the Love-Wisdom Essence of the universe. It is the Love-Wisdom essence which we seek for our own illumination and at-onement.

The mystics who strived to attain such spiritual alignment with this force called it by many names. To the Hebrew seers, it was known as Skekinah. To the Christian Gnostics, it was Sophia. To the new age disciple, it is the Cosmic Christ. It is the essence of pure divine energy, expressed through love and wisdom within this universe. Since Metatron has often been charged with the sustenance of humanity, we can begin to see possible correlations.

The educator and overseer of this solar system and all life within it is the Cosmic Christ or Metatron. Much of the special evolution which the earth stimulates in humanity is learning to develop and express the qualities of love and wisdom more effectively. It is learning to deal with the dense conditions of energy—learning the creative possibilities of limitation while at the same time learning to transcend those limitations through the appropriate expression of love and wisdom.

Never before has humanity been in a position to receive the ancient wisdom teachings to the degree that they are becoming available. This availability is increasing as we move closer to the Aquarian Age. It is because of this general availability that special preparations had to be made so as to insure their receptivity upon the planet, while lessening the opportunity for their abuse. Because of the kind of energy that will influence the earth as we move into this new cycle, special preparation had to be made on a more cosmic level to insure that these energies would be expressed within an environment of love, wisdom, and dedication to the good of the whole.

One legend teaches that this process was inaugurated by Metatron—the Cosmic Christ at the time of the end of Atlantis. This high civilization that evolved over 850,000 years ago was a society in which great knowledge of the energies of the universe was available. That knowledge and the energies associated with them were abused, resulting in a number of great cataclysms upon the earth, the last of which occurred "in the year 9564 B.C., according to information given to Solon by the Egyptian Priests."[2] There were groups that survived it, and they carried the ancient teachings and wisdom to safety in various parts of the world.

Many of the ancient legends about an earthly paradise stem from early periods within the life of the Atlantean civilization. Many of the legends of the sinking and decimation of the world also stem from this Atlantean cycle in the evolution of humanity. In Biblical scripture this is reflected through the tale of Adam and Eve in the Garden of Eden, and the flooding of the world at the time of Noah, respectively.

The original fall of man was the original alignment of our spiritual essence with the forces of materialization, so that we

---

[6] Schure, Edouard. *From Sphinx to Christ* (Harper and Row, San Francisco, 1982).

could enter into physical existence. Although a sacrifice, it provided and prepared a way for an expanded expression of spirit once we graduated from this dense realm. This added the element of gravity to our energy expression, weighing us down. There was great risk in this. If we became too deeply involved with these deeper energies, it might not be possible to rise and evolve properly. Humanity did become too involved with the energies and beings of materialization, and thus we were running the risk of becoming entrapped in the realm of matter.

This is reflected often throughout New Testament scriptures. Luke 12:15 reads, "And he said to them, `Take heed and guard yourselves from all covetousness, for a man's life does not consist in the abundance of his possessions.'" One of the most frequently quoted scriptures and least understood is found in Luke 9:23–25. When examined from the perspective of humanity becoming ensconced in matter, it takes on much greater depth. "If anyone wishes to come after me, let him deny himself, and take up his cross daily and follow me. For he who would save his life will lose it; but he who loses his life for my sake will save it. For what does it profit a man if he gain the whole world, but ruin or lose himself."

One theory of this entrapment centers around the Atlantean Epoch, although there is no actual evidence that such a period or civilization truly existed. In this theory, the entrapment was reflected by the imbalanced expression of knowledge and energy during the Atlantean epoch of humanity. This can be compared to a scuba-diving treasure hunt. Humanity opened to an awareness of treasures, and we followed a lifeline down to that treasure chest below. Unfortunately, the rope did not quite reach. In order to obtain that treasure, we would have to release our life line to the spirit and free dive down. We then became so involved in the treasures of the physical realm that we forgot where that life line was. We became so focused on gathering physical experiences, we forgot our true home—our true essence. We lost the direct consciousness of the more subtle realms surrounding and interpenetrating with our life. Humanity became rigid, separate and was filled with conflict and inertia. Humanity, as a whole, ceased to manifest the qualities of truth, love, and wisdom.

Theosophical and Anthroposiphical teachings have expanded upon this. Humanity is comprised of more than just a physical substance and energy. We have bands of more subtle energy that comprise our essence. Most metaphysical traditions refer to these as the Divine, Monadic, Atmic, Intuitional/Buddhic, Mental, Astral, and the Physical/Etheric. These "subtle bodies" of humanity surround and interpenetrate the physical, and can provide access to various levels of consciousness and planes of life. The last of these to evolve into a manifest part of the human energy system was the etheric body. The etheric body serves two primary functions: (1) it grounds the consciousness to the physical life, and (2) it serves to filter out the other energies and awareness of the other dimensions surrounding us and affecting us. From the Atlantean period to the time of the birth of modern Christianity, this band of energy was not as tightly linked to the physical body, and it was much easier to use the ancient techniques to extend the physical consciousness into the more ethereal realms.

By the time of modern Christianity, the etheric was so dynamically linked to the physical, that new energies and processes would have to be initiated in order to touch those more ethereal realms and levels of consciousness. Fortunately though, through the birth of Christianity, it could now be done in a fully conscious manner.

The traditional manner of initiation into the more ethereal essence of life was for the initiate to be placed in a sleep condition for approximately three and one-half days. The master would serve as facilitator and draw the consciousness out of the physical body, and open the spiritual realms to the individual. At the end of the prescribed time, the individual would be "called back into the body," with an illumined consciousness of the true spiritual dimensions. The individual would then have direct knowledge of the Love-Wisdom Essence (Metatron/the Cosmic Christ) of the spiritual worlds, and could "bear witness" to them. The last to undergo this traditional method is the one we know of as John the Beloved. John and Lazarus of Biblical scripture are one and the same. John is the initiate name of Lazarus. "This sickness is not unto death" (John 11:4) means that it is the ancient initiatory process of "induced sleep."

An examination of the Biblical references to John and Lazarus will clarify this link further for those wishing to elaborate. Since then the etheric energies of humanity have become too tightly wound with the physical life processes to safely permit this method of initiation. At the same time though, because of the implanting of the Cosmic Christ energies directly into the earth itself, such methods are no longer necessary. The individual life force has been given impulses that can enable a fully conscious union with the supersensible worlds surrounding us. This is what will be explained and revealed throughout the rest of this text.

Even if only perceived as a metaphor or a construct to explain what otherwise may be unexplainable or occult, it opens us to new possibilities. It helps us to begin to see relationships between events, between people, between all expressions of life. It helps us to see that everything in the universe affects everything else. Everything we do affects everyone and everything else, and everyone and everything else affects us on both mundane and spiritual levels. It counterbalances a theological approach to life that is fatalistic and often irresponsible. It places the responsibility for our life and our evolution and growth within our own hands.

Humanity always has some energies to serve as a counterbalance. The counterbalance to the process of involution and entrapment within the physical is the process of evolution and education. As mentioned, Metatron (i.e., the Cosmic Christ) is the educator for our solar system, and thus the physical earth and all life upon it is bathed in the educational energies of Love-Wisdom, designed to assist the individual in unfolding a divine consciousness, one that is tied to the rope of the Christ. It is designed to unfold the potential within all lives who are using the Earth as their schoolhouse.

Those that work to assist humanity—regardless of position within the hierarchy (including the Christ) are bound by set spiritual laws. They can only assist as much as we allow them, beyond their own expressions. This spiritual law allowed for the Christ to stand outside of the Earth environment and project energies onto it to stimulate all evolving life to rise. The seat of this projection is reflected by the sun.

The evolutionary process on Earth requires involving ourself with its forces. These earth forces, though, cannot be assimilated by our physical consciousness and turned into higher Wisdom. Only by reestablishing the life of the soul in connection with the Divine essence could our experiences be assimilated and give propulsion to our growth. The Cosmic Christ could not interfere directly nor deprive us of our free will to grow through learning.

Greater beings came to earth from time to time to assist us as teachers and to bring light, but they were often limited as they were not truly a part of humanity's evolutionary life stream. It was through their assistance that the ancient Mystery Schools were established, and that the ancient teachings survived the cataclysms of the Atlantean epoch. Many of the mythologies of the world reflect the assistance given humanity by greater beings.

The more highly evolved of humanity began to concentrate efforts toward a more direct linking with the Love-Wisdom essence of the universe. These are the Ancient Mystery Traditions as we know them today. Over the centuries as individuals grew in wisdom and light, the energies of certain streams of humanity grew stronger, and the opportunity to bridge the gulf between humanity and the Cosmic Christ grew. As each new individual grew into that awareness, the bridge between the Christ and all evolving life began to be formed. Since most of humanity still was unable to connect for themselves, a magnificent process was set in motion to enable the Christ to cross over and connect more directly with humanity.

It was the teaching of the ancient mystery systems which provided the impetus for the formation of this bridge. Their training opened greater and greater numbers of humanity to enlightened energies, each adding to this bridge to the Divine. This is not to say that all knew what the dynamics of the process were or what they were leading to, but it does show that there was a method to this process that extended to the evolutionary core and time of all life.

Through the master we now know of as Jesus, and with the aid of Metatron, in the form of the Christ, this bridge and linkup with the Divine was to be completed. Through the consciousness and vehicle of Jesus, who underwent extensive training in the mystery traditions, the aspects of Love, Wisdom, Devotion, and Idealism would become impregnated into the physical, etheric, and spiritual bodies, and the life of the Earth itself. As we will see, at the time of the "Baptism" of Jesus, the consciousness would vacate the physical body, enabling the Christ energies to take possession and work directly upon the Earth itself.

At the time of the crucifixion and the "giving up of the ghost upon the cross," the Christ essence would be placed within the cross of matter, touching the heart of the planet itself. The Christ, instead of being an outside regent that projects energies onto the earth, would now become the Planetary Logos, working and touching all of humanity for ages to come. The Christ energy filled the heart of the earth and touched the etheric realm surrounding it, infusing it with Love, Wisdom, and Devotion. Thus, the Christ energies would become an intrinsic part of the etheric make-up of all life from henceforth. With every incarnation, these Christ energies would stimulate the divine spark within the heart of all of us to an even greater degree.

The Christ entered the evolutionary life stream of humanity and would now be able to influence it more directly. The Archangelic Christ essence became a part of every living being upon the planet. This is further reflected through Paul's words in Galatians 2:20: "It is now no longer I who lives, but Christ who lives in me. And the life that I now live in the flesh, I live in the faith of the Son of God, who loved me and gave himself up for me."

It is this archangelic essence (Son of God) which plays upon each of us in a manner that can be enhanced, accessed, and amplified in a very powerful manner. The Christ energies now affect all life on the planet, stimulating a quickening in a cyclic manner that facilitates the self-initiatory process. It is this cyclic play of energies that will be discussed in Part Two of this work, along with rituals to assist in enhancing its effects.

Having been fully introduced and anchored within the Earth through the life and ministry of Jesus, the Christ set about to accomplish the development of a new etheric pattern of energy for humanity that would offset negative influences and allow a fully conscious communion with the spiritually divine realms of life. What had been held exclusively within certain groups would now become accessible to all who were willing to apply the effort and dedication. Now, more than ever, humanity was ready for a re-emergence and reexpression of the Ancient Mystery Teachings.

As we will see throughout the rest of this text, the coming of the Christ created a new impulse for humanity, one that would compensate for our loss of vision of the communion with the forces of Nature and the Divine. The mysteries would be restored to their former glory and regardless of the "censorships" of humanity, they would remain accessible to all.

What then was the historical impact of the Christ and the one we know as Jesus? Did Jesus truly become the Christ? And if so, how did this really occur within the course of events as we now know them? This is what we will explore, but evidence comes from many sources—external and internal, and thus the real truth can not fully be discerned without new perspectives, intuition, and some knowledge of the esoteric tradition as it operated at this time within the evolution of humanity. We must remember that the process involved so much more than what may appear on the surface.

"Gods do not think as men think. The thoughts of men are images; the thoughts of Gods are living beings!"

Rudolph Steiner

Chapter Two

THE HISTORICAL JESUS AND THE MYSTICAL CHRIST

"The true life of Jesus was the actual happening, historically of what before him had happened only in initiation. . . .
The life of Jesus is thus a public confirmation of the
mysteries."

Rudolph Steiner

The thread of the life story of Jesus is one that has been examined,
reexamined, outlined, and determined historically without great
difficulty. It has, for the most part, been the primary focus of the
Christian church over the past nineteen centuries. There are plenty
of documents that can prove there was a man named Jesus, who
lived at or around the time determined, and that he was a healer
and teacher who had a following.

Whether or not Jesus was to become the Christ or overshad-
owed by the Christ, and accomplished all that is said of him, must
still be determined, but there are ways of bridging the gulf of igno-
rance. This can occur through understanding the true historical
aspects of the time, and the man known as Jesus, in conjunction

with new perspectives on the documents which are held as the key to the true significance of this event (i.e., the Bible, especially New Testament texts), through the application of one's own intuition, and, finally, through knowledge of the esoteric traditions operating in the evolution of humanity and in the world at the time of the birth of Christianity.

In determining the historicity and veracity of anything, the documents must relate actual facts, be genuine, integral and trustworthy. A document is considered genuine if written by the author whose name it bears, and if written in the period of history contemporaneous with or immediately following the events it records. It is integral and complete if it comes down to us in substantially the same form in which it was first written, i.e., without alterations or insertions by later writers or copiers, in a manner that alters its historicity. A document is trustworthy when it records truthfully the information based on a certain knowledge. The author must be knowledgeable of the facts.

There is a critical principle that must also be considered in determining the historicity of anything. When a document is accepted as genuine, integral, and trustworthy by contemporaries or near contemporaries of the author, it should be accorded the same value by succeeding generations, unless evidence is brought forward to show why it should be rejected. In such case the burden of proof rests with those who contest the historical value.

The thing that must be kept in mind is that the historicity of a document may not be the same as the historicity of the events related in the document. The New Testament could be entirely fictional, for example, and this would not in any way affect its historicity as a document. The validity of the document must also come under scrutiny. This is even more important when the documents are not necessarily written by eyewitnesses, or recorded at the time of the events, as occurs with New Testament documents.

In determining the veracity of anything, we can use both internal and external evidences. Internal evidence of the veracity of documents upon which individuals place historical value involves an accurate depiction of the political, geographical, sociological, and cultural situations of the time. The language used, the style of expression or idiom, the choice of words must fit the period in which the document is written.

External evidence of the veracity is determined through other documents where it is stated implicitly that such and such is true or that so-and-so wrote the document in question. Many of the documents to support the historicity of the New Testament writings concerning this time are listed in the appendices of this book.

From fragments, and from citations in early writers, we learn that other accounts of this time—besides the four canonical gospels—began to be circulated among the early Christians. These have come to be known as the Apocryphal "Gospels." Some of the earliest writers rejected these as not having been written by "eye witnesses and the apostles." Others refer to them as a guide to the esoteric teachings and reflections of the one known as Jesus at this time.

There are predominantly eleven other "gospels," and they were also rejected by the established church as spurious. What we must understand also is that any hostile testimony toward original documents can be of particular value as a form of "external evidence" of historicity, and thus it is important that the individual begin to apply his or her own examination and intuition to these writings. These eleven Apocryphal Gospels are:

Name	Written	Rejected by
Gospel of the Hebrews	ca. 100	Eusebius
Another Gospel of Matthew	ca. 150	Eusebius/Origen
Gospel of the Egyptians	ca. 150	Origen
Gospel of the 12 Apostles	ca. 150	Origen/Epiphanius
Gospel of Phillip	ca. 150	Epiphanius
Gospel of Thomas	ca. 150	Origen/Eusebius and Gelasius
Gospel of Peter	ca. 190	Eusebius/Gelasius
Gospel of James	ca. 200	Origen/Gelasius
Another Gospel of Matthew	ca. 300	Gelasius
Gospel of Infancy of Christ	ca. 300	Gelasius
The Assumption of Mary	ca. 400	Gelasius

The four canonical gospels of the New Testament have become the primary basis of modern Christianity. It is very likely that these gospels were chosen because they were the more respectable derivations. They were less exotic and more representative of the entire Roman empire: the gospel of Mark being representative of the West, Matthew of the South, Luke of the North and John of the East.[7]

The book of Matthew was written approximately 90 A.D., the Book of Mark was written somewhere between 75 and 80 A.D., and the Book of Luke was written close to the end of the first century, according to the Greek Codices and other extant literature. The Book of John was composed sometime around the end of the first decade of the second century. If we are to assume that the death of Christ occurred around 33–36 A.D., then the final forms of the Gospels of Matthew, Mark, and Luke were not composed within 20 years of the death. This throws great doubt upon the accuracy and validity of them.

Dating Biblical events is difficult. Even within the gospels there are two different accounts of the birth. Matthew records the birth around 7–4 B.C., circa the reign of Herod and the Massacre of the Innocents. Luke, on the other hand, records Jesus being born around the time of the Roman census which would have been 6–7 A.D. It is very likely that the crucifixion occurred around the year 36 A.D., and Jesus would have been in his early forties. This fact, is supported by John 8:57, where the people say to Jesus, "You are not yet 50."

Unfortunately, for many millions, the New Testament is supposed to be the divinely inspired Word of God, as if it were dictated to the authors by God, Himself, in some sort of spirit communication. The truth is, "none of the manuscripts we have are the originals, or can be demonstrated to be exact copies of originals. . . . The authors themselves are frequently in disagreement with one another, in their ideas and convictions, and in the matters they record."[8] We must also understand that many of the documents are letters, written with no thought for public publication. Because of this, much of what we have today is to a great degree an idealized interpretation created by and for the various schools of Christianity.

There is a great degree of extant literature surrounding the historical aspects of the Christian Scriptures. "No other work of antiquity has been so well handed down, i.e., by so many and such old manuscripts, as the New Testament. Speaking only of Greek

---

7 Schonfield, Hugh J. *The Original New Testament* (Harper & Row, San Francisco, 1985), p. xvii.
8 Ibid., p. xx.

manuscripts, we distinguish papyri (from the oldest writing material), majuscule or uncial manuscripts (using only capital letters), minuscule or cursive manuscripts (using capital and small letters) and lectionaries (collections of passages for liturgical use). The number of manuscripts is increasing continually and now surpasses 4000:

Papyri (100–300 A.D.) – 50
Uncial (300–800 A.D.) – 208
Minuscules (800–1300 A.D.) – 2370
Lectionaries (300–1300 A.D.) – 1603
(*Encyclopedic Dictionary of the Bible*, 1438).

If we add to this the immense number of translations of Biblical scripture, we are left in a quandary of determining much of the accuracy of the texts. Much of the scripture has been deleted, books censored, and whole sections altered through the centuries—many by papal decree. Each translation has the capacity of being colored with words and phrases in accordance with the interpreter's point of view.

Beginning on page 26 is a chart of many of the translations that have come down to us in modern times. We must also consider, too, that in the past twenty years even more interpretations of the scriptures have occurred. How, then, do we determine the legitimacy of the scriptural writings, or, by focusing upon such, are we missing the forest for the trees? The answer lies in examining Christianity from the historical perspective as a Mystery School, one in which great foresight was applied.

Through Metatron, as the Christ, entering into the earth sphere directly to give new impulse to humanity, the process was initiated in a manner that would succeed in spite of "censorship of teachings," in spite of the "possibility of alterations and deletions," in spite of the possibility of conscious manipulation and alteration of the teachings. In order to take the mysteries out of the hands of the privileged and select, the entire life process of Jesus and the Christ would have to become an analogy of the mysteries. All preparations, all events, the ministry itself—every aspect in the life of Jesus Christ—parallels an experience of the initiatory process into the Archangelic Mysteries.

Thus what could not be discerned from the actual teachings could be by example. Through Paul comes the interpretation of the ministry and death of Jesus as events which sprang from God. This is reflected in such scriptures as I Corinthians 15:47. It is later supported by Peter in Acts 2:23 and Romans 3:25. Luke and Matthew's accounts of the birth reflect Divine intervention and higher significance than just a mundane event. The role of Jesus in light of the resurrection, rooted in the ancient myths of all the dying and rising gods and goddesses, thus has its greatest magic in revealing a process for higher initiation.

In spite of the subsequent censoring, the major events in the life of Jesus Christ have carried through. Knowing these major events is all that is necessary for anyone wishing to open to an initiatory experience. There was enacted, through the description of this life and its events, what had previously only been enacted in the Mystery School Initiation Rituals. The rituals in the second half of the book will show how to use those major events to open to such experiences today.

Where, though, does the occult aspect of Christianity fit into all of this? Unknown to the general Christian community, Christianity is as much occult in philosophy as it was orthodox. Jesus distinguished between the things that he could say openly to all and the things which he could only hint at, the things which the few could handle but the many could not. The Mysteries of the Kingdom of Heaven were to be opened to all, but they were to be done in a manner that would prevent them from being profaned and still be accessed without the more traditional Mystery School training.

After Jesus' death, there would develop a split in his followers. This resulted in two types of Christians: one of the occult or esoteric practice, and one of the more orthodox and moralistic kind. The first involved direct experience and knowledge of the spiritual and natural laws and their practice within life, and the second focused upon "vicarious atonement and good works." In the struggle between the two, the latter eventually won out, since much greater numbers were versed in it than the hidden aspects. This would ultimately lead to the abolishment of the occult mysteries of the Christ.

The gulf that ensued would widen, but the hidden aspects would never die out. The orthodox elements continued to employ literal interpretations to the teachings of the Christ, and the more esoteric references were lost to the few who were able to understand and pass them on to others. It is these that embody the true spirit and essence of Christianity. As we grow beyond the literal teachings, duty becomes desire, and the problems and confusion surrounding the literal will dissolve.

We will find the answers to our questions through an exploration of the hidden aspects of Christianity. The scriptures were not meant to be oracles, but rather a guide for the individual to discover his or her own answers based upon *experience*. "Occultism is more than a science to be pursued objectively; it provides also a philosophy of life derived from its experience, and it is this philosophical, or even religious, aspect, that attracts most of those who devote their lives to it . . . (the seeker) is no longer dependent upon (blind) faith. He has had personal experience and out of that experience, he tends to formulate a religious belief in which he himself aspires to share in the work usually assigned to saints and angels as the ministers and messengers of God."[9]

Reading between the lines. Looking beyond the physical. Seeing past the obvious. Searching behind the literal. This is where truth will be found. This is how truth becomes an active part of life. The literal is an easy way out. It is a way of avoiding emergence from the cocoon of our life.

Approaching Christianity from a literal or strictly historical perspective has disastrous results. The literal invites confusion. The historical has too many disconnected threads. There are too many discrepancies, too many impossibilities, to many contradictions to open one to true understanding.

Great difficulties can arise from a literal reading of the New Testament. Many claim an immaculate conception and virgin birth, while others declare it an impossibility. The genealogies of Jesus as given within the Gospels of St. Matthew and St. Luke are different, so how could they apply to the same person? After all, Matthew traces the lineage through Joseph, which becomes entirely meaningless in the case of a virgin birth. St. Luke traces it through Mary. If Jesus were God, how could Satan tempt him?

The events of the night before Jesus' crucifixion are too numerous and too mindboggling to have occurred within a single night, as a literal reading would imply. The Last Supper. The agony in the garden. The betrayal by Judas. The hailing and questioning before Caiphas. The hailing and questioning before the Sanhedrin. The hailing and questioning before Pilate. The questioning in the Hall of Judgment. The visit of Herod. The return to Pilate. Pilate's

[9] Fortune, Dion. *Sane Occultism* (Northamptonshire: The Aquarian Press, 1981), p. 11.

speeches and washing of hands. The scourging and mocking of Jesus. The long and painful carrying of the cross to Golgotha. There are too many events to have occurred within such a short time.

This is not to say they did not happen, but not within the time scheme presented. What is the answer then? The answer lies in the occult aspects. By examining the events from a universal perspective, and as a mystery school tradition and teaching, we can begin to place the events in a perspective that opens one to great devotion and illumination.

So much is unacceptable in its literal form that the idea receives support that the authors were spiritually instructed men, writing the events in a manner to encourage instruction—as in the tradition of the ancient mystery schools. They wrote to preserve and to conceal from the more base, and yet reveal to the worthy and the dedicated the Love-Wisdom which they had personally experienced.

The Bible is a mixture of truths, symbols, and allegories. Those that wrote it did so in the finest tradition of the Mystery Schools. They concealed the inner knowledge behind the literal, for they knew that such knowledge would awaken great spiritual, intellectual, physical, and psychical powers. The Christian Initiates were well aware that if such teachings were revealed openly, the powers invoked and awakened would be profaned and subject to grave misuse.

We must approach it from a historical outline, but we must learn to read the events from an intuitive and occult perspective. In this way, only, do the true mysteries unfold. "And the disciples came and said to him, 'Why speakest thou unto them in parables?' He answered, saying unto them, 'Because it is given to you to know the mysteries of the kingdom of heaven, but to them it is not.'" (Matthew 13:10–11).

OUTLINE OF THE ENGLISH BIBLE

Biblical scripture began with the Hebrew Old Testament and the Greek New Testament. Earliest translations were in the Greek and Aramaic languages.

Third to Second Century B.C. Septuagint Greek Old Testament
Fourth Century A.D. Jerome's Latin Vulgate Bible
700–1000 Anglo-Saxon Paraphrases of Latin Vulgate

1384 Wycliffe's Bible
1522–1534 Luther's German Bible
1526–1530 Tyndale's Translation of New Testament
1528 Pagninus' Latin Bible
1535 Coverdale's Bible
1537 Matthew's Bible
1539 The Great Bible
1556 Beza's Latin New Testament
1560 Geneva Bible
1568 Bishop's Bible
1582–1610 Rheims Douai Bible
1611 King James Bible
1749–1750 Challoner's Revision
1881–1885 English Revised Version
1901 American Standard Version
1946–1952 Revised Standard Version
1957 Complete Lamsan Aramaic Bible

Since 1957, there have been a multitude of translations from most major denominations across the country, with more each year.

AN OCCULT LOOK AT THE HISTORICAL PERSPECTIVES

The period from 200 B.C. to 200 A.D. was one of drama and tension. "There was an eager exchange of ideas, much questioning of positions both social and political, and in the background there was a brooding sense of climax as if the peak of human destiny would soon be reached. Was there to be extinction or was there something beyond? Inevitably, prophets, astrologers, soothsayers flourished and mystics of many kinds . . ."[10]

In the century and a half before Christianity, The Roman Empire of Augustus embraced many languages and cultures. It was a complicated world in which religious concerns, beliefs and practices were central to individual lives, families and communities.

Palestine was a land of many nations, languages, and interests. It was filled with mixed and hostile peoples whose interests were often so divided that harmony and peace were seemingly

---

[10] Schonfield, p. xxi.

impossible. There were in fact many groups of the Jewish faith, although not all were Hebrews. The Hebrews in Palestine were Hebrew since the origin of the time of the great exodus from Egypt and even before.

There was a difference between the Palestinian Jews and the Diaspora, those who had been scattered from around Babylonia. The genealogy of Jesus was to show that he fulfilled Jewish prophecies (in Isaiah) about the Messiah's descent. The Jews at the time were expecting a Messiah who would be a descendent of King David. This is reflected in the Gospel of Matthew 1:17, which says, "So all generations from Abraham to David were fourteen generations, and from David to Babylon fourteen generations, and the deportation to Babylon to the Christ fourteen generations." This suggests that the Messiah would come through a descendent of the Jews who had been affected by the Diaspora.

In the midst of them were the groups known as the heathens, whose customs and rituals were gaining prominence. The Jews living outside of Palestine were more tolerant of pagan practices than those who resided in the Holy Land. But even with those of the Holy Land, there were many sects within the parent body of Judaism, one of which would develop into Christianity.

To the northeast were the nomads, as well as the Syrians and Graecians. To the east and west of Palestine the Egyptians, Phoenician and Graecian rites were prominent. In the very heart of Palestine, the Greek language and influence was dominant. In upper Galilee were the Gentiles. Gentile was really a generic term referring to anyone who was not Jewish. They were greatly disliked by the Jews, often because the Gentiles would make fun of the Jew's speech and ridicule their language. The educated throughout Palestine spoke the Greek language, while the Hebrew language gave way to the Aramaic.

Palestine and Jerusalem were places of great extremities and diversities. There was great wealth and great poverty—existing side by side. Mystical and heathen cults lived together. As a result, Judaism was undergoing its own problems. "Religious currents at the time were diverse. . . . One can distinguish three broad categories of religious belief and observance. First, there was the traditional religion of the family and community gods . . . second, there were the so-called 'mystery cults' . . . which had their mythic roots in local fertility rites. . . . Finally there was the way of life which sought human fulfillment and blessedness through the pursuit and practice of philosophic wisdom. . . . Nature religions were diffused throughout the Mediterranean. Most popular were the cults of the Great Mother, i.e. Isis in Egypt, Mithras of Persia. They offered in rites of initiation an experience of the Divine which evoked deep emotions of awe, wonder and gratitude."[11] Most people of the area were touched by, or even involved in, all three, to some degree.

We often depict Jesus touring the countryside, preaching and healing, but a look at the scriptures reveals there had to be a strong realization of the conditions of the time, i.e., Matthew 26:5, Matthew 7:15–16, Luke 18:1–5. Disease and crime were rampant. There was great fear of evil and demons. Violence was common. Begging, superstition, and spys were everywhere.

". . . among the calamities of that black period, the most trying grievance was the degenerate spirit, with which the first men in the Senate submitted to the drudgery of becoming common informers; some without a blush in the face of the day; and after by clandestine artifices. The contagion was epidemic. Near relations, aliens in blood, friends and strangers, known and unknown, were,without distinction, all involved in one common danger. The act recently committed and the tale revived were equally destructive. Words alone were sufficient, whether spoken in the forum or amidst the pleasures of the table. . . . Informers struggle, as it were in a race, who would be first to ruin his man; some to secure themselves; the greatest part infected by the corruption of the times."[12]

In Judaism, there were two major sects, and they held opposing ideas and hatreds for each other. The largest group was the Pharisees. The priests, the scribes, and the laity comprised the Pharisee sect. They believed in and followed Mosaic Law, and even the interpretations of the scribes were considered valid. They placed traditional religion above politics, feeling they could live with any government that did not restrict religious freedom. "They accepted the Doctrine of God's cooperation in human acts . . . free will and moral responsibility . . . and that the Messiah would restore the divine dynasty and free the Jews from foreign dominion."

---

[11] Walker, Williston. *A History of the Christian Church* (New York: Charles Scribner's Sons, 1985), pp. 6–8.
[12] Tacitus. *Annals, Bk VI,* vii.
[13] Kittler, Glenn. *The Dead Sea Scrolls* (New York: Warner Books, 1970), p. 28.

The second sect was the Sadducees. They were not numerous, but were influential because they comprised the nobility, the wealthy, and the higher ranking priests. They did not believe in retribution or resurrection. They held the belief that there was a place in the earth where the dead went—without judgment. They did not believe in spirits or angels or answered prayer or Divine Providence and Guidance. They did accept free will.

It is puzzling to students of religion that the third sect of Jews in existence at this time—the Essenes—are never mentioned in the New Testament while the Pharisees and Sadducees come under criticism throughout. The discovery of the Dead Sea Scrolls has stirred numerous questions concerning their role in Judea at the time of Jesus. What is known about them comes through the scrolls and through other writers in the area, such as Philo of Alexandria (circa A.D. 20), Pliny the Elder (circa A.D. 70), and Josephus, who wrote between 75 and 85 A.D.

The Essenes had a more severely disciplined life than the other two sects. They were Jews by birth, from the Hebrew Line, and they held greater affection for each other than the other sects. They rejected pleasures as evil, but esteemed conquest over passions to be virtuous. They often neglected wedlock, but they often chose out other's children while fit for learning to train them in the Essene ways—much in the manner of the more modern Shakers. When wedlock did occur, it was between two individuals who were compatible on all levels of development, and the match was overseen by the High Initiates and Adepts within the group.

They held extraordinary piety for God. "In those days, when there had been more and more people in Carmel—the original place where the school of prophets was established during Elijah's time, Samuel's, these were called then Essenes. They were students of what you would call astrology, numerology, phrenology, and those phases of that study of the return of individuals—incarnations." (Josephus). They were a sect established to prepare the way, to educate and train the Messiah.

Essene comes from a word "asaya" meaning "doctor" or "healer." They were trained in many of the healing arts, and were often the ones first sought out by other peoples in the area. They were the true physicians in the area. They knew the secrets of nature and they had the ability to utilize energy in all of the healing arts. One current belief, as yet not verified, is that they were skilled in the use of sound and music and voice as a healing modality, and they were often called the "soft-spoken ones" because of their great ability to use their voice to impact, and with the energies of others. There is implied within this a knowledge of using sound and the power of the "Word" in the tradition of the ancient mystery systems.

In Biblical times, Samuel formed the School of Prophets. He was the great initate-singer of his day, and through his school he passed on the teachings and techniques.[14] The Essenes were the last remnant of the Brotherhood of the Prophets organized by Samuel, and more recent evidence is linking their schooling with the earlier Pythagorean Mystery School Tradition. The Essenes had two primary centers—one in Egypt beside Lake Maoris and the other in Palestine near the Dead Sea. They also had individual communities established throughout the area.

According to both Josephus and Philo, there were several thousand Essenes living in Palestine.[15] It is very likely that Jesus met and even associated with the Essenes to some degree. As to why they do not show up within Biblical scripture, there are several possibilities. One is that the gospels tend to focus only on adversaries. Also the name "Essene" is often the subject of scholarly debate, and thus their influence under other sectarian names may have occurred.

"The Essenes were divided into two groups, the Householders and the Temple Initiates. The Householders married and set up homes in villages and cities in the usual way of life . . . preparing themselves through strict spiritual discipline for the sanctity of parenthood, with the object of attracting advanced egos from the heaven world who would further the work of the Order and of humanity in general.

"The more esoteric group comprised Initiates who had taken a vow of perpetual virginity and held themselves unspotted of the world, living, usually, in isolated monastic communities where they could devote their whole life to the things of the spirit. Some of these, however, might also be found in the towns and cities when a special work was to be done . . .

---

[14] Andrews, Ted. *The Magical Name* (St. Paul: Llewellyn Publications, 1991), p. xii.
[15] Charlesworth, James H. *Jesus within Judaism* (New York: Doubleday), p. 61.

"Mary and Joseph belonged to the highest initiatory Order, hence the greater was their sacrifice in going out into the world to become affiliated with the lesser degree of the Householders."[16]

It was common for an Initiate woman of the many ancient mystery traditions (pagan and Jewish) to make an appeal to a higher soul in order to receive it into the womb and thus bring a prophet, teacher, or semi-divine being into the world. Many believe this could have been the intention of Mary. The soul, chosen for a divine mission, comes from the divine world, freely and consciously. In order that it can enter an earthly life, a chosen vessel is necessary. This is the calling of the mother from the elite—an Initiate herself—one who by her moral and spiritual bearing, by the purity of her own soul and life, by the high development of her senses would attract in her blood and flesh the soul of a redeemer or prophet.

Jesus would come from a long history of Jewish prophets, individuals who had been dedicated to their God by their parents. The individuals of this line were often referred to as "Emmanuel" which means "God within."

The Archangelic Christ spirit is so great a power that it could not incarnate within the womb of a woman or within the body of a child. An adult body would be needed, one strengthened and trained to contain and house the full force of a Solar Archangel. For reincarnationists, this would be a highly evolved soul in which there would be developed perfect harmony on physical, etheric, astral, mental, and spiritual levels. When this preparation had been achieved, then the Cosmic or Archangelic Christ could incarnate and use the physical vehicle.

The Rosicrucian tradition, along with other occult studies, refers to the highly evolved soul that elected to assume this task through rebirth as Jesus—the one known as Zoroaster. (To some the significance of the three Magi at the birth implies the awareness of the initiates of the Zoroastrian tradition being aware of this reincarnation.)

Regardless, though, of the degree of initiation that the soul may have gone through in other lives, regardless of the fact that the incoming soul may have been an ancient master, the soul would

[16] Heline, Corinne. *The Blessed Virgin Mary* (Santa Monica: New Age Bible and Philosophy Center, 1986), p. 61.

The Angel appears to Mary, telling her she would bear a child.
Engraving by Gustave Doré

still have to reconquer the higher self and expand it by renewed effort. All souls are bound by certain universal laws. Reincarnation darkens the consciousness, demanding that it be reignited and expanded upon. Every soul, every prophet must be initiated. The higher self must be awakened and made conscious of its strength. There had to be a harmonizing of the physical, etheric, and astral with the spiritual. This development, to be accomplished at the highest level, must be done within—without others being aware of it. This would be the task of the one we know of as Jesus during the years prior to the "Baptism."

Mary probably only knew in the beginning that a highly evolved soul would come through her. The extent of the mission and the power that would manifest could only be revealed when the soul itself was prepared and awakened to it. Not even the high Essene Initiates or other mystics of the area could tell Jesus what his mission would be. That had to come from *within*—not from without—a lesson for us all. Each alone has to discover his or her mission.

RIVAL CLAIMS TO DIVINE "SONSHIP"

More than twenty claims exist concerning individuals invested with Divine Power to contest the verdict that Jesus Christ was the "only son sent of God." Twenty messiahs, saviors, and sons of God, according to tradition, have in past times descended from heaven and taken upon themselves the form of men. They clothed themselves in human flesh and furnished incontestable evidence of a divine origin by various miracles, marvelous works, and excellent virtue. Many are claimed to have had virgin mothers and to have come into the world around the time of the winter solstice. Through their lives, they laid the foundation for the salvation of the world and then ascended back to heaven. A partial list of these follow:

Krishna (Hindustan)	Bali (Afghanistan)
Buddha (India)	Thammuz (Babylonia)
Osiris (Egypt)	Quetzlcoatl (Mexico)
Odin (Teutonic)	Mohammed (Arabia)
Zoroastra (Persia)	Jao (Nepal)
Indra (Tibet)	Adonis (Greece)

Prometheus (Graeco-Roman)   Eros (Druid)
Attis (Phrygia)   Thor (Scandinavia)
Mikado (Sintoos)   Baal (Phoenicia)
Beddru (Japan)   Adad (Assyria)

Although these claims exist—and there are many parallels—stories and myths were often adjusted to "accommodate" the divine process. We will see that the manifestation process of the Christ goes beyond these in a manner that is tremendously awe-inspiring.

OCCULT PREPARATION IN THE MANIFESTATION OF THE CHRIST

There are some important considerations in understanding this dynamic process. First, the vehicle would have to be strong enough and developed enough or the Solar Word would not be able to manifest. Even if Jesus were a highly evolved soul to begin with, there would still have to be tremendous preparation. The Essenes are credited with overseeing much of this training and education. The hidden years of travel would account for much mystical contact. Jesus would have to be familiar and learned in the mystical teachings of many lands so as to re-express them in a manner attainable by all of humanity. Much of this training occurred during the "missing years."

Jesus would also have to be familiar with the customs, habits, deceits, hypocrisies, temptations, and weaknesses of the people of many lands. He had to learn to deal in allegory, analogy, metaphors of many nations and trades, in order to relate to all people. He had to be developed in the use of the power of words and sounds. These abilities, once developed into mastership, would then be given an impetus greater than anything humanity had ever experienced when the Christ manifested.

The ancient schools of Wisdom dealt with primarily four stages of initiation:

1. Preparation and Instruction
2. Purification
3. Achievement or Illumination
4. Higher Vision

The first two always occur simultaneously in the life of the individual. The third and fourth may occur at different times. The preparation and purification involved the early training of the Master Jesus. The Illumination would occur at the time of the Baptism. The Higher Vision and its synthesis for humanity would occur in the three-year ministry that followed. The Christ would work those three years to help lead others through those steps of initiation and leave a path for all of humanity to follow thereafter.

It is important to understand the import of the process of Baptism in the true esoteric sense. Baptism, as we now treat it, is not what was truly experienced in the Ancient Mystery Schools. The modern Baptism is more aligned with what can be called the "Dedication in the Temple"—the dedicating or rededicating of the soul to a new spiritual path and endeavor. A true Baptism in the manner of the ancients would only be performed after very strict preparation and purification. The immersion in the water, in accordance with strict spiritual guidelines, will loosen the etheric web around the physical body, allowing for the consciousness to withdraw into the astral body in full consciousness, there to explore the more spiritual and ethereal realms.

A true baptism in this sense—if performed without proper purification and preparation—will create physical, emotional and spiritual breakdowns. It will loosen the etheric web and may open one to some spiritual "sight," but because the body has not been properly prepared, the nervous system will eventually short circuit. The time frame will vary, but it usually takes no more than five to six years for the deterioration to set in. Correcting such damage can be difficult and time consuming. We must be careful about the labels we apply.

Baptism in its truest sense is a ritual of tremendous initiation. It is a dedication ceremony that mimics a sacred rite still "hidden" from most. This is not to imply that the ceremony commonly used today has no power or spiritual force attached to it. As we will see in the second half in the section on the "Rite of the Winter Solstice"—the dedication ceremony has an esoteric significance as well. It is tied to one of the seven Feminine mysteries that the Christ restored.

At the time of the Baptism of Jesus, the Christ descended into the vehicle of the one called Jesus. The force of the Christ was given greater power by its union with the Holy Spirit—symbolized by the dove in this scriptural scene. This was crucial. In the Ancient Mysteries, the Holy Spirit is the Mystery of the Eternal Feminine, and occult tradition tells us that it is called by the name *Iona* upon the Astral Plane. The force of this love aspect—the force of the renewed Feminine upon the planet—would affect the astral/emotional energies of humanity. It is what would assist the Christ in creating tremendous conversions. It would help transform and vivify the souls of all whom he touched.

Until the time of the Baptism, Jesus' true name was Yeshua. At the time of the Baptism, he would come to be known as Yeheshua in the Aramaic language. In the Hebrew alphabet, every letter had significance. Its name, its meaning, its sound and even its numerological correspondence had great significance. The 22 letters of this alphabet was known to the Hebrew seers as the 22 steps to wisdom. The "H" is a Hebrew letter "Heh," meaning "window." As discussed earlier, a true Baptism opens a fully conscious vision of the spiritual realm. A window to let in the light of God would thus be opened. This subtle change in his name would let those who were schooled in the mystical arts know that he was a true master, although it would not let them necessarily know that he was now the Christ incarnate. This would have to be discovered by each in turn.

Christ is baptized by John
Engraving by Albrecht Dürer

This is the Illumination, the third step in the initiatory process. Before the next step could be taken—the Higher Vision and Synthesizing for Humanity (the actual ministry)—there would have to be the "Temptation." Although essentially god-like, the Christ was bound to the laws of evolution once the physical form was assumed. This meant that even he would have to pass the "Temptation" phase that follows all great illumination.

For humanity it is the facing of our lower self, the transmuting of our lower passions entirely. It is a process often termed in metaphysical parlance as the "Meeting of the Dwellers on the Threshold." It is all of those things that we have painted over, shoved to the back of the closet and pretended didn't exist. It is every negative emotion and thought ever created by us, in this lifetime and from every lifetime. We must face the energy of what we have put out into the world, love ourselves in spite of it and transmute it once and for all. We must transmute the "Guardian" which bars the way to the spiritual world by expelling from the soul and transmuting the last vestige of our baser emotions. Only then can we fully cross the threshold to true spirituality.

The Christ had no lower self, for the Christ had never walked upon the earth. The vehicle of Jesus had been purified and cleansed of his "Guardian." Humanity, on the other hand, had a collective "Guardian," a miasma of negativity that hindered the sight of the spiritual. This collective negativity and imbalance was alive within the magnetic aura of the earth itself. This collective "Guardian" would be faced, so that the process of higher initiation for all of humanity could be accelerated and the "Guardian" dispelled. By the Christ facing the collective "Guardian," the glue that bound it together would be loosed, facilitating the process for each individual to extract his or her own and transmute it once and for all.

It is this process that is reflected in the scriptures concerning the withdrawal into the desert, following the Baptism. There the Christ would encounter three temptations by the "devil," the collective Guardian. The three temptations are the three things that most strongly trip humanity up. The invitation by the devil to turn the stones into bread is the temptation of the lower senses that must be overcome. The devil then offers him kingdoms and all the world which is the temptation of power that must be overcome. The third invitation of the devil for the Christ to throw himself off the top of the temple in Jerusalem is the overcoming of fear that must be faced. (Keep in mind, though, that these temptations and the explanations given may reveal even deeper significance to those wishing to explore them more fully.)

The period of the "Temptation" was the time in which the Illumination of Jesus with the mission and energy of the now-overshadowing Christ consciousness occurred. It was during this time in the desert, those "forty days" following the Baptism, that it was revealed that it was necessary to make accessible to all what had until then remained the privilege of a few. He was about to preach the "Gospel of the Kingdom of Heaven"—a mystical and ancient term referring to the mysteries—about to place the Great Mysteries within reach of the simple. He was to interpret for them the teachings of the Initiates. To do this he added an inner light, the Power of Love, and the strength of action—the Divine Feminine manifesting through the Christ.

THE OCCULT OVERVIEW TO THE MINISTRY PROCESS

The actual ministry of the Christ Jesus corresponds to part of the fourth stage of the ancient initiatory process—Higher Vision and Synthesis. The Higher Vision of the Christ would now have to be synthesized and enacted in the events of the time, so that the initiatory process could become more available to all of humanity. Just as all the masters and teachers had to undergo the four stages (preparation and instruction, purification, illumination and achievement, higher vision and synthesis), the teachings of Christ Jesus to those around him would also take these stages:

Preparation and Purification

This was the backbone of much of the teachings of the Christ, for without proper preparation and purification, the higher illumination could not be achieved nor sustained. It is this moral aspect that has become the primary focus of modern Christendom.

The moral code was the most radical principle taught, although its true significance was lost on many. The basis for a number of the secret doctrines that will be explored in the following chapter pertained to his moral code. The matter of morality was given great emphasis. By it, Christ Jesus measured the standard and quality of character and nature of those he admitted to his secret teachings. He used it to determine their fitness.

The moral code was an ancient moral code with a very real Mystery element to it. He did not create it. It was not unique with him. It had existed in the Mystery Schools for many ages. It provided a means of behavior and action that would bring about a more personal experience with the Divine. It was considered understandable and applicable only by those of spiritual development and mystical unfoldment. The task was to preach it in a subtle form and establish it as a common code among the common people. In order to do so, it would take the power of the Christ.

The old civic and religious morality in Palestine at this time touched various aspects of life and were not generally Jewish. They were influenced by many cultures and peoples. A person's primary duty was to the community, and that duty was not based upon any divine commandment, but upon civic commandment. To many, only the mortal, physical self could commit the sin. The soul within the physical body was always pure, but it was imprisoned within the physical body. Immoral behavior involved a challenge and breaking of civic code more than divine in spite of the religious tradition. Immoral and "sinful" acts did not bring upon the perpetrator any divine condemnation in the civic sense, but it was believed that if the body suffered sufficient torture, it was considered that just compensation had been made. The exception was blasphemy, which could only be truly compensated for in death. In that case, the physical body had gone too far. To many, it was always the physical body that committed the sin.

The spiritual and behavioral code that would be established by Christ Jesus was actually quite different. At the time, it was considered extremely radical and thus often served to inflame the more "civic" minded people. The code of Christ Jesus, though, did have an element of the moral code of the Jews, but it went so far as to open to all the mystery of personal responsibility in the evolvement process:

1. Morality constituted a duty to the Divine and not to the community. It was a private matter between humanity's inner self and God. The moral codes were not mere public matters. It was not the principle of cooperation with one's fellow human or the helping of one's worldly brother or sister, but it was the saving and evolvement of the soul that was key. When the latter was accomplished, the former would automatically occur.

2. The Christ Jesus would introduce subtly the duality of humanity—in a different sense than the old morality. The human being was more than a mere body of earthly elements with a spiritual soul imprisoned within it. The Christ would work to develop the realization that just as humanity had an outer self with all of its urges, sensations, and susceptibility to influences, they also had an inner self which could control the outer. This inner self was partially associated with the soul. Many of the parables and healings were a means of demonstrating that the appropriate inner force could control the outer. ("Jesus asked him, 'What do you want me to do for you?' 'Rabbi', the blind man said, 'I want to see.' Jesus said in reply, 'Be on your way! Your faith has healed you.' Immediately he received his sight and started to follow him up the road." Mark 10:51-52.)

3. It was not taught nor implied that the physical body was anything more than a mortal frame—wholly unimportant to the scheme of things, other than as a vehicle by which the inner self can learn and grow to greater union with its soul and thus with God. ("If thy right eye offend thee, Pluck it out and throw it away." Matthew 5:29.)

   An understanding of the words and language of the time will show that there really was no intimation that his system was intended to bring salvation to the physical body of humanity. Many of the teachings were couched in words and phrases, indicative of much more than a mere literal interpretation. They are words and phrases common to most mystery traditions—indicating an esoteric significance for those who could recognize such. Some of these are:

the little child	the door
the straight gate	lamp and light
the narrow path	raising the temple up
the marriage	true riches
the saved	the seed and the garden
born again	the mountain
the Kingdom of God	the mysteries

All of these are ancient terms associated with the process of initiation and can be found in the scriptures of many of the ancient mystery systems of the world.

4. Salvation of the soul was not really taught. All references are misinterpretations, a misunderstanding of the secret principle he was teaching. To Christ Jesus, the soul was immortal, perfect, divine, and linked to the consciousness of God. The salvation emphasis referred to the inner self which constituted the individuality, the distinct character of the perpetual self. It is that aspect humanity is developing and unfolding so that when alignment with the soul is achieved consciously, we become what in esoteric parlance is termed "Masters of Evolution"—more than we ever were in the beginning. It was because the untrained public could not distinguish between the soul, the inner self, and the physical self that the real message was not discerned.

    This inner self, unlike the soul, is not essentially immortal save by its own developed virtues, morality, and spiritual unfoldment. It is the free will aspect—that part of us that is free to choose and free to attain. It is this which we are working to resurrect. Humanity's inner self (individuality) would be developed and saved. It was the duty of the individual to bring the inner self into attunement with God, as an entity worthy of perpetual existence and perfection. It is the inner self that commits the sins that constitute the violations of moral law—not the physical body. ("But I say to you that anyone who so much as looks with lust at a woman has already committed adultery with her in his heart." Matthew 5:28).

5. More important than establishing and maintaining a civic code whose purpose was to make a livable society or idealistic nation, it was necessary to salvage one's inner self through duty to the Divine. Change must first come from within if it is to be permanent. Imposed from without, it would not be permanent nor entirely effective. ("Seek ye first the Kingdom of Heaven and all shall be added unto you.")

The Christ Jesus worked in two ways in the Preparation and Purification process in the ministry. The first was through open meetings, demonstrations, and performances in front of multitudes. The second was through secret meetings with those who would carry on the work.

It is safe to assume that there were probably two types of people admitted to the secret meetings. There were those anxious to know the facts and who demanded signs and demonstrations. They were sincere in as far as they went in their desire to master the principles taught, but they were not always ready to follow the spiritual precepts or change the course of their personal lives. These were eventually eliminated. This is demonstrated at various points within the scriptures, the most prominent example being the rich man who would not give up all his possessions and follow the Christ. (Mark 10:17-25).

The second were those who accepted in sincere faith all of the truths and who cared little for demonstrations. The virtue of their improved lives was reward enough. This is most evidenced by the accounts of Mary Magdalene.

Illumination

The Christ Jesus recognized that there was a hierarchical development within humanity on the earth. He had no intention of "tossing pearls before swine," and yet he did intend to reveal the Great Mysteries and place them within reach of all. He therefore spoke and taught according to the development of the groups, but, having the Power of the Word, he couched his teachings in terms and phrases that would create a resonance—a response—upon the level at which the individual could receive it.

His teachings and parables contained words and gestures that reveal much about the true mysteries for one who desired to know and was willing to put forth the efforts. They can be divided into six major categories (as per Corinne Heline in her *New Age Bible Interpretation*). This is quite significant in that six in the Hebrew Qabala is the number for the Heart and initiation into the divine consciousness. It is the center upon the mystical tree of life that has to do with the source of healing and miracles. It is the level of Christed consciousness.

1. *Parables of the Old and New:* These are those teachings of the Christ concerning the change of order and the new energy being enacted for ages to come.

    Parable of New Wine and Old Wine (found in Luke, Matthew and Mark)
    Parable of Treasures New and Old (Matthew 13:52)
    Parable of the New Patch on the Old Garment (Luke, Matthew and Mark)

2. *Parables of the Preparation for Discipleship:* These depict the qualities and dedication necessary for initiation.

    Parable of the Pearl of a Great Price (Matthew 13: 44–46)
    Parable of the Hidden Treasure (Matthew 13:44–46)
    Parable of the Mustard Seed (Mark and Luke)
    Parable of Leaven (Luke 13:20–21)

3. *Parables as Symbols of Discipleship:* "The seven parables are lessons pertaining to the teachings on humility, compassion, and service—three columns found in every initiatory Temple." (Corinne Heline, *New Age Bible Interpretation,* Vol. V; p. 56.) Four of these were spoken in mixed multitudes, and explained to the Apostles. The other three were given to the Apostles in private. The division of four and three is mystically significant, with dynamic associations to many of the mystery Temples. The four is the foundation upon which the pyramid of spirit is raised.

    Parable of the Chief Seats (Luke 14:7–11)
    Parable of the Pharisee and the Publican (Luke 18: 9–14)
    Parable of the Laborers and the Hours
        (Matthew 20: 1–16)
    Parable of the Talents (Matthew 25: 14–30)
    Parable of the Pounds (Luke 19:11–27)
    Parable of the Good Samaritan (Luke 10: 25–37)
    Parable of the Sower (Mark 4:3–20)

4. *Parables of Obstacles Toward Attainment:*

    Parable of the Unmerciful Servant (Matthew 18:35)
    Parable of the Young Ruler (Matthew 19: 16–30)

Parable of the Rich Fool (Luke 12:13–21)
Parable of Lazarus and the Rich Man (Luke 16: 19–31)
Parable of the Prodigal Son (Luke 15: 11–32)
Parable of the Lost Coin (Luke 15: 8–10)
Parable of the Lost Sheep (Luke 15: 4–7)
Parable of the Rejected Cornerstone (Matthew, Mark,
    and Luke)

5. *Parables for the Teaching of Regeneration:* These involve the higher teaching of the process of alchemy, discipleship, and testing upon the initiatory path.

Parable of the Barren Fig Tree (Matthew 21:17–1)
Parable of the Last Judgment (Matthew 25: 31–46)
Parable of the Tares (Matthew 13: 24–30)

6. *Parables of Initiation:* These are the teachings of deeper esoteric significance. They are for those who have found the path of discipleship and are ready for the deeper work which will lead to true attainment.

Parable of the Wise and Foolish Virgins
    (Matthew 25: 1–13)
Parable of the Great Supper (Luke 14: 16–24)
Parable of the Wedding Garment (Matthew 22:11–14)
Parable of the Wedding of the King's Son
    (Matthew 22: 2–10)

Through the parables of the Christ, definite steps in occult development and unfoldment are revealed. Though seemingly concealed from most, uncovering its gold now requires individual effort alone. They provide illumination for "the Way of Evolution (for the masses) and the Way of Initiation (for the few)." They show what can be attained through the initiatory process. Unlike other Mystery teachers and saviors, though, the Christ initiation was no longer an external process, but is an inner experience, achievable by the individual. The hidden Christ Mysteries are still available to all.

> "And their eyes were opened, and they knew him; and he vanished out of their sight."
>
> Luke 24:31

Chapter Three

THE CHRIST MYSTERIES

"I am the Light of the world. No follower of mine shall ever walk in darkness; no, he shall possess the Light of Life."

John 8:12

The Bible is a manual for occult development. That which we call the New Testament is a manual of occult initiation for all within the New Age. Every event and every aspect in the life of the Christ Jesus has an occult significance in the initiatory process. Within its teachings are concealed the inner Mysteries.

The Christ Mysteries reveal the divine principles and the natural laws of the universe and they teach how to unfold the power to work with them. These Mysteries are neither "weird" nor incomprehensible. The word itself refers to the secret revelations—an initiation into something that is a great truth and yet has been concealed.

Why are the Christ Mysteries concealed—as with all the mysteries of ancient societies? Some may argue that the sole purpose of Jesus incarnating and for the manifesting of the Christ through him was to reveal, not to conceal. It must be remembered that great truths can be destroyed by giving them common circulation. They are taken for granted when placed into the category of everyday facts that are easily acquired and easily comprehended without effort or worthiness.

Christ Jesus recognized this. Casting pearls before swine results in the loss of those pearls. Veiling the Mysteries of life and the universe by utilizing words and phrases of intense universal power could bring the truths to the people without casting them away. This reveals a great insight into human psychology. It was obviously recognized that it is human nature to value something at what it costs to obtain it. Christ Jesus held the truths aloft, and yet within reach. It was simple, and yet difficult, to attain.

As mentioned in the beginning, the search for the occult is the search for the interconnectedness and hidden divinity within all things. It is the destiny of humanity to conquer matter. This quest for the hidden spirit is a search for our innermost self—the point of greatest reality. It is not a path into which all of our troubles are dissolved, but rather it is a path to bring that light which is hidden in all things and all people into outer expression.

For the unenlightened and the unawakened person, the whole idea of an occult life is either a mystery or ridiculous or both. For the mundane or profane individual, the procedure of unfolding higher potentials and capabilities was and is mysterious. The ancient teachings add great knowledge to the life experience of the individual. Such knowledge gives power which demands responsibility. The ancient teachings that lead to the manifestation of higher vision and destiny can so completely transcend all customary experience that one's center of perception can be easily disrupted.

For this reason, in more ancient times the initiation into higher truths was under the strict guidance of a teacher. Today, because of the availability of the Christ energies and mysteries, we can win for ourselves the conditions for higher initiation and heightened consciousness. This does require a secure perception of the hidden energies of life, and it presupposes careful observation, discrimination, and judgment of those energies. The purpose for the spiritual initiatory path is to assist us in looking beyond the physical limitations of life, to learn the creative possibilities of limitation, while at the same time transcending them.

The Occult Christ Mysteries help us to rediscover the wonder and awe of the Power of God, and how that power lives within us. Part of what the Christ Mysteries do is throw us back upon ourselves for our answers and our miracles. Not from books or teachers, although they will serve their purpose—but from the well of truth that lies within. Rather than looking for some light to shine down upon us, we must find the hidden light within to shine out from us.

What follows throughout the rest of this chapter are skeletal guidelines to but some of the occult significances within the true Christ Mysteries. They will help to demonstrate some of the more easily identifiable esoteric threads running through modern Christian scripture. It will help to demonstrate the cryptographic aspect of occult teaching that demands looking beyond the surface indications for the hidden Light. It may also provide the inspiration for individual exploration to even greater depths. Some of these aspects, along with others, will be explored in greater detail in the second half of this work, when we examine the hidden Christ energies operating through the Sacred Cycle of the Seasons.

THE OCCULT TEACHINGS OF THE CHRIST

Within the contents of modern Christian scripture can be found the threads to ancient studies of occultism. It has ties to astrology, psychism, the chakra system of the body, the precepts and problems of the path of discipleship and initiation, the process of holistic healing and therapeutics, the natural laws of the universe upon which all life operates, the masculine and feminine principles in the universe, and in humanity, a guide to the alignment and achievement of power in the seven spiritual worlds of life, and so much more. The scriptures are a manual of great metaphysical and spiritual knowledge necessary for true unfoldment.

The scope of this work will only touch upon some of them, opening the door for more in-depth exploration by the individual. The work of the Christ Initiate is to take the responsibility of one's life into one's own hands. Through the skeletal framework of the mysteries given, and through the exercises at the end of Part One and throughout Part Two, one can open more fully to the true occult significance of this magnificent manual of metaphysics.

The Secret Doctrines in General

1. The Christ Jesus taught the trinity—the triune nature of humanity. This is comprised of the body, the individuality, and the soul, on one level. On a higher level, it involves the masculine, the feminine, and the divine child born of the complete union of both aspects within us. (Matthew 6:19–22, Matthew 3:16, John 3:34, Luke 4:18).

   The Trinity in the modern Christian perception—often considered the most original and sacred of the mysteries (as in the Father, Son, and Holy Ghost)—was not adopted by the church until the 12th century. Later, in the 16th century, the church fathers in the Lutheran Council would proclaim it as fundamental. We must thus distinguish between the trinity of modern Christendom from the Sacred Triangle, or Trinity of the Ancient Mysteries.

2. The Christ Jesus revealed the strange secrets of the human mind, particularly in its influence on the health of the physical body. This will be explored further when we discuss the Natural Laws of the Universe that the Christ Jesus taught to his disciples. (Matthew 6:22–23)

3. The Christ Jesus taught the urges and impulses of the physical body and how these are passed on to the inner self to decide and choose the response. Thus the inner self, in accordance with the decisions and choices and their resulting actions, had to assume responsibility for its actions and thoughts. (Matthew 5:27–30)

4. The Christ Jesus taught that the physical body could not be held responsible for its acts since it did not possess any degree of consciousness. It could not be made to suffer at a future time, as it did not have a future time. The physical was continually changing, and by working with those changes, certain methods of healing could bring about quick changes in the physical and material nature of the body. There are more than twenty examples of healing within the scriptures, each reinforcing or demonstrating a method by which the healing of the body could be instigated. It does imply a more holistic approach, one involving the manipulation and conscious direction of energy from more than just a purely physical level.

5. The Christ Jesus taught how the inner self is independent of the physical. (Mark 6:34–44)

6. The Christ Jesus taught how consciousness could be projected to a distant point and made visible or observe the situation. Projection of consciousness or of the self was taught as a first step in a mystical life process that necessitates a greater mastery of fundamental natural and spiritual laws of life. These 12 fundamental Natural Laws taught by Christ Jesus will be explored later within this chapter.

7. The Christ Jesus taught how to call upon the essence of a distant being and bring it into one's own presence, to make it tangible or visible—as in the time of the Transfiguration. (Luke 9:28–36)

8. The Christ Jesus taught the disciples and Apostles the Power of the Word, especially when applied to the Law of Prayer. The prayer given as an example—The Lord's Prayer—has an esoteric significance, containing a seven, nine, or twelvefold meaning.

9. The Christ Jesus taught also within the scope of the "Power of the Word" that doing or saying "in his name" meant in the name of the Christos, and involved a technique for invoking the full power of the Solar Archangel into play. It is a formula whose explanation and practice would form part of the mystery of the "Word."

10. Christ Jesus taught the process of alchemical transmutation. The changing of the water into wine, the feeding of the multitudes, the "Last Supper" involve the esoteric process of the alchemy of spirit—the transmutation of the grosser into the finer.

11. The Christ Jesus taught the principle and power of faith.

12. The Christ Jesus taught the increasing of the human aura whereby the radiations of the divine consciousness through it could heal and cure.

13. The Christ Jesus demonstrated and taught how prayer and sound had sympathetic effects upon consciousness. (Matthew 6:5–15, Matthew 7:7–12).

14. The Christ Jesus taught the doctrine of immortality. (John 14:1–4).

15. The Christ Jesus taught the ancient doctrine of reincarnation. (Galatians 6:7).

The Natural Laws of the Universe

We live in a universe of energy. This energy operates within us and around us in accordance to basic laws and principles. By learning to work with these laws and principles, the individual would find that life is more fulfilling, more abundant, and more prosperous. The individual discovers that he or she is not at the mercy of life "circumstances." Learning to use or work with these laws and principles propels the individual along the path to higher destiny and opens the great reservoir of universal energy.

These laws and principles operate whether the individual is aware of them or not. By becoming aware of them and working with them, the individual could control that which had seemed "uncontrollable." These laws and the energy they direct are neutral and impersonal; they exist and work for everyone regardless of belief or disbelief.

All of the ancient Mystery traditions taught the use of certain laws and principles that controlled the energies of the universe. Each expressed the laws and principles in accordance with the society of their day, adjusting and adapting them in the manner best received. To the Egyptians they were known as the "Hermetic Principles." To the modern Christian aspirant they are termed the "Twelve Natural Laws."

In Occult Christianity, twelve was an important and powerful number. Twelve, in the ancient science of numerology, is a universal number. It represents the quadrant of 3. Three is the number of the Divine Child—the Christ manifested upon the earth. The four threes that comprise twelve are the Christ manifesting through the four elements that comprise physical life—fire, air, water, and earth. Twelve often signifies rest and completion at the end of a cycle. It is the spiritual number of understanding, of the feminine wisdom gained through sacrifice.

There were twelve Apostles. As we will see, these twelve Apostles are aligned with the twelve signs of the zodiac. The Holy City of Revelations has twelve gates. In the New Age disciple, the traditional seven chakra system will become the twelve chakra system, the twelve spiritual centers and powers within humanity. There are also twelve characteristics to be developed in the New Age disciple and twelve expressions of energy that assist in the development of such qualities. Thus it should not be surprising to discover that the Christ Jesus taught twelve Natural Laws of the Universe:

1. *The Law of Thought:* "The eye is the body's lamp. If your eyes are good, your body will be filled with light; if your eyes are bad, your body will be in darkness. And if your light is darkness, how deep will the darkness be?" (Matthew 6:22–23)

   This law teaches us that what we focus upon is what we set in motion around us. Your mind creates the good and the bad within your life. Your ideas determine what is to be created. All energy follows thought! Where we put our thoughts, that is where the energy flows.

2. *The Law of Supply:* "Ask, and it shall be given you; seek and ye shall find. Knock and it shall be opened unto you." (Matthew 7:7)

   This law teaches us that where there is no demand there is no supply. We must build for ourselves an awareness that there is an infinite supply for us within the universe, but we must also ask for it. Abundance is a consciousness of wholeness.

3. *The Law of Attraction:* "Wherever your treasure lies, there your heart will be." (Luke 12:34).

   Like attracts like. Energy is magnetic as well as electric. What we put out, we get back. Similar vibrations and energies are drawn to each other; they resonate with each other. These energies may be physical, emotional, mental and/or spiritual. We must learn to ask ourselves, "What is there within our consciousness that is drawing the circumstances of our existence?"

4. *The Law of Receiving:* "What I say to you is this: Make friends for yourselves through your use of the world's

goods, so that when they fail you, a lasting reception will be yours. If you can trust a man in little things, you can also trust him in greater; while anyone unjust in a slight manner is also unjust in greater. If you cannot be trusted with elusive wealth, who will trust with lasting?" (Luke 16:9–11).

This is often one of the most misunderstood laws, especially in a society in which the "martyr" aspect of a religion has become so infused. We must learn to give and to *receive!* Many refuse gifts that could start a process of abundance simply because they feel "unworthy" of it. Giving is wonderful, but so is receiving. If we refuse to receive the little things in life (i.e., the compliments, the assistance of others when offered, simple expressions of gratitude, and so forth), the universe will not send us the bigger things we wish to manifest or receive within our lives. Thus they are always elusive. As we learn to receive the little, it starts a magnetic pull, drawing the greater into our lives.

5. *The Law of Increase:* "Give and it shall be given to you. Good measure pressed down, shaken together, running over, will they pour into the folds of your garment. For the measure you measure with will be measured back to you." (Luke 6:38).

We must have faith and awareness that increase is in the world for us. We can learn to express this faith by giving thanks before the receiving occurs. Veiled within this law is the other half of the "Law of Receiving." We must learn to receive, but we must also learn to *give.* The two together create a cycle of increase that perpetuates itself.

6. *The Law of Compensation:* "Whatsoever a man soweth, that shall he also reap." (Galatians 6:7).

This is sometimes referred to within metaphysical circles as the law of karma, or cause and effect. It refers to the manifestations of actions and situations in our life from the use of free will in the past. It is neutral, compensating us for the good and the bad. Every action has an equal, but opposite, reaction. What we put out, we get back. To the ancient Hermeticists it is the law that states: "Every cause has an effect; every effect has its cause; everything happens according to the Law; chance is but a name for Law unrecognized; there are many planes of causation, but nothing escapes the Law." Understanding this helps us to understand that we are connected to all things, all people, all times, and all places.

7. *Law of Non-Resistance:* "But I say unto you that you resist not evil." (Matthew 5:39).

This is the law that teaches us to "go with the flow." Things happen in God's time, not ours. Resisting and fighting against the negative establishes a link with it— it creates resonance which activates the law of attraction. We must learn to recognize learning in all people and all situations around us. It is sometimes called the law of synchronicity—things happen in the time and the means that is best for us if we allow them to. We do what we have to do and then allow events to play themselves out.

8. *The Law of Forgiveness:* "Forgive and you shall be forgiven." (Luke 6:37).

Unless we learn to truly forgive and recognize all things as learning opportunities, we stay tied to the "karma" of the situation. When we refuse to forgive, we align ourselves with, and share on subtle levels, the karmic implications. This is especially true of ourselves. We must learn to forgive our own idiosyncracies and not berate ourselves for our mistakes. This will trigger the Law of Attraction in a negative manner. Sometimes the only way we grow is through difficult lessons. Inside each of us is a child, and we must decide whether to ridicule and blame that child or to forgive it, nurture it, and teach it in new ways.

9. *The Law of Sacrifice:* "Straight is the gate and narrow is the way which leadeth unto life, and few there are that findeth it." (Matthew 7:14).

Sacrifice operates in all things, but we must learn not to associate sacrifice with pain and suffering. Parents often sacrifice for their children, and derive great joy from it. When we sacrifice we give up one thing for another. Sacrifice is not negative; it teaches higher discipline and can be joyful. Learning to set aside one aspect of life that another may be achieved, teaches us responsibility, discipline, and appropriate expression and development of the creative free will.

10. *The Law of Obedience:* "At that time Jesus said to them, 'Render unto Caesar the things that are Caesar's, and render unto God the things that are God's.'" (Mark 12:17).

    As long as we are within the physical, there will be certain natural laws that must be obeyed. Ignoring the Natural and Spiritual Laws manifests a variety of imbalances and problems. Thus it is necessary to learn as much about those laws operating in our life as possible. There is no dishonor in obedience if the command is just. Obedience to the inner self and the laws that govern it brings new freedom and new patterns of energy within one's life. It has its place in both the physical and the spiritual realms. It is what brings harmony to life.

11. *The Law of Success:* "The works I do so shall ye do, and greater works still." (John 14:12).

    We are denied nothing but that which we deny ourselves. Obstacles and tests help us to awaken our innate powers. We are meant to succeed. Success is ours with right effort and right application of the Laws of Spirit and of Nature. The divine forces are available to those who help themselves. The unfoldment of our potentials does not occur in artificially contrived situations but through the applications of the laws within our day to day life circumstances. The laws of the divine universe deny humanity nothing.

12. *The Law of Love:* "Jesus said to him, 'You shall love the Lord thy God with thy whole heart, thy whole soul and thy whole mind. This is the greatest and first commandment.

The second is like it: You shall love thy neighbor as thy-self. On these two commandments the whole law is based, and the prophets as well.'" (Matthew 22:37–40).

This is the greatest law of all. It overrides all of the oth-ers. It overcomes karma and all life conditions, but we must extend love unconditionally to ourselves and to others. It opens the entire universe to us. One of the eso-teric significances of this law is that proper application of it will activate what is called the third eye or brow chakra—the two-petalled lotus (reflected within the two-part commandment). It is the key to the incarnation of the Christ, the sacrifice from a Solar Regent to a Plane-tary Logos, for the implanting and stimulating of the divine Love-Wisdom spark in all of humanity. It is the key to awakening the Divine Feminine.

All of the "miracles" of the Christ Jesus were to demonstrate what all of humanity had the potential to unfold within them-selves. The word "miracle" means a "wonderful thing." This "wonderful thing" does not imply any violation of natural laws but rather the proper application of them in all areas of life!

THE OCCULT SIGNIFICANCE OF THE APOSTLES

There was a definite hierarchy among those who would receive the teachings of the Christ Jesus. First there were the twelve Apostles. Then there were the 144 disciples who would work with these twelve. (In Luke 10:1, we read "After this, the Lord appointed a further seventy-two and sent them in pairs to every town and place he intended to visit." The "further seventy-two" implies that a pre-vious seventy-two had been prepared and sent forth. This 144 would ultimately be broken into groups of twelve, overseen by one of the twelve Apostles.) Then, of course, there was the multitude-whom he taught.

The Apostles and the 144 disciples were trained in the ancient doctrine of stewardship. The Apostles were not to consider them-selves the personal recipients of an individual blessing. They were being given a task to dispense the truths and the Mysteries as "stewards." They were not to hold the secret knowledge and wisdom within their own consciousness like a personal possession. One of the earliest mystical principles that all must learn—to be worthy of the higher knowledge and understanding—is to do so only as a channel of the Divine. Any attempt to hold such knowledge secretly and failure to dispense it to the worthy—even if not used selfishly—would constitute a failure to meet one's obligations and responsibilities. This was considered a greater "sin" than using the knowledge too frequently for personal benefit.

The Christ Jesus divided the program of earthly activities into twelve sections, each overseen by one of the Apostles. Twelve disciples and students from the 144 were selected to work for each. Thus, there was a microcosmic aspect of his own teachings. The Christ Jesus had twelve primary persons, and each Apostle would then become the "Christ Figure" for his section. In esoteric lore, there were also twelve female "Apostles," overseen by the highest female Initiate of the time—Mary. This will be examined further in the next chapter on the "Feminine Mysteries."

As mentioned earlier, all events within the life of Christ Jesus, and all aspects within the scriptures, are allegories and symbols of greater significance. Even the Apostles have a hidden significance to them as well. They were not only historical figures, but they were selected in a manner that made them living "allegories" of aspects of ancient occult mysteries.

From the multitudes that surrounded him, Christ Jesus chose the Twelve Apostles to comprise his inner circle. They were not the ignorant "fisherman" as so often assumed, but each had a degree of esoteric training that made them ready to receive the teaching of the Higher Mysteries of Christ Jesus. Thus, within each one can be found much esoteric significance for those who will put forth the effort to examine them from a non-historical perspective.

In the following occult correspondences to the Apostles, I have used the original twelve—including Judas Iscariot. Although, after his demise, he would be replaced by the one known as Matthias, it is important to understand that Judas also represented an attribute of humanity and an important aspect of the initiatory process. He is a dynamic symbol of the lower man which must be killed off or it will betray the higher self. Matthias, who replaces Judas among the twelve, is the redeemed man.

The Twelve Apostles represent varied qualities and characteristics, symbolic of the universal creativity operative within humanity and indicative that the initiatory path is open to all types. They must be treated symbolically and historically, for they served a dynamic function in the revealing of the mysteries to all people. Understanding the hidden significance of them can reveal much about one's own path of initiation.

The key to understanding some of the occult significances of the Apostles is understanding the astrological correspondences. It is difficult to understand much of the hidden meaning of Biblical scripture without some astrological background. The ancient seers lived in close communion with the stars, and the celestial beings associated with them. The imagery and symbols within the ancient scriptures, parables, and teachings are tied to the symbols and images of esoteric astrology. It is difficult to separate them—impossible if true comprehension is to be achieved.

ASTROLOGICAL SIGNIFICANCE OF THE APOSTLES

Astrological Sign	Apostle	Common Symbol
Aries	James	Pilgrim's Staff
Taurus	Andrew	Traverse Cross
Gemini	Thomas	Builder's Square
Cancer	Nathaniel	Large Knife
Leo	Judas/Matthias	Lance
Virgo	James the Just	Club
Libra	Jude-Thaddeus	Lance
Scorpio	John	Chalice
Sagittarius	Philip	Staff with Cross
Capricorn	Simon	Saw
Aquarius	Matthew	Purse
Pisces	Peter	Keys

(These aspects will be explored a little further in the second half of the book, in relation to the Celebration of the Winter Solstice within the Christ Mysteries.)

ESOTERIC ATTRIBUTES OF THE APOSTLES

The Apostles were also symbols of specific qualities, and they also represented attributes that could be developed by following specific courses of action or working with specific cosmic principles of energy expression:

Apostle	Attributes & Qualties	Cosmic Principles
Peter	Action; Faith	Activity
James	Aspiration; Hope	Will
John	Regeneration; Prayerful; Love	Wisdom (Sophia)
Andrew	Humbleness; Strength	Attraction
Thomas	Skepticism; Discrimination	Contraction
Matthew	Service; Spiritual Will; Strength of Custom	Crystallization
Philip	Spiritual Knowledge	Reflections and Relationships
Nathanael	Intuition; Imagination; Dreaming	Addition and Increase
James the Just	Methodical; Growth of	Expansion Spirit
Jude-Thaddeus	Courage	Construction
Simon	Zeal; Rebellion; Catalytic	Repulsion
Judas / Matthias	Passion; Redemption	Destruction

REPRESENTATION OF THE APOSTLES

Apostle	Kind of Person Represented
Peter	The active and busy
James	Those aspiring to anything
John	The prayerful individuals
Andrews	The humble upon the planet
Thomas	All of the skeptical people
Matthew	All servants or those who provide services
Philip	The commonplace person
Nathanael	The dreamers of the world
James the Just	All who are methodical and mental in life
Jude-Thaddeus	All who live life courageously
Simon	All who are rebellious
Judas/Matthias	The passionate and all who have betrayed or have been betrayed (also all who set things right)

Within the inner circle of the twelve apostles there was also an internal hierarchy of development. Corinne Heline divides these into three categories of preparation and development in discipleship and initiation:

1. *The Master's Degree* (James, John, and Peter)
   These three saw the Transfiguration and they also accompanied the Christ Jesus to the Garden of Gethsemane to assist in the final preparations. The qualities associated with them are faith, hope, and love. We are told in Corinthians that "Now abideth Faith, Hope and Love. But the greatest of these is Love." Love is the quality associated with the Apostle known as the "beloved one" of Christ Jesus or the one "whom he loved." These are also symbolic of the three pillars of the New Age Temple.

2. *The Fellowship Degree* (Andrew, Thomas, Matthew, Philip, and Nathanael)
   These individuals would not take the final initiations until after the death and resurrection, but they were more developed and schooled in the esoteric tradition than those of the latter degree.

3. *The Degree of Apprenticeship* (James the Just, Jude-Thaddeus, Simon, and Judas Iscariot)
   Although we are differentiating in the degree of initiation and development of these individuals, we must keep in mind that those different stages would be unnoticeable to most people. The Apostles were all schooled in esoteric study. The Christ Jesus was serving as their initiator, and was preparing all to carry on that initiatory process in their own unique ways. It is likely that those of this degree had little experience in the actual teaching process themselves, and thus can be classified as apprentices. They were schooled in the esoteric tradition, but had not had the opportunity to apply it practically to the outer world.

OCCULT ASPECTS OF THE SERMON ON THE MOUNT

No study of the Christ Mysteries would have any validity without some examination of the esoteric aspects of "The Sermon on the Mount." Within it is the outline of the entire focus of the Christ teachings. It is through this sermon that the Christ brings forth the new laws, based upon *Love* and not fear. All of the admonitions within this sermon require a new and more powerful expression of love to be fulfilled. This sermon was given around the time of the summer solstice, the culmination of the cycle of the Christ energies in the Sacred Year of the Soul, as we will explore in the second half of this book.

The admonitions toward specific expressions of love are impossible without certain qualities. These include complete self-mastery, the complete dedication and consecration to the spiritual life. It requires "resisting not evil"—thinking not of the wrong suffered, but rather, thinking of the course of action that will best help the individual who commits the wrong. It is love expressed through justice that is tempered with mercy. It demands helpfulness on all levels—understanding, kindness, encouragement. Bitterness over past deeds must be vanquished or it will create ties that will bind those holding the bitterness to future entanglements—in this life or the next.

All of the teachings and events in the life of the Christ Jesus have an exoteric (outer) and an esoteric (inner) significance. Many understand and can see the significance intellectually, but the Christ teachings were meant to awaken the heart so that the inner significance could be lived by the individual. This magnificent sermon provides the three greatest methods and clues to the awakening of the heart—the reexpression of Love as a dynamic force within the world (the Divine Feminine):

1. The Beatitudes

2. The Golden Rule

3. The Lord's Prayer.

The Sermon on the Mount
Engraving by Gustave Doré

All have an occult significance often missed by the casual reader or student. They each can be explored upon many levels. We will examine the Beatitudes specifically to demonstrate how they can veil much esoteric teaching of the Ancient Mysteries. (The Lord's Prayer will be touched on lightly in the next chapter on "The Resurrection of the Feminine Mysteries.") The entire Sermon on the Mount is in its most complete form in the book of Matthew, chapters 5 through 7. The Beatitudes are found in Matthew 5:3-12. We will give the basic keynote or quality associated with each of the beatitudes, its planetary correspondence in astrology, its level upon the Tree of Life of the ancient Hebrew Qabala (see Page 67) and a brief explanation:

"Blessed are the poor in spirit: for theirs is the kingdom of Heaven."

Keynote = Humility
Planet = Earth
Tree of Life = Malkuth (the Kingdom)

Malkuth is at the base of the Tree of Life. It is the recipient of all the energies of the universe flowing down into it from the rest of the universe. It is the microcosm and thus it is the task of the aspirant to "climb the tree of life"—to lift oneself from the energy of the Kingdom of Earth to the Kingdom of Heaven.

"Blessed are they that mourn for they shall be comforted."

Keynote = Comfort
Planet = Moon
Tree of Life = Yesod (Foundation)

The moon is a symbol of the subconscious—that part of us which controls the emotions. The subconscious knows there is more to life than what is consciously perceived and consciously experienced, and thus it often mourns for higher experiences. It can open us to an awareness of those higher experiences through our dreams, our psychisms and intuitions. These form a foundation that can comfort us in our outer life circumstances. It can help us to understand that there is more to life—even if it is not understood.

"Blessed are the Meek for they shall inherit the Earth."

Keynote = Receptivity to the Higher Teachings
Planet = Mercury
Tree of Life = Hod (Splendor/Glory)

Meekness is not to be confused with timidity. Meekness is an openness, a receptivity to new knowledge and truth. As we open ourselves to truth and to new knowledge, life flows more fully and we have the opportunity to apply the knowledge so that we can control our lives and thus "inherit the earth."

"Blessed are they who do hunger and thirst after righteousness, for they shall be filled."

Keynote = the creative use of passions
Planet = Venus
Tree of Life = Netzach (Victory)

Our passions and emotions can cause us to hunger and thirst for that which may not be beneficial. As we learn to apply the creative drive of our passions appropriately and direct them in a controlled, rather than lustful, manner, we fill ourselves with the creative life forces, love, and idealism.

"Blessed are the merciful, for they shall obtain mercy."

Keynote = Abundant mercy and divine compassion
Planet = Jupiter
Tree of Life = Chesed (Mercy)

The amount of abundance in any area of our life is equal to the amount we give out. The more we give, the more we receive. This is part of natural law, as previously discussed. It involves the Law of Compensation and the Law of Receiving, in conjunction with the Law of Attraction.

"Blessed are the pure in heart, for they shall see God."

Keynote = Purity and transmutation through Love
Planet = Sun
Tree of Life = Tiphareth (Beauty)

In the earlier section on the parables, we briefly discussed the significance of the number six. In the Tree of Life, the sixth level is Tiphareth, the level of Christ consciousness—achieved only through purity and the alchemical process of transmutation. Tiphareth is the level of consciousness within humanity that activates healing energies—one of the most dynamic gifts demonstrated by Christ Jesus. When one awakens the heart center fully—as represented astrologically by the sun and qabalistically by Tiphareth—the higher vision of the Divine opens to the individual.

"Blessed are the peacemakers, for they shall be called children of God."

Keynote = Strength through Harmony
Planet = Mars
Tree of Life = Geburah (Severity and Strength)

Working for peace requires discipline and strength. We each must learn to bring peace and harmony to ourselves and thus to the world. This is accomplished by a strong assertion of the divine Will-force within. Its application requires harmony or the discipline and strength will become ascetic and cruel. We must develop our strengths like they were children—with firmness and gentleness. The result will be peace.

"Blessed are they who are persecuted for righteousness sake, for theirs is the kingdom of heaven."

Keynote = Higher understanding of sacrifice
Planet = Saturn
Tree of Life = Binah (Understanding)

All of life serves a purpose. The path of the aspirant or the disciple is filled with choices and decisions, and sometimes sorrows and burdens. As we learn to understand their hidden significance, the clarity of the path we are walking becomes crystallized. We can see the kingdom to which it is leading. This also implies the hidden law of karma. A true disciple chooses to accelerate his or her growth by taking on the tests and lessons of life more

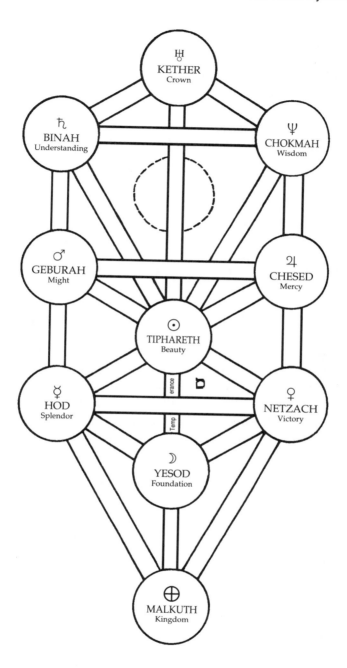

Mystical Tree of Life of the Hebrew Qabala.

fully. The meeting of karma is expanded, so that the individual may take on ten lifetimes' worth of work within the course of one. Such a task may seem a burden, but it is right that all karma be met. As we meet our responsibilities, we earn the right to the Kingdom of Heaven.

"Blessed are ye when men revile you and persecute you, and shall say all manner of evil against you falsely, for my sake."

Keynote = Self-mastery and the Power of Faith
Planet = Neptune
Tree of Life = Chocmah (Wisdom)

Neptune is known as the planet of divinity. It is a symbol of the unconscious mind, that which we are striving to become more conscious of. As we develop faith—not as a belief but as a power in the universe—we open ourselves to a mystical vision of the divine. In the Qabala Chocmah is the level at which we attain to true spiritual wisdom. At this level of consciousness, the energy is so strong and so pure that nothing negative can ultimately manifest. Thus, although on the surface things may not be going well, its ultimate effect will be dynamically positive. Regardless of one's life conditions, this is the promise that in the end it will all work itself out, and the blessings will come. This is that stage upon the path of discipleship where the individual can see the inner wheels of the universe in movement and have the vision of where all events are leading, regardless of how they may appear. He or she can see behind the clouds of life or beneath the waters of the world.

"Rejoice and be exceedingly glad, for great is your reward in Heaven."

Keynote = Synthesis and union
Planet = Uranus
Tree of Life = Kether (Crown)

As the aspirant and disciple upon the spiritual path begins to synthesize the spiritual with the physical, the rewards are great. Uranus in Greek mythology was united with Gaia. Uranus is heaven and Gaia is earth. They are wed. Kether is opposite Malkuth. This is the crown of discipleship in the Christ Mysteries. It is the highest expression of universal love and intuition, the linking of the soul so as to liberate oneself from the lower personality.

OCCULT AND PSYCHIC PHENOMENA
OF THE SCRIPTURES

Much criticism is leveled at those who are working within the metaphysical, psychic and spiritual fields. The psychic sciences are still often ridiculed, scoffed at by many of the more orthodox and fundamental literalists of modern Christianity. Demonstrations of psychic phenomena are often accused of being the work of the "devil" or some other negative and unseen agency. What these literalists often do not understand is that these same phenomena were demonstrated by the Christ Jesus. The apostles and disciples were taught the use of various energies in order to perform these "wondrous" acts. The following is a partial catalogue of psychic phenomena found within New Testament Scriptures. (The Old Testament is also replete with examples, but the focus of this work is upon the manifestation of the Christ Mysteries.)

Clairvoyance
Matthew 3: 13–17
Luke 1: 39-45
John 4: 4-42
Acts 16:9

Control of Aura
Matthew 14: 34-36
Mark 9: 2-8
Matthew 14: 22-33

Psychometry
John 4: 16-19 Luke 2: 36-40
Matthew 20: 17-19
Acts 6:5
Acts 8: 5-40
Acts 21:8

Control of Elements
(alchemy, levitation, etc.)
Matthew 14: 22-33
Luke 8: 22-25
John 2: 1-12
John 6: 1-14
John 6: 16-24
Acts 5: 19-21

Prophecy
Luke 1:67-80

Counseling
John 4:16-26
Acts 5: 3-6, 9-10

Spiritual Gifts
I Corinthians 12: 1-30

Higher Communication in Dreams
Matthew 1: 20-25
Matthew 2:13
Matthew 27:19

Spirit and Angelic Communication
Matthew 26:53
Matthew 28:9
Mark 16:20
Luke 1: 1-38
Luke 4: 10-11
Mark 16:20
John 14: 26
Acts 11: 12-15
Acts 4:31
Acts 8: 26-30
Hebrew 1: 13,14

Healing by Magnetized Articles
Matthew 14: 34-36
Acts 19:11-12

Gifts of Healing
Matthew 9:27-30
Matthew 9: 32-33
Matthew 8: 28-32
Matthew 17:14-21
Matthew 9: 2-7
Matthew 8: 14-15
Mark 8: 22-25

Gifts of Healing
Mark 10: 46-52
Mark 1: 40-44
Luke 17: 11-19
Luke 9:2
Luke 10:9
Luke 7: 1-10
Luke 8: 43-48
John 9
John 11: 1-44
John 4: 46-53
John 5: 8-9

This list is by no means complete. Many phenomena and forms of mediumship can also be found. This includes forms of trance and seances, the appearance of spirit lights, the phenomenon of apportation, independent spirit voice, materialization, fire mediumship, and much more. The occult phenomena of the spiritual path is reflected within the teachings of the Christ Mysteries. To many these phenomena are not understood, but as more people begin to open to the metaphysical realms and teachings, as more begin to explore the ethereal realms and become familiar with them, the "spookiness" of such phenomena will disappear. It must be kept in the mind of the spiritual disciple, though, that the manifestation of the phenomena is not the goal. The goal of the true disciple is the *truth*—and it is the development of these occult abilities that assist us in the discovery of the truth within our lives.

"I am the way and the truth and the life . . . "

John 14: 6

Chapter Four

RESURRECTION OF THE FEMININE MYSTERIES

"A great sign appeared in the sky, a woman clothed with
the sun, with the moon under her feet, and on her head a
crown of twelve stars."

Revelation 12:1

Part of the function of the true Christian Mysteries was to restore
the Divine Feminine. Every mystery school taught the balance of
the male and female within the individual. Only by accomplishing
this could the divine child within be born. Unfortunately, the
scriptures, as we have them, are relatively thin in regard to the
function of the feminine energy in general, but also of the female
initiates in particular.

Students of the more traditional mystery systems rendered
homage and reverence to the feminine aspects of life as equally as
the masculine. Within the Mystery Schools were many myths of the
Divine World Mothers: Isis of Egypt, Tiamat of Babylonia, Gaia of
Greece, the Navajo Changing Woman, Nu Kwa of China, and many
others. Every society has its catalogue of myths and tales in which

were veiled the mysteries of life and the universe. Every society has a plentitude of myths and tales of the Feminine aspects of life. There is no shortage of magnificent female persons and goddesses.

Intuition and imagination are the two vital principles of the Feminine. They, in turn, give birth to fertility and divinity. In the Western world, during the latter days of the pre-Christian era, the pagan religions were being abused. The mystery ideals were being misunderstood and unbalanced through an increasing centeredness in the outer brain consciousness of humanity. Humanity was overstimulating the masculine elements of its nature.

The early Christian Initiates knew that living the Christ Mysteries would awaken the Feminine once more in the ages to come, opening increasing numbers to higher vision and illumination. The Feminine typifies the awakened and illumined soul—the only kind of soul in which the divine within ourselves may be borne.

The teachings of Christ Jesus served a purpose of restoring a balance between the masculine and feminine aspects of life, within the individual and within the world. The leaders of Palestine—especially those who were schooled in some of the esoteric principles—must have recognized this within the Christ teachings. And in a society that was extremely patriarchal—as Judaism was at that time—it created a threat.

As mentioned earlier, the Sadducees and the Pharisees were the two predominant sects of Judaism. The mysteries were being held by the privileged and few. Then along came the Christ Jesus who made the mysteries available to all, and on top of this, focused upon the teachings of the Feminine. The Love-Wisdom aspect stressed through the teachings of Christ Jesus is the Feminine Principle upon which true illumination manifests and the kingdom of heaven is achieved. Love is a major aspect of the Feminine. It is little wonder that the leaders of Judaism were so confounded and angered.

It is the Feminine which enables us to attune more to the subjective side of life. It is this hidden phase that Christ Jesus came to restore. Although the scriptures are relatively scant in regard to female persons, the teachings are filled with revelations of the Feminine mysteries. As we live the Christ Mysteries, the Feminine within us comes to life naturally, regardless of whether we can identify it as such or not. Living the "Golden Rule" as found within the previously discussed Sermon on the Mount is the means to awaken the Feminine aspect of our lives. It awakens the subjective side. It gives birth to an increasing awareness of how lives and events are intertwined.

There have been many symbols, images, phrases, and metaphors from all of the ancient traditions that are tied to the feminine energies of the universe. Many of these same images and symbols are found within the teachings of Christ Jesus, thus providing clues to the feminine teachings of the scriptures. Not all of the following are found within Christian Scripture, but many are. (We must keep in mind also that there was often, in the early centuries of the church, a great deal of censorship of material.) The vase, the bride, the moon, the sun, various planets, caves, volcanoes, rivers, lakes, lioness, serpents, cows, mares, whales, crows, herons, doves, fig trees, corn, marigolds, and many more are found within all traditions and apply to some aspect of the feminine force within the universe. To ancient and modern astrologers, the Earth is a female planet—hinting that all of humanity has come to learn more about the Divine Feminine.

There are parables and teachings in the scriptures that use these same images and symbols, indicating that Christ Jesus was teaching some aspect of the Feminine. Some accounts of the birth of Jesus place the Holy Family in a cave and not a stable. The parable of the bride. The wedding feast at Cana. The fact that most of the travels and teachings of Christ Jesus occur around water, a universal symbol of the Feminine Forces of the Universe, is profoundly significant. Christ Jesus fought the patriarchal society, calling their leaders hypocrites, for one is not illumined without the expression of the Divine Feminine Wisdom. It is this Mother Wisdom that helps us to recover the child, and Christ Jesus spoke often of children.

The Christ Jesus breathed new life and expression into the ancient images and teachings of the Feminine. He stirred the imagination and the creative forces of those he touched, and these feminine aspects restore our individual sense of power and control over our lives. The scriptures are an allegory for the redemption of the Divine Feminine. "Be ye Loving (compassionate) as your Creator in Heaven is Loving (compassionate)." (Luke 6:36).To the modern mystic, Matthew Fox, this signifies much about the redemption of the Divine Feminine: "True redemption is always about compassion—an awakening of passion with God and all God's creation and children."

It is this aspect that we will outline through this chapter. We will explore some of the major occult teachings about the Feminine within the Christ Mysteries. We will explore the major events in the life of Christ Jesus as an allegory of the Seven Feminine Initiations and the Seven Masculine Initiations, along with other events that teach particular aspects of the Feminine Mysteries. We will examine specific scriptures and their significance in awakening the Feminine Forces within our lives. We will also examine the importance of the major female characters within the scriptures—particularly the highest female Initiate of the time, Mary the Mother of Jesus.

THE HIDDEN FEMININE WITHIN THE LIFE OF CHRIST JESUS

As mentioned earlier, all of the events in the life of Christ Jesus have a significance other than historical. The major events were an enactment of the Mysteries that previously had only been done in ritual within the Mystery temples. The entire life was a living example of the Mystery Teachings. Thus, anyone willing to put forth the effort could begin the process of exploring the Mysteries, simply by beginning with the major events.

Most of the ancient traditions taught the balance of the male and female, the positive and the negative, the yang and the yin, the electric and the magnetic, the rational and the intuitive. It is by bringing the male and female together that the divine child within us is born. Both aspects have their function and purpose in the unfoldment and evolution of humanity. Both aspects exist within us all, and each must find the means of harmonizing them within the individual life circumstances. Each must learn to experience and express them.

We will explore, in the second half of this book, the cycle of Christ energy as it plays within our lives and affects us with each passing season. As we will see, the Christ energy creates a quickening of all life in a particular manner—one in accordance with the changes of the season. Thus, there is a season in which the Christ energy facilitates our awakening and directing of our feminine energies, and there is a season in which the masculine aspect of us is more accessible. There is also a season for preparation, and a season for blending the two.

Seven, in the ancient mystery traditions, was a sacred number. It was a symbol of the individual rising from the material plane, striving for the spiritual. It represented the spiritual path that leads back to the Source. It is a sacred number because inherent within it lies the answers to the mysteries of physical life. The creative process of the universe was six days, the seventh being the day in which it was all synthesized—the Sabbath or Day of Rest. It is the number of knowledge of the world—physical and spiritual. (The four and three which comprise the seven reflects this. The four is the physical, and the three is the spiritual, which rests upon the physical foundation.)

There have been many correspondences associated with the number seven. There are seven days in a week. There are seven colors in the rainbow. There are seven major planets. There are seven senses (hearing, taste, touch, smell, sight, common sense or synthesis, and intuition). There are seven major systems to the body. There are seven chakric centers of the body. Metaphysics teaches that humans have seven bodies, six more subtle than the physical. In scripture we learn of the seven gifts of the Holy Spirit (the Feminine active within humanity). Thus seven is often called "The Holy Number."

THE SEVEN FEMININE CHRIST MYSTERIES

The following mysteries will be elaborated upon in the second half of the book, in the chapter on "Rite of the Winter Solstice."

1. *The Annunciation*
   The announcement to Mary by the Archangel Gabriel
      that she will give birth to Jesus.
   Manifests a glorified vision and illumination that
      arises from balancing the masculine and the feminine.
   Reflected astrologically by the Moon in Taurus.

2. *The Immaculate Conception*
   The conception of the child Jesus.
   The spiritual power of new vision is impressed upon
      the body.
   Reflected astrologically by the Moon in Taurus.

3. *The Holy Birth*
   The birth of the child Jesus.
   Manifests a birth of the creative will; awakens new
   power.
   Reflected astrologically by Mars in Capricorn.

4. *The Presentation in the Temple*
   Jesus is blessed and dedicated to God according to the
   Law of Moses
   The aspirant dedicates his/her own unique life to the
   spiritual.
   Reflected astrologically by wherever the sun is.

5. *Flight into Egypt*
   The family flees in response to Herod's decree.
   The temporary veiling of the inner life which occurs in
   the development of all aspirants because of outer
   world influence.
   Reflected astrologically by Saturn in Libra.

6. *The Teaching in the Temple*
   Jesus at age twelve, separated from parents and found in
   the temple at Jerusalem talking with the teachers.
   Manifests an expanding consciousness through the
   blending of the heart and mind.
   Reflected astrologically by Mercury in Virgo.

7. *The Baptism*
   The baptism of Jesus at the hands of John the Baptist.
   The initiation of opening to full, conscious sight and
   the full understanding of discrimination, indicated by
   the temptation which followed.
   The Baptism is reflected astrologically by Jupiter in
   Cancer.
   The Temptation aspect is reflected astrologically by
   Mars or Uranus in Scorpio.

THE SEVEN MASCULINE CHRIST MYSTERIES

(These will be elaborated upon in the second half of the book, in the chapter on "Rite of the Vernal Equinox." The feminine allow for a development of gifts and energies, and the masculine assist us in honing and expressing them properly.)

1. *Transfiguration*
   Christ Jesus reveals true archangelic essence to Peter, James, and John.
   Manifests ability to raise the consciousness and touch the Divine, regardless of time or space.
   Reflected astrologically by Mars or Uranus in Scorpio.

2. *Triumphal Entry*
   The Christ Jesus comes into Jerusalem , riding an ass, while the people wave palms and sing hosannas.
   Reflects the attainment of soul wisdom through having raised the consciousness and expressed the Feminine.
   Reflected astrologically by Mercury in Aquarius.

3. *Feast in the Upper Room*
   The ritual of the last supper with Christ Jesus and the Apostles.
   The teaching of the alchemical process
   the transmutation of energies through the balance of the male and female.
   Reflected astrologically by the balancing of the sun sign with its polar opposite in the wheel of the zodiac.

4. *Garden of Gethsemane*
   The period in which Christ Jesus retires to the garden and faces the ultimate commitment to sacrifice and selflessness.
   The part of the initiatory path where the disciple surrenders the last of personal will for Divine will, sometimes called the dark night of the soul—ultimate commitment to compassion.
   Reflected astrologically by Venus in Pisces and Saturn in Capricorn.

5. *The Trial*
   The trial of Christ Jesus before the Sanhedrin, Pilate, and Herod.
   The facing of the temptation to use one's higher vision and power for self or in selfless love.
   Reflected astrologically by Saturn or Neptune in Scorpio.

6. *The Crucifixion*
   The hanging of Christ Jesus upon the Cross and the ensuing death.
   Demands ability to face cruelty of others, renouncing all but what is our endeavor to spiritual realization.
   Reflected in astrology by Venus in Pisces.

7. *The Resurrection*
   The Christ Jesus overcomes death.
   The disciple learns the realization of immortal love and life, learning to consciously bridge sleep and wakefulness, life and death.
   Reflected astrologically by the Sun in Aries.

THE OCCULT FEMININE
IN THE SYMBOL OF THE CROSS

There is much significance associated with this dynamic symbol. Many assume it is a symbol of Christianity alone. The cross was a symbol used in almost all societies around the world. Its meaning varied somewhat, but the commonalities are stronger. The true cross for the Christ Mysteries is the equal armed cross. It is a symbol of a balanced union of the masculine and feminine energies.

The horizontal bar of the cross is a symbol of the Feminine, and the vertical bar is the symbol of the Masculine. Unfortunately, the "Calvary Cross" associated with modern Christendom maintains a shorter horizontal bar than the vertical—a reflection of the patriarchal attitude still fending off the powerful significance of the Divine Feminine. Part of the esotericism of the Crucifixion is the sacrificing of the Masculine (in the form of Christ Jesus) so that the Feminine can regain its rightful place within the modern world.

The "Way of the Cross" is the path of Initiation within the Christ Mysteries. The Fourteen Stations of the Cross found within modern Catholicism have much occult significance—much more than a representation of final events in the life of Christ Jesus. It reflects the activity of the spiritual fires of the creative life force (kundalini) and its ascent up the spine on one level, and on other levels it reflects much about the Feminine Mysteries. To the Christian Gnostic, it is through the Feminine that humanity finds the "saving blood of the Christ." (This is reflected in the following outline of these stations. After each fall, the Christ Jesus has a meeting with a woman. He draws upon the Feminine for greater strength.)

THE STATIONS OF THE CROSS*

1. Christ Jesus condemned to death
   (Dedication to Initiation)

2. Christ Jesus takes up his cross.
   (The path of Initiation)

3. Christ Jesus falls the first time.
   (Symbolic of human frailty)

4. Christ Jesus meets his mother.
   (Ideal of the exalted Feminine)

5. Simon helps carry the cross.
   (Simon's dedication to discipleship)

6. Veronica wipes the face of Christ Jesus.
   (Transmutation of the Feminine)

7. Christ Jesus falls a second time.
   (Symbolic of failure through desire)

8. Christ Jesus speaks to the weeping women.
   (Sorrow for the degradation of women)

* Extracted from *New Age Bible Interpretation* by Corinne Heline.

9. Christ Jesus falls a third time.
   (Symbolic of the material mind)

10. Christ Jesus is stripped of his garments.
    (Renunciations)

11. Christ Jesus is nailed to the cross.
    (Development of stigmata)

12. Christ Jesus dies on the cross.
    (Initiation consummated)

13. Christ Jesus is taken from the cross.
    (Liberation from the body)

14. Christ Jesus is laid in the tomb.
    (Path of further Initiation)

THE FEMALE INITIATES OF THE CHRIST MYSTERIES

When most people examine the scriptures, at first glance it may appear as if the women followers of Christ Jesus were sadly ignored. Upon closer examination, we find that women play a predominant role within the Christ mysteries. Women at this period in history—in this area of the world—held a generally inferior position to males in the society. Because of this, the influence of Mary the mother of Jesus and the other women initiates is often difficult to discover.

This also has significance for the placing of the mysteries before all people. The feminine role—which Christ Jesus taught and demonstrated—is powerful, but also very subtle. The Feminine must be searched out and manifested within each of us—just as it must be done within the scriptural writings. Although much of the detail of the women followers of Christ Jesus is not explicit in the canonical books of the New Testament, in extant and apocryphal writings many of the missing pieces can be found. Traditional concepts of the Feminine sensitivity, taught in all the esoteric traditions, is also found in modern scripture. The women we do know about often exert a strength and a courage that enables them to risk taking new steps in their lives—and they appear to do so more easily than the men. The first witnesses to the resurrection are Mary Magdalene, Mary the mother of Jesus, and Joanna. The intuitive, feminine aspect made them more sensitive to the hidden power of the event. This is even more emphasized when the Apostles do not believe their story. The masculine aspect cannot see as clearly.

Joanna is described in the writings of Luke as a strong woman. Her husband was a highly placed court official of Herod, and she left her husband to follow this new path. She left the old masculine energy to give assertion to her own.

There are other women that demonstrate that inner strength that allows them to run the risk of taking new steps within their lives. Salome, the wife of Zebedee, presents her two sons to Christ Jesus, to be his disciples. (These are James and John.) She will eventually follow her own way in the Christ Mysteries. There were "other women who used their resources to help Jesus and his disciples" (Luke 8:1-3), and one named Suzanna was such. Mary, the mother of Mark, opened her home in Jerusalem to the Christ Jesus and his disciples. It was in her home that the Last Supper would take place. She is a dynamic symbol of the feminine energy operating through the plane of service."Luke speaks of prophetesses like Hanna and the daughters of Philip; and women entrepreneurs . . . slaves who have gained their freedom . . ." and other strong women who supported the Christ Jesus (Elisabeth Moltmann-Wendel, *The Women Around Jesus*).

When mentioned in the scriptures, they are often given in the traditional three of the ancient mysteries. The Feminine expressed itself in three aspects: virgin, mother, and wise woman. The story of Mary has three levels to it: as a virgin in the Immaculate Conception, as the mother of Jesus and as the wise woman of the Mysteries, the highest female Initiate of the time. It is three women who first learn of the resurrection. Anna (the mother of Mary), Elizabeth (her cousin), and Mary, herself, are tied together as three degrees of prophetic development. Of the women mentioned by name at the cross of Christ Jesus in the Book of Mark, there are three: Mary Magdalene, Mary the mother of James the younger, and Salome.

We are told within the scriptures of the women looking on at the death of Jesus, but there is no mention of men observing the strength that derives from the feminine energies of life. This is reflected also within the denial by Peter. The masculine expression of love was not enough to withstand the pressures of the outer world. The inner feminine love is strong enough.

The scriptures also demonstrate the power of the Feminine and its innate sensitivity—even when one is not aligned with the Christ teachings. This is strongly revealed in the case of Pilate's wife. Her innate sensitivity urged her to give sage advice to have nothing to do with the Jesus situation.

It is often wondered why so many women in the scriptures had the name Mary. The more exoteric aspect is that it was a popular name at that time among the wealthy and those of higher society. On a more esoteric level, it has great importance in drawing attention to the significance of the Feminine Mysteries. The name has two pre-dominant meanings: "myrrh," or if traced further back, "from the sea." The Mystery Traditions of many societies used the water element—the sea—as a symbol of the Divine Feminine. All life comes forth from the sea. The Great Ocean of the Divine gives birth to the universe. Out of the waters of life come new being. In most esoteric traditions, at a certain stage of development the individual would take upon himself or herself an "Initiate Name." This name would reflect the energies most reverenced and honored by the individual. The women in the scriptures—just as with the men—were often already schooled in varying degrees of esoteric tradition.

We must remember that, aside from the historical aspect of the scriptures, everything within it has an esoteric significance. The fact that we are time and again confronted with the name "Mary" should make us want to explore further.

The women followers of Christ Jesus had an interrelatedness and an "occult" aspect that can be discerned by those who will put forth such effort. More than one esoteric tradition teaches that Mary, the mother of Jesus, had her own group of disciples with whom she worked more directly in their training and evolvement. The Rosicrucian Tradition refers to there being two "Feasts in the Upper Room," being held in chambers side by side. One involved the innermost circle of Christ Jesus and was overseen by him. The other involved the innermost circle of the female disciples, and this was overseen by Mary, the Blessed Mother—the male and female brought together to receive the last teaching on the alchemical processes of life.

Among the women followers of Christ were Martha and Mary.
Engraving by Gustave Doré

It is hard to determine who the twelve female disciples were. There are many women mentioned, and each has a symbolic significance. Their specific roles, though, are not as clearly defined as their male counterparts. This reflects the difference between the intuitive and the rational—the female and the male energies respectively.

Anna was the mother of Mary, and she was trained in the ancient Essene tradition, as was Elizabeth, Mary's cousin, and mother of John the Baptist. Mary's visit with Elizabeth, early in her pregnancy, reflects the feminine tradition of many other societies in which the Mysteries of birth and the sacred truths of the pre-natal period are shared, woman-to-woman.

There are tales and legends about an Essene named Judith who would oversee the early training of Jesus in the Essene tradition. There is also Mary Magdalene. She is a dynamic symbol of the transformation and life that begins with proper expression of the Feminine forces. She is a symbol of the movement all can make from the lowest to the highest, and thus she is a model for the Christ Initiate.

We also learn from the scriptures about Martha and Mary of Bethany. They are sisters. Mary is the idealist, and is a symbol of the inner. Martha is more practical and reflects an outer expression of the Feminine. Both aspects are needed—the inner and the outer, and thus they are always shown together. Legend tells us that they traveled with Joseph of Arimathea, helping him to carry the Grail Chalice to new lands.

We have mentioned Mary of Jerusalem, the mother of Mark. She was well-to-do and opened her home to Christ Jesus and his disciples. It would be in the upper rooms of her home that the Last Supper would occur. She is a symbol of the feminine energies operating within the field of service.

There is mention of another Mary, the wife of Cleophas who was the brother of Joseph. She has come to be a symbol of strength and courage upon the path. One by the name of Marianne can also be found associated with the Christ Mysteries. She was the sister of the Apostle Philip. One legend tells that she would make the bread (an ancient symbol of the feminine energies) for the "Feast in the Upper Room." The wife and daughter of Philip are also mentioned, but little is known, other than that they were around. The same is true for Peter's wife, Petronilla, and his mother-in-law.

The last of the specific women mentioned in the scriptures appears when the Christ Jesus is carrying the cross up to Golgotha. This is Veronica, who wipes his face, leaving his imprint upon the cloth. Veronica is a symbol of the etheric energy of the human which must become more sensitized (more attuned to the Feminine) if the Christ energy is to impress itself within the life of the individual. Only then is true sight restored.

On this same path up to Golgotha, the Christ Jesus speaks to a group of weeping women after his second fall. This reflects a recognition and sorrow for the degradation of the Divine Feminine, but it also indicates that strength must be drawn from the Feminine if the complete path of initiation is to open to the individual.

Through the writings of Paul and the book of Acts, we learn much about women who would become disciples and initiates of the Christ Mysteries after the death and resurrection. Some of these are Priscilla, Claudia, and Lydia, the first woman disciple of Paul. We learn about Lois, the grandmother of Timothy and Eunice, his mother. Apocryphal texts provide insight into others such as Phoebe, Thecla, and the wife of Simon of Cyrene.

The Feminine Mysteries live on strongly, silently, developing and conceiving perpetually within the world. They were not relegated to a subservient level in the true occult Christ Mysteries. Rather they were honored and reverenced and nurtured within all who strove to be born again, for birth never occurs without the masculine *and* the feminine. One cannot exist without the other.

THE MYSTERIES OF THE BLESSED MOTHER

Mary is the highest female Initiate living at the time of the Christ Jesus. Around her are the keys to the true Feminine Mysteries associated with the Christ teachings. These will be explored more fully in the chapter on "The Rite of the Winter Solstice," for this is the time of the year in which the Christ energies playing upon and within the planet can facilitate the awakening of the Feminine energies within ourselves.

She is shown in the traditional three aspects of the Divine Feminine: the virgin, the mother, and the wise woman. She was dedicated by her parents, Joachim and Anna, to the spiritual life through the Essene tradition, just as they were. She is a dynamic symbol of the illumined soul—the only kind of soul that can give birth to the divine child within.

Both Mary and Joseph were type-patterns of the spiritual expression of the feminine and the masculine through the lesser mysteries of the initiatory path. This is the path that was to be taken by the Apostles and the other disciples, prior to the death of Christ Jesus. Mary would go further. She would undergo the Great Initiations within the course of her life—achieving levels beyond the Apostles.

These Great Initiations are sometimes referred to as the Initiation by Water, Fire, Air, and Earth. The water initiation refers to work upon the emotions. If our emotional waters are controlled, they reflect—opening spiritual sight. This was indicated by the Annunciation.

The fire initiation involves conquering the desire aspects of the soul. Fire can be destructive or creative. It can inspire or it can burn. This initiation requires learning to control the inner forces of our own creative fires—the kundalini—so the highest expression of light can come forth. This was reflected in the life of Mary through the Immaculate Conception.

The air initiation involves control and conscious illumination of the mind. It is the Christing of the mind by which time and space are transcended. It awakens the "Power of the Word." It is reflected in the life of Mary at Pentecost.

The fourth Great Initiation undergone by her is that of earth. This involves the process of transmutation of the physical atoms of energy through spiritual power. It is mastery over everything physical. Many are the tales of masters and divine beings who do not age or who choose to appear in a certain form. This is an aspect of the earth initiation. It is reflected through the Assumption within the life of Mary.

This High Initiate aspect of Mary is reflected through the "Way of the Cross." Mary would be the only follower to walk the entire road to Golgotha with Christ Jesus. This symbolizes that she was the only one able to experience it at its highest and truest level. She had prepared her whole life for this.

Apocryphal and canonical texts reveal her communication with the angelic hierarchy throughout her life. She now works to assist humanity in awakening the Feminine and to work in cooperation with the Angelic Hierarchies for the evolution of all.

While the Christ moved from an external Solar Logos to an indwelling Planetary Logos, Mary moved from the indwelling Feminine prototype to the now-external Divine force. With the birth of the Christ Mysteries, the process of switching the polarity of energy expression began. Where the masculine was expressed in the outer and the Feminine through the inner, now the Feminine is beginning to be more expressed within the outer life of humanity and will continue to do so. This combination of energies descends upon us in accordance with the cyclic nature of our seasons and the months.

The influence and magnification of the Feminine upon the planet follows a monthly cycle that can be celebrated. (This monthly cycle has ancient ties to the menstrual cycle of women everywhere—the ebb and flow that occurs in the course of a month.) Each month of the year gives us the opportunity to celebrate an aspect of the Divine Feminine as they were expressed through Mary within the Christ Mysteries:

JANUARY—*Feast of the Nativity*
  Keynote — Birth of the Higher self; Better things to come
  Symbol — Dawn
  Flower — Hyacinth

FEBRUARY—*Feast of Purification*
  Keynote — Dedication to the spiritual
  Symbol — Gate
  Flower — Snowdrop

MARCH—*Feast of Annunciation*
  Keynote — Soul Power and New Vision
  Symbol — Root
  Flower — White Lily/Marigold

APRIL—*The Sunrise Ceremony*
  Keynote — Life, death, and immortality
  Symbol — Grape
  Flower — Primrose

MAY—*Feast of Transmutation*
  Keynote — Blessings of Nature

Symbol — Corn-sheath
Flower — Rose

JUNE—*Feast of Love*
Keynote— Higher expression of love
Symbol — Rose
Flower — Iris/Rose

JULY—*Feast of Visitation*
Keynote — The sacred truths of birth
Symbol — Fountain
Flower — White Lily

AUGUST—*Feast of the Assumption*
Keynote — Transmutation
Symbol — Chalice
Flower — Sunflower

SEPTEMBER—*Feast of Mary's Nativity*
Keynote — Healing, illumination, and peace
Symbol — Temple
Flower — Golden Rod

OCTOBER—*Feast of the Illumined Heart*
Keynote — Transforming of karma held within the heart
Symbol — Shrine
Flower — Rosemary

NOVEMBER—*Feast of the Dead*
Keynote — The Dark Mother and the benediction of the dead
Symbol — Beacon
Flower — Chrysanthemum

DECEMBER—*Feast of the Immaculate Conception*
Keynote — Idealism of the mystical child
Symbol — Mirror
Flower — Poinsettia

THE AUTHORITY OF THE BLESSED MOTHER

There is often much discussion of the influence and role of Mary in the development of the Christ Mysteries after the death of Christ Jesus. Esoteric tradition teaches that Mary oversaw the activities of the Apostles and the other disciples, as a silent head. In the society at the time, women could not take the outer more dominant role. This was the task of the Apostles. It was her task to oversee all that occurred.

Our greatest clue to this occurs when Christ Jesus is hanging upon the cross. As mentioned, Mary walked the Way of the Cross with Christ Jesus. She, alone, had the ability to understand the full significance of the events. Even John, the one whom Christ Jesus loved and who was the highest Initiate of the Apostles, is not described in the scenes along "The Way of the Cross" up to Golgotha. Thus, as highly initiated as he was, he was not on the level of Mary.

In the Book of John, chapter 19, verses 25-27, we discover much. In it are the third of the "Seven Last Words" discussed frequently within the orthodox Christian Churches: "Near the cross of Jesus there stood his mother, Mary, the wife of Clopas, and Mary Magdalene. Seeing his mother there with the disciple whom he loved, Jesus said to his mother, 'Woman, behold thy son.' In turn he said to the disciple, 'Behold thy mother.'"

This contains much hidden significance, having levels of meaning. The most obvious, and most commonly assumed, was that they were being placed in each other's care. With Mary, though, now as the highest Initiate, she was being given the authority over the conception and development of the Christ Mysteries. She was to assume authority over the Apostles, and the Apostles were to see her as such. Her role would be in the background as guide and inspiration and teacher—the traditional role of the Mother—but upon spiritual levels.

There are, of course, other significances to these phrases. What is important to our scope is the understanding that the Feminine must be kept strong and vital within the teachings. It is interesting to note that, in this piece of scripture, there are three women initiates at the cross, and only one of the Apostles. Again it reflects that the women were able to experience the full spiritual significance of the event, while only the one male disciple could at the time. (We also have the significance again of the "three" women.)

This entire scene in the book of John reflects much about the role of Mary in the future development and unfoldment of the Christ teachings. It has strong parallels to the first major event described in the writings of John—the Marriage at Cana in chapter two. "Marriage" was one of the "clue" words used in many esoteric traditions. It has hidden within it the occult significance of alchemy, and the bringing together of opposites through love.

In the marriage event at Cana, Mary informs Christ Jesus that there is no more wine. Jesus response is "Woman, how does this concern of yours involve me? My hour has not yet come." Mary does not respond other than to tell the waiters to do whatever Jesus asks. She knows that Christ Jesus will follow the prompting of the Divine Feminine. Christ Jesus goes on to change the water into wine—the alchemical transmutation.

In this scene, as in the one at the foot of the cross, there is the presence of the Mother, the use of women and the mention of the hour. Now that the hour has come, Mary has been given the role. The Divine Feminine has been given the authority and Christ impulse for humanity and for eternity.

It would be negligent to speak of the authority of Mary and the impulse of humanity toward a greater activation of the Divine Feminine within all without mentioning the event in her life known as the Assumption. In the Assumption, Mary is assumed, body and soul, into the realms of the angelic hierarchy. This can be interpreted in various ways, none of which is entirely incorrect.

Just as with the "giving up of the ghost," the Christ would begin a process of becoming the "indwelling spirit " of the planet, infused within all life and the etheric patterns of energy of the earth, the Assumption of Mary reflects a similar kind of position. The Christ who had operated outside the earth, would now operate within, affecting humanity in cycles from the internal patterns of the earth energies itself. The Feminine which had been hidden within humanity would now operate from the outer, being brought more to life.

Mary is described as working now with the angelic hierarchy, stimulating their influence upon humanity in a more dynamic manner than ever before. She is known as the "Queen of Angels" in the Catholic tradition. She works to amplify and intensify the cooperative efforts of angelic hierarchies with humanity. In the next half of the book, we will learn about the angelic hierarchies influencing and affecting humanity through the rhythms of the yearly cycle and through the various signs of the Zodiac. It will be the influence of Mary that will guide the ministrations of angelic hierarchy, month by month, in accordance with the Christ energies playing upon and affecting humanity season by season. This monthly angelic ministration, overseen by Mary, has ancient ties to the Divine Feminine and the monthly cycle that women experience throughout their lives. Now all of humanity has the feminine energies cycling more dynamically in more powerful rhythms each month.

The Divine Feminine as a new authority upon earth is found within one of the greatest and most powerful prayers within scripture. Often referred to as Mary's Canticle or the "Magnificat," it is found in the first chapter of the Book of Luke. It is filled with great esotericism and it contains an esoteric formula to call forth the Divine Feminine within all:

> "My soul doth magnify the Lord:
> And my spirit rejoices in God my savior,
> For he has regarded the lowliness of his handmaid.
> And behold, from henceforth all generations shall call me
> blessed.
> For He that is mighty doth great things for me and holy
> is His name.
> And His mercy is from generation unto generation to
> them that fear him.
> He hath showed might with his arm.
> And he hath scattered the proud in the conceit of their
> heart.
> He hath put down the mighty from their throne and has
> exalted the lowly.
> He hath filled the hungry with good things; and the rich
> he hath sent away empty.
> He hath received Israel his servant, being mindful of his
> mercy.
> As he spoke to our fathers, to Abraham and to his seed
> forever."
>
> Luke 1: 46-55

Within this canticle are words and phrases that invoke the Divine Feminine. It has ties to the foundations of the Christ Mysteries and the preparation for their revelation since the time of Abraham. The predominant teaching of esoteric Christianity is the teaching of "Polarity of the Masculine and Feminine." It was this mystery that Melchizedek taught to Abraham, and that the Christ would pass on to the disciples, and to the world.

Chapter Five

RITUAL OF THE CROSS
AND THE STAR

The cross and the star are the two predominant symbols of the Christ Mysteries. In the Christ Mysteries themselves, they are the symbols of the "Great Overcoming." The cross is the earth signature of the Christ and the star is the soul signature. The cross is the probationary path of the student and the star is the symbol of the completion of discipleship.

The cross and the star are both symbols of great antiquity, found in most cultures throughout the earth. The star was the great light of the divine that guides and awakens humanity—the seat on the universe of the gods, goddesses, angels and archangels. The symbolism of the Star of Bethlehem reflects this aspect. On one level, it is the light of the Christ hovering over and blessing the one known as Jesus, who would make it possible for the Christ to walk the earth for three years. The star in the Christ mysteries is the inner light of the soul which we are trying to manifest within our lives. It comes to life through the esoteric path of discipleship, the path of the cross.

The cross has great symbolism in all of the ancient mystery traditions. It is the symbol of archetypal humanity. It reflects the harmonizing of the four elements and their union, necessary for the highest expression of the soul. The point of intersection in the cross is the "sacred center" of life. It is the point of communication between the higher and the lower. It is the point at which the spiritual and the physical meet. It is the point of greatest energy and creativity. It is the point where new birth occurs. This is even more significant when we consider that the vertical pole reflects the masculine energy of the universe and the horizontal pole the feminine energy. Whenever the two unite, new birth occurs.

Unfortunately, the Calvary Cross has come to be the symbol for modern Christianity. In this form of the cross, the horizontal bar is shorter in length than the vertical, again reflecting the predominance of the Masculine Energy of the universe. The true form of the cross for the Christ Mysteries is the equal-armed cross; a balanced intersection of the male and female. As humanity learns first to balance the poles of energy (equal-armed cross), then to give expression to its higher gifts, the cross as a symbol of the Christ Mysteries will change. The two intersecting poles of the cross will form the parallel, twin columns of true Christ Initiation—the twin columns of the Christ Mysteries through which the New Age initiate will enter the inner temples.

THE CROSS AND THE STAR OF THE CHRIST MYSTERIES

The following visualization and meditational exercise has a dynamic effect upon the individual, particularly in awakening a sensitivity to the true Christ energies as they play upon and within humanity. It stimulates and strengthens the auric field, and, if persisted with over the course of a year, will awaken inner abilities and open the individual to awarenesses beyond the senses, but in a fully conscious manner. It is excellent in the practice of supersensible meditation.

In this kind of meditation, the individual penetrates into deeper levels and experiences of archetypal energies—in this case, those associated with the Christ Mysteries. In many forms of meditation, the practitioner does not take the efforts far enough. Initially, when the individual begins to meditate, he or she focuses upon an image, a sound, a picture, a seed thought, etc. This, in turn, triggers a release of energy associated with it, into the consciousness of

The Cross and the Star of the Christ Mysteries

the individual. The meditator often receives vibrant images or impressions.

As the individual continues over the course of days and weeks with this same symbol, the images received in response diminish in their intensity and vibrancy. At this point the individual changes to another symbol to meditate upon. This then triggers a fresh release of energy into the consciousness. This, in turn, continues until the vibrancy diminishes, and then the individual changes again. The individual never gets beyond the surface level of energy associated with the archetypal force behind the symbol.

THE RELEASE OF ARCHETYPAL ENERGIES
THROUGH MEDITATION

The Static Intervals provide an opportunity for the energy system—physical and subtle—of the individual to assimilate and become acclimated to the archetypal energy released into his or her life. As the individual continues meditating on the symbol—even though nothing "seems" to be happening—the next level of intensity of the archetypal force will be experienced. This continues until the individual opens to a fully conscious experience of the Archetype.

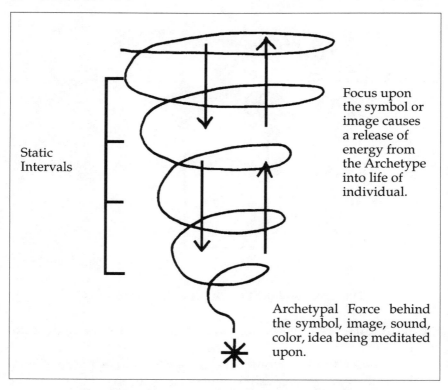

Focus upon the symbol or image causes a release of energy from the Archetype into life of individual.

Static Intervals

Archetypal Force behind the symbol, image, sound, color, idea being meditated upon.

Symbol, image, sound, idea being meditated upon.

The meditator needs to understand that in the process of opening consciously to the full experience of the Archetypes of the Universe, persistence is needed—especially during those static intervals. These are critical periods.

Focus upon any image, symbol, or idea in the meditational process causes a release of the archetypal energy connected with that symbol into the life of the individual. This energy is the source of meditational imagery, new insight, consciousness, and so forth. This energy is invoked by the individual through the meditation symbol. This energy must be assimilated by the individual. His or her own unique energy system must become acclimated to this new release of archetypal energy.

Often there will arise periods where the meditation seems fruitless. Little vibrancy is experienced, as it was when the symbol was first meditated upon. This is a static interval—a period in which the individual's system is becoming acclimated to the energy already released. This must be done before the next, deeper level of intensity can be released by the individual. If the meditator persists, this static interval will pass, and an even more intense experience of the archetypal energy will occur. This continues until there occurs a fully conscious awareness and union with the Archetypal Force itself.

Most will not persist past the first static interval. They become bored or believe that nothing is being accomplished. It just is not being recognized. Thus, the individual moves to another symbol entirely, and new "experiences" occur. If persisted with, these too will reach a point of static interval. This kind of meditation allows only for a surface experience of the archetypal force behind the image and symbol.

This is not to say that such meditation does not serve its purpose, but there should be at least one symbol that we persist with over an extended period. As we learn to touch more deeply the archetypal force of even one symbol, it magnifies the effects of other meditational work.

The following meditation exercise is one that, if persisted with, will open the purity of the hidden Christ Mysteries to the individual in the course of one year—particularly if used with the rites of the seasons, described in Part Two. It will open illumination into all aspects of one's life. It will increase the activity and vibrancy of one's dreams. It heals and balances the auric field. It balances the male and female within the individual. It awakens illumination and it stimulates higher forms of intuition. It accelerates the process of awakening discipleship and initiation into the true Christ Mysteries.

THE CROSS AND THE STAR

This meditation has great symbolic significance and impact upon the life of the individual who employs it with consistency. It is based upon the image shown on page 95. It is comprised of three aspects: the black cross, the seven red roses, and the star. It is important to understand the significance of all aspects before employing the visualization and meditation.

The black cross is a powerful symbol. It is meditated upon in its equal-armed form—the balance of the male and female. The black cross is a symbol of the physical body and physical life consciousness. It is the dynamic symbol of the overcoming of the physical or lower nature. It is the discipline of the probationary path that brings stability and harmony to the physical life.

As the lower self is brought into harmony and control, the individual will give birth to higher expressions of energy. This is reflected in the seven red roses. Seven has always been a mystical number, one often associated with higher knowledge, expressed within the physical life. Within Biblical scripture can be found various references—from Isaiah to St. Paul—concerning the seven gifts of the Holy Spirit.

As we walk the probationary path and open to true discipleship, our inner potentials will manifest. These potentials or gifts—represented by the roses—can be anything that we wish them to be. Often they are the gifts we have most wished to develop. It is important, though, to remain constant in what gifts the roses will symbolize for you. Do not change them from week to week, or month to month. Maintain the significance and emphasis upon them for at least a one-year cycle of the Christ energies.

Seven Gifts of Holy Spirit
Wisdom in discourse (words of wisdom)
Words of knowledge (power to express knowledge)
Gift of faith
Gift of healing and miracles
Gift of prophecy
Gift of discernment of spirit
Gift of languages

Seven Gifts of Light
Wisdom
Understanding
Counsel
Might
Knowledge
Fear of the Lord
Piety

Seven Gifts of Enlightenment
Love
Joy
Peace
Patience
Gentleness
Goodness
Faith

The roses can represent whatever you wish—from great prosperity to higher intuition. (You are not bound to the examples above.) Decide what seven "gifts" you most wish to manifest and express within your life. What things are most important to you and to where you are going? Give this careful consideration, as this exercise sets the archetypal energies in motion within your life that manifest opportunities to develop and unfold such gifts. Many times these "gifts" may manifest in a backdoor fashion. For example, someone wanting to manifest *patience* as one of his or her gifts, may unfold circumstances over the course of the year that will try and test the individual's patience, thereby developing it more strongly.

These gifts do not just "magically" appear. They unfold through the course of our daily lives. Initiation and unfoldment does not occur in artificially contrived situations but through the acting upon opportunities and application within our normal life circumstances. We can visualize and put emotional energy into this, but unless we do something physical to help their unfoldment and express them, they will never manifest. We must learn to manifest the more ethereal energies within the course of our physical lives. And even if these gifts were developed within a past life, they still must be redeveloped and reexpressed on an even higher level.

Meditation

The seven red roses are to be visualized in a circle at the point of intersection of the two bars of the black, equal-armed cross. Visualize each rose unfolding upon the cross—each gift coming to manifestation within your life as you control and direct the lower physical self.

Within the circle of the seven red roses, visualize the star shining. Its energies feed the roses so that they live more vibrantly within your life. Visualize the emanations of the star shining from the very heart of you, through the gifts of the roses out and beyond every aspect of your physical life, symbolized by the black cross. (Again refer to the picture on page 95.) The star is the Christ energy that lives within the heart of all physical life upon the planet and which gives greater impulse and opportunity to express the divine within our individual lives.

The image is an abstraction of the divine within us that serves as a call signal to bring it into greater manifestation.

Allow the image to overlay and penetrate the physical body. This impacts greatly upon the auric field, strengthening and energizing it.

The circle of red roses, surrounding the inner star, should be imaged as encircling one's own heart, where resides the divine spark within all. As you visualize and form the equal-armed cross of balance and polarity, allow each rose to begin to appear and unfold. As each unfolds, singly, think of the "gift" associated with it that is also now unfolding within your life. Continue with this until you have unfolded seven red roses within a circle at the intersection of the black cross. Then visualize a star within the circle of the seven red roses. Visualize it as nourishing and feeding constantly the force of the Christ into your life and into the manifestation of your highest potentials. Visualize this process occurring while awake or asleep—conscious or unconscious—growing stronger within you each day.

Don't limit yourself to the meaning and significance of this image as described within this work. Use it as a foundation, and apply as much individual significance to this image as possible. Allow it to grow in its meaning, and thus its energy.

Take at least ten minutes a day to focus upon and concentrate that image. This allows it to overlay and penetrate the physical body and your life.

Points of intersection are points in which there is great energy, and thus the roses manifest at the point of intersection of the male and female bars of the cross. Performing this visualization and meditation at times of the day in which there is an intersection will enhance its effects. Dusk and dawn are intersections between night and day. Prior to going to sleep and before arising from the bed in the morning are also intersections that separate the waking and sleeping life.

This exercise, when performed as the last thing prior to sleep, has a dynamic effect upon the dream state. It makes the dreams more vibrant and colorful—as well as more significant in revealing growth patterns.

One year of performing this exercise every day will open up levels of perception that are difficult to match through other forms of meditation. It must be done every day, though. Guard against "forgetting" or believing that "skipping one or two days won't hurt." Consistency is the key.

This exercise has the ability to open a conscious vision of the spiritual background of the physical world. Usually this first reveals itself through dreams. It awakens a new awareness and experience of the physical world. It enhances discrimination and can lead to greater opportunity to commune with the spiritual realms. It leads to intuitive cognition of the world on many levels, with an increased ability to synthesize one's life experiences.

Most importantly, it opens the truth of the Christ Mysteries operating upon the planet, and allows the individual to participate in such on a more magnificent scale. Our individual will is transformed into an "organ" of spiritual perception that brings the Love-Wisdom aspect of the Universe alive in all things.

The heart is often described anatomically as a hollow organ "placed obliquely within the chest." At the heart, though, of the Christ Mysteries is the Love-Wisdom which is to be awakened within the heart nature of humanity. The cross and the star are the symbols for the awakening of the higher force and expression of the heart energies. Humanity is the Temple of God and the Heart is the Holy of Holies. It is the inner room and sanctuary in which moves the Divine. Through this meditation, the individual may awaken the Christ which lives within the heart!

"In Israel's Holy of Holies can be heard the soft flutter of angel's wings, the whisper and rustling of curtains, and in the midst the flame of the Covenant—God in His World."

Manly P. Hall
Man—Grand Symbol of the Mysteries

PART TWO

THE INITIATORY RITES OF THE SEASONS

"To everything there is a season and a time for every purpose under Heaven. A time to be born, and a time to die; a time to plant and a time to harvest. A time to kill and a time to heal; a time to tear down and a time to build . . ."

Ecclesiastes 3: 1-3

"The physical body and its needs are geared to the rhythm of days. The soul body replenishes its forces in harmony with the seasonal rhythm of the year. The spirit nourishes its being in accordance with the rhythmic sweep of the reincarnational cycle."

Corinne Heline

"Heard melodies are sweet, but those unheard
Are sweeter; therefore, ye soft pipes, play on;
Not to the sensual ear, but, more endeared,
Pipe to the spirit ditties of no tone . . ."

John Keats

Chapter Six

THE ANGELIC POWER
OF THE SEASONS

"The rounded world is fair to see,
Nine times folded in mystery:
Though baffled seers cannot impart
The secret of its laboring heart,
Throb thine with Nature's throbbing breast,
And all is clear from east to west.
Spirit that lurks each form within
Beckons the spirit of its kin;
Self-kindled every atom glows
And hints the future which it owes."
                    Ralph Waldo Emerson
                                Nature

Every society has taught, at one time or another, the sacredness of
the seasons. The ancient mysteries involved teaching the rhythms
and cycles of nature and spirit, and how to align with them more
harmoniously. Part of our task in unfolding our highest potential
involves aligning all of our energies with the energies and rhythms

of the universe. We must learn to recognize them, align with them and then utilize them to enhance our own life circumstances.

Within the schools of the ancient Mystery Traditions the students would learn of the sacredness of the seasons and the power that was available at such times. Each season brings with it a corresponding change in energy that plays upon humanity in very real, albeit subtle, ways.

There are many ways of looking at the year. We can look at it as beginning January 1 and ending December 31. We can look at it as following the planting and harvesting rotation; beginning with the spring, moving through the summer and fall, and culminating with the winter. In many of the ancient societies, the year followed a different course, a course that has great significance and import to Occult Christianity. The year would begin with the autumn equinox, move to the winter solstice, the spring equinox, and then culminate with the summer solstice.

This latter method of viewing the year focuses upon it as it plays out in the energy of the soul of the individual. Each year is considered a "Year of the Soul," because each year provides opportunities for new soul growth, if one aligns to the natural rhythms.

In general, the four-day period leading to and including the end of one season and the beginning of the next was considered a time of "Holy Interval." It was an intersection of two energies, creating a vortex that would thin the veils between the spiritual and the physical, and function dynamically within the lives of the student of the mysteries. At these times, certain energies can be accessed that cannot be reached at other times of the year. This four-day interval, marking the ending and beginning of the different seasons, is a time when the spiritual forces ascend in their play upon the earth. Each season marks a time when a particular manifestation of the spiritual force of the universe becomes dominant and influences every atom of life upon the planet.

The "Year of the Soul" is a year of concentrated growth and change for the individual who aligns and utilizes the energies available. Everyone has years in which there occurs greater soul growth than at other times. It is the task of the student of the Christ Mysteries to make each year a "Year of the Soul."

The beginning of the "Year of the Soul" is the autumn equinox. Each seasonal change then brings with it a new spiritual impulse that plays within our lives through nature—touching each of us at the atomic level of our energy. It touches the soul, providing opportunity for growth. In the fall, the energies play upon humanity, facilitating receptivity to a new spiritual impulse to our lives. It is then dedicated in the winter, and resurrects itself into a new form of expression within our lives in the spring. It is then fulfilled and consummated in the summer.

At each turning point of the year, the gates of the inner spiritual temples and worlds open up to the earth and release a fresh outpouring of spiritual force upon the earth. The more we become aware and celebrate such times, the more we can take advantage of those forces to accelerate our growth and enhance our lives.

Behind all physical phenomena lie specific archetypal spiritual forces, which is why the physical sciences were sacred in more ancient times. Nature was the way in which the Divine spoke to humanity. The ancient wisdoms included religion, science, art, and astronomy. The movement of the stars and the changes of the seasons all reflected specific interplays of energy between the divine worlds and the physical.

The atomic structure of all life is affected with each change of the season. This quickening gives play to conditions in each person's life for uniquely personal opportunities for growth, expression, and transition. Communication with other beings and dimensions occurs with greater ease and occurs more widely. Knowing which energies are in play with each season and how they manifest within the earth environment is the first step to learning to direct them and manifest their effects more dynamically within our lives.

The life of every man and woman corresponds and is reflected through the seasons. Winter is the time of holy birth. Spring is the youth of expression. Summer is adulthood, and autumn is the time of harvest and recapitulation. It is the time of shedding the old for the new.

Egypt is a primary source for the modern Western Mystery Tradition and the importance of the seasons within the Christ Mysteries. The Biblical person of David spent time in Egypt while evading Saul. Joseph was sold into slavery into Egypt and rose to tremendous heights of glory. Moses studied in Heliopolis, the City of the Sun. In Egyptian life, the sacredness of the seasons was preeminent. The sacredness of the season revolves with the movement of the earth around the sun within a year's time span. Through the Greek and esoteric Hebraic traditions—with their Egyptian influence—we still have access to understanding the application of the Christ Mysteries to these sacred times.

The Year of the Soul within the Christ Mysteries holds as its keynotes: birth, death, resurrection, and ascension. Since the "giving up of the ghost" upon the cross, the Christ energy, now a part of the energy fabric of the earth itself, manifests in the life of humanity, in accordance with the natural rhythms of the earth. The Christ energies amplify the effects of the normal rhythms, and will continue to do so, following this cycle until humanity has evolved past the need for the physical.

The four seasons sound forth a call to come higher. They are times for giving birth to new expression of our divine energies, higher clairvoyance and initiation. They are times which serve to help awaken and utilize the Christ energies for dynamic impulse within our own growth process.

AUTUMN EQUINOX

Autumn is the time in which the Christ energies influence humanity in a manner that facilitates the process of purifying one's life and for the planting of new seeds and endeavors. The nature of the now indwelling Christ force affects us in varying ways with each season, manifesting subtle changes and opportunities for those who are aware. The fall season is a time to determine new values, and to make new decisions and goals. It is a harvesting and assessment time for what has passed in the previous year, and it is a time for setting new goals for the coming year. It is a time in which the energies influencing all of humanity are most appropriate for purifying the mind and for transmuting that which would hinder the full and highest expression of the Divine Feminine. This enables the energies that are set in motion through the rest of the year to be fully taken advantage of.

The autumn season holds an energy that aids in purifying and transmuting the lower, for overcoming obstacles and in preparing our creative life forces for regeneration. It is a time for harvest and spiritual recapitulation. It is a time for shedding the old to prepare for the new. It is a time of transition and to initiate transition. If attuned to properly, it manifests opportunities for needed changes and needed purification.

The fall season sets in motion an energy that facilitates communion with the angelic hierarchy that can build over the course of the year. (As we will explore later within this chapter, many of those of the angelic hierarchy work with the rhythms of the seasons and through the various signs of the zodiac to facilitate the growth of humanity.) This season also provides opportunity to balance the physical and the spiritual. Our dreams often reveal much during this season about measuring and determining our values. The season also brings some degree of testing one's judgment. There is a reaping of past sowing, along with opportunity for sowing next year's harvest. Whatever seeds are sown in the fall season will come to fruition by the following fall.

How these energies will interact specifically in the life of the individual will vary; thus it is important to be as "watchful" of events in one's life at this time as one can. These energies perform in such a way that, during the three days prior and the day of the autumn equinox, everyone's etheric bodies are drawn back into alignment with the physical. This provides opportunities for healing, balancing, and greater strengthening of the physical. It also opens the etheric realm to more conscious sight. It is a time of preparation so that the gifts of the Divine Feminine can be conceived more easily within the winter season, asserted and expressed through a new vibrancy of the masculine in the spring, and then united with the Divine Masculine to give birth to the Divine Child within us during the summer.

WINTER SOLSTICE

As the sun moves into the sign of Capricorn in the northern hemisphere, the winter season begins. This movement brings with it a change of energies that touches all life. The indwelling Christ energies of the planet now work to bring the etheric and astral energies of humanity and the planet in alignment with the physical.

This is a time of the year when love is preeminent. The Christ energies converge upon humanity to awaken the feminine energies within us all. Because of the alignment that occurs at this time, along with the awakened feminine energies, many of those of the angelic hierarchy draw nearer to the earth. They are beheld and sensed by many—if only through the dream state. This will be explored later in the chapter on "The Rite of the Winter Solstice."

The energies of the winter solstice and those of all the festivals celebrated at this time of the year are connected to humanity's life of healing, new birth, and the heart chakra. It is a season that deepens the life feeling which flows to us through the astral, and it can release opportunity to bring peace to the soul and new birth to inner potentials. It strongly plays upon the hearts of all.

This is a time of year in which the inner light is kindled in spite of outer darkness, and thus it is a powerful time for revelation through dreams and meditations. It is a time to go within ourselves to free ourselves from separateness. It is a time in which the feminine energies are stirred in all life upon the planet, so that their seeds can sprout within the darkness and begin their growth toward the light.

The Christ energy descending upon us at this time of the year brings opportunity for healing and the expansion of consciousness for those who would open more fully to it. It is a time that opens perceptions of what must still come upon us in the growth process. It opens a vision of what we must still face within ourselves if we are to give birth to the higher.

This is actually a time for withdrawal from outer activities, so that we can give birth to the light within our own darkness. To bring new life from the darkness of the womb is the goal of this season, and the purpose of the quickening of the Christ energies at this time upon humanity. These universal rhythms converging upon us are keyed to enable one who is seeking to awaken the interior gifts and light.

This energy is most appropriate for learning how to balance our emotions and to use our astral energies constructively. This is a time to cleanse the heart and the astral so that the profound feminine mysteries can unfold within our lives—the birthing capabilities within each of us. The energies at this time stimulate introspection and inspire seriousness for greater depths of meditation. Anyone wishing to succeed in meditation and dreamwork, or those who have difficulty with them, could choose no better time to initiate efforts along these lines.

This is a time where doors open to approach the angelic hierarchies. It is a time in which the universal and Christ energies facilitate illumination, forgiving and forgetting petty resentments and great wrongs, and it is a time for new initiation.

VERNAL EQUINOX

As the sun moves out of the sign of Pisces (water) and into the sign of Aries (fire), that which we were cleansing and giving birth to through the winter can now be given greater expression. The shift of energy upon the earth at this time of the year marks a time for greater expression of the masculine energy within all of us. It is a time to unveil and assert our creative aspects more dynamically and productively—a time to resurrect the Feminine from the darkness.

The creative force within each of us is stirred into greater outward expression. Aries is the sign of creative fire, of new beginnings. Much esoteric significance has been attributed to this time of the year—from the resurrection of Tammuz in Sumeria to the resurrection of the Christ within the Christian Tradition.

The keynote for this season is creation and expression of the new. It is an excellent time to initiate new endeavors and to manifest opportunities for such within our life. (This will be explored more fully in the chapter "The Rite of the Vernal Equinox.") It is a time in which the energies propelling us are excellent for initiating a new order to one's life. Its energies are strengthening and developing in the physical. It facilitates initiating change and the beginning of the balancing of the masculine and feminine within us.

In Western Orthodox Christianity, sorrow and mourning has come to be associated with this time of the year. Focus has been upon "Crucifixion" whereas it should be upon "Resurrection" which reflects the true energies playing upon the planet now. There is an impulse to resurrect our lives—if only out of the doldrums of winter. It is the time to focus upon the conscious transmutation of our lives. The living waters of life (Pisces) are flooded with new radiance (Aries), and if the cleansing and preparations have been accomplished through efforts in the previous two seasons, this new radiance can effect changes in all avenues of life. It awakens the "Magic green fire" of Gaelic legends—the alchemical force. This force is now even stronger upon the planet because of the Christ influence.

SUMMER SOLSTICE

The summer solstice marks the high point of the "Year of the Soul." For a brief time, all four planes of life are aligned with the physical—the spiritual, mental, astral, and the etheric. Because of this, there is a more direct flow of spiritual energy available to us within the physical. It is a time that provides opportunity to consummate a phase of our spiritual growth. It is a time in which separateness can yield to unity—in any area(s) of our lives.

The summer solstice is a time when the forces of nature reach the peak of their annual cycle, and the Christ energy stirs their magnificent play within our life. The keynote is transformation and transmutation that instills greater spirituality. The energies available to us at this time of the year facilitate communion with our angelic brethren—more easily and more intimately.

This is the time of the blending of the male and female within us for greater expression and a higher birth. The glyph of the sign of Cancer provides much insight into the esoteric significance of this blending. The winter is a time of stimulation of the feminine within us, and the spring is a time of the masculine. Summer is the time of bringing the two together to give birth to the Holy Child residing within each of us. This is a time to ascend to a new form of life expression for us—if we utilize these rhythms.

This is the time of the Mystic Marriage—the linking of the male and female, the bridging of the pineal and the pituitary (crown and brow chakras)—to open ourselves to new realizations of our true essence. If understood and accessed properly, these natural impulses will stimulate tremendous illumination. Autumn releases the forces of purification and preparation, and winter the forces of love—the feminine. Spring releases the force of will—the masculine power—but summer releases the "Power of Light!" It is a time of the *light within* that only occurs through the renewing of the mind. Light brings beauty and vision, and it is both of these which are keynotes of the summer.

In the quest of the spiritual student, there must be alignment and attunement, not only to the energies of an entire incarnation, but to those of the yearly cycle. Within the Christ Mysteries, attunement to this cycle is necessary for higher initiation. Each season, as we will explore through the other chapters within this second half, is aligned to specific Christ Mysteries and serves to help us recognize that Christianity was intended to be a Modern Mystery School. The individual, by attuning to these mysteries and to their rhythms throughout the year, brings his or her physical and spiritual energies into alignment, and can thus use that alignment for illumination, revelation, and true unfoldment.

YEARLY CYCLE OF ENERGIES WITHIN THE BODY

All of the ancient traditions teach of the masculine and feminine energies that exist within each of us. The task of the spiritual student was to learn to balance and express them creatively within their life circumstances. The early alchemists taught that true illumination and at-onement would be formed from a union of the sun and the moon—that is—a union of the masculine and feminine energies. On one level, this can be seen as a union of the subconscious and the conscious. On another level, it is the union of the centers of light within the body—the chakras—specifically those of the pituitary (brow) and the pineal (crown). Within these two crown jewels is divine work consummated!

The pineal gland is the seat of the masculine energy of the individual. This is known in esoteric tradition as the Sun-Seed. It is the active part of our energy system—necessary if our divine capabilities are ever to be expressed within the physical world. For its full power to be experienced and expressed, the individual must be sufficiently dedicated and spiritualized—and wise enough to know how to activate and use it.

In the course of a year, the masculine energy flows throughout the body, making an annual circuit—similar in many ways to the path of the sun through the heavens. As it moves throughout the body, it activates and stimulates other energy centers and currents—in accordance with the various seasons.

After the summer solstice, it begins to flow and move, so that by the time of the autumn equinox, the masculine energy has reached the heart chakra center of the body, helping to attune the energies of the physical body to the rhythms and energies of

Nature and of the Christ, as they play upon us and within us at this time of the year.

After the autumn equinox, the masculine energy begins to move. By the time of the winter solstice, it has reached the solar plexus center of the body, stimulating it into greater activity. In the ancient mysteries, this center was termed the "manger" of the human body, or human temple. It is the point of lower birth and illumination which must always come before the higher birth.

By the time of the vernal equinox, the sun or masculine energy is moving upward, again touching the heart center. In the autumn, it stimulates the heart for a cleansing, but by spring it is stimulating the heart center for a higher expression of its creative forces.

By the time of the summer solstice, the masculine force of the body rises once more to its uppermost position, located at the pineal, to provide greater opportunity for higher illumination. Paying close attention to one's own rhythms, focusing meditation at these times in directed manners—as we will learn—this circuit is radiated with new life and powers that restore vitality and vibrancy to the body, soul, and spirit.

We have feminine energies within us as well. Just like the masculine, they also make a circuit throughout the body. The feminine energies do not follow the course of the sun, but rather the moon. Each phase of the moon brings a shift and movement of the feminine energies within the individual. It renews itself month by month, but in the course of a single year, this feminine energy can be accumulated through various practices, to give a dynamic power and force to one's life on all levels.

The seat of the feminine energies is the pituitary gland. It will follow a circuit monthly, reflecting the path of the moon around the earth and through the twelve astrological signs. At the new moon, the feminine energy is found at its home in the pituitary gland (brow chakra). At the quarter phase following the new moon, it moves down to the throat chakra, stimulating this center of higher expression.

At the time of the full moon, the feminine energy reaches our center of generation (the base or sacral chakra). This is a critical time. It releases tremendous amounts of energy into the system of the individual. If unaware, this lunar seed power can be easily dissipated and lost through misuse of energies. Through proper meditation, it can be conserved and then lifted once more to the pituitary during the rest of the month. If this is done over the course of the year, a tremendous reservoir of energy accumulates which can then be used for great alchemical changes.

At the quarter phase following the full moon the feminine energy is drawn back up to the throat chakra, hopefully more energized through its contact with the lower center. Then once more at the time of the new moon it reaches its home at the pituitary.

Many ancient traditions and societies have used the time of the summer solstice to link the male and female together. The feminine energies accumulated over the previous year are united with the masculine energy over the previous year. Through special meditation techniques, the energies are linked at the point of the third ventricle of the brain, the bridge between the pineal and the pituitary. A rainbow bridge is formed that opens up full spiritual consciousness and illumination.

This is the point of the higher manger—the higher birth. The masculine and feminine energies—through the pineal and pituitary glands—are parents in a union that creates new life for the individual—physical and spiritual. The divine Christ Child within us is born.

ANGELIC POWER OF THE SEASONS

All life is hierarchical. Humanity often does not recognize this due to a myopic view of life. Part of the purpose of the Christ Mysteries was to open this sight: "The spirit of the Lord is upon you; and therefore he has anointed you. He has sent you to bring glad tidings to the poor, to heal the brokenhearted, proclaim liberty to captives, recovery of sight to the blind, strengthen those who are bruised and to announce a time of favor from the Lord. And today in your hearing and in your hearts it is fulfilled." (Luke 4: 18–22). Assisting the Christ in this and all endeavors are those celestial beings of light known as the angelic hierarchy.

This view of life is extending more each year, and those who are willing to accelerate their growth and evolution will have the responsibility of extending awareness from individual life rhythms to the more universal. This will entail a greater understanding and working with those life forms and energies that extend far beyond humanity itself.

As discussed, the Christ Mysteries involve recognizing the Christ as an indwelling planetary Logos, quickening and touching humanity with the rhythmic cycles of the seasons. The Christ works inwardly, affecting humanity, but there are those assisting him in a more "external" fashion.

As the great Solar Archangel, the Christ has assistance from others of his hierarchy. Four of these serve as governors of the four seasons. They assist the Christ during each season so that the energy is experienced by humanity in the most beneficial manner. These four are:

Michael—Autumn Season
Gabriel—Winter Season
Raphael—Spring Season
Auriel—Summer Season

These four and their specific functions in the Christ Mysteries will be explored in the following four chapters when we discuss each season particularly.

There are others of the angelic hierarchy that are also working to assist humanity. They do so in accordance with the rhythms of the seasons and the rhythms of the months—thus they do so in a manner that works with the laws of polarity—the balancing of the male and female—the essence of the Christ Mysteries. Their activities have been carried on since humanity first inhabited the earth; unfortunately few are, or have been, aware of their functions. Their activities were taught to the students of the mysteries in many societies, but to the general public they were less identifiable, or were attributed superstitious characteristics.

The impact of these celestial beings has grown since the birth of Christianity. With the Christ working intimately with the earth, the sensitivity of humanity to the ministrations of the angelic hierarchy has increased. This is enhanced even more by the governorship of much of their activity by the one Christianity calls the "Blessed Mother Mary." It is she who now oversees their activities, assisting from the outside in·amplifying their energies upon humanity—as the Christ works from the inside.

Mary is called by orthodox Christians the "Queen of Heaven and of Angels." The Assumption of Mary was in part the lifting up of her energies, the initiation into an "assumption" of this role in

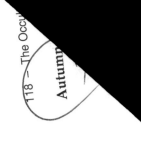

the universe and in the Christ Mysteries.
important for the true student of the Christ
stand the occult significance of the angelic hie

   Astrology is a guide to the interaction o
from the higher kingdoms within our own live
us in subtle, but real, ways, through their
through their governing energies and force
charts reveal the relationship between indivic   ....ary and
celestial entities and yourself.

   The zodiac on one level is a symbol of twelve creative ministrations of the celestial beings known as angels within our lives. The
twelve signs of the zodiac reflect twelve great "patterns" of angelic
influence. These beings of light called angels work through the
signs of the zodiac during the course of year, to effect changes of
energy upon the planet and all life. As the individual becomes more
attuned to those rhythms, the communion with the beings behind it
increases, and the individual's life is filled with blessings. These
angelic beings diffuse their energies through the universe and our
solar system through the signs of the zodiac and the planets. The
more we align with them, the more we can utilize their influence.
Learning to do so is part of the task of the Occult Christian.

   Just as the seasons reflect the play of Christ energies in particular patterns upon all life, the months within the season (and their
astrological signs) reflect angelic influence that assists in directing
the released Christ energy in ways that can be more effectively
used by the individual. Each month brings its own corresponding
energy change—in accordance with the change of the season.

   Each season has its predominant energy pattern. Each month
within that season also has its pattern, directed by the angels of the
signs falling within the particular season. Those of the angelic hierarchy who work through a cardinal sign of the zodiac assist the
individual in generating the power of the particular season into his
or her life. Those of a fixed sign in the zodiac assist the individual
in concentrating that newly generated energy, and those of the
angelic hierarchy which work through a mutable sign of the zodiac assist the individual in distributing the energies of the season
into the most appropriate areas of his or her life:

(purification and preparation)

1. The angelic hierarchy working through the sign of Libra assist in generating greater energy for purification and preparation.

2. The angelic hierarchy working through the sign of Scorpio assist the individual in concentrating the energies of purification and preparation, according to individual goals and purposes.

3. The angelic hierarchy working through the sign of Sagittarius assist the individual in distributing the purification and preparatory energies to wider areas within one's life.

Winter (giving birth to feminine energies)

4. The angelic hierarchy working through the sign of Capricorn assist the individual in generating more feminine energy.

5. The angelic hierarchy working through the sign of Aquarius assist the individual in concentrating the generated feminine energies.

6. The angelic hierarchy working through the sign of Pisces assist the individual in distributing the newly generated and concentrated feminine energies.

Spring (expression of the masculine energies)

7. The angelic hierarchy working through the sign of Aries assist in generating more dynamic expressions of masculine energy.

8. The angelic hierarchy working through the sign of Taurus assist the individual in concentrating the newly generated masculine energy.

9. The angelic hierarchy working through the sign of Gemini assist the individual in distributing the generated and concentrated masculine energy more productively.

Summer (union of the masculine and feminine)

10. The angelic hierarchy working through the sign of Cancer assist the individual in generating the ability and opportunity to unite the feminine and the masculine.

11. The angelic hierarchy working through the sign of Leo assist the individual in concentrating the force of the united energies of the feminine and masculine.

12. The angelic hierarchy working through the sign of Virgo assist the individual in distributing and expressing the new birth of energies culminating from the union of the feminine and masculine forces.

It is important to understand the intimate relationship and influence upon us through the angelic hierarchy of the various signs of the zodiac and the months in which they are most active. Everyone is influenced in varying degrees by them. Signs of the zodiac in which we have a lot of planets, or particularly those associated with our birth, our ascendant and our moon will have a greater influence upon us as well. We will be more susceptible to the influence of the angelic hierarchy at such times. Thus we need to be aware of how each group directs energies into our lives to assist us in our evolution, and particularly in unfolding the true Christ Mysteries.

ANGELIC HIERARCHY OF THE AUTUMN

Angels of Libra

This group of the celestial hierarchy work to assist individuals in unfolding their latent divinity. Its symbol is a scale—the balance—the lesson of polarity in the Christ Mysteries. They work upon the astral and etheric bodies of humanity. They oversee what is often called the "Trial Gate of Choices." They assist humanity during this month to awaken intuitive perception as to the balance of the individual's life. They work with the time of probation in this preparatory and purification season. They bring to the forefront conflicts in spirit and personality. In the undeveloped person, the energies are experienced and expressed as unbalanced fiery passion. To the more advanced, their energies stimulate the ability to weigh opposites and attain balance through higher expressions of love. They assist the individual in opening and moving through human love to devotion and aspiration and on to higher understanding. They awaken the search for balance within the individual.

Angels of Scorpio

These beings of light work to keep the human spirit strong. They provide instruction and assistance to the individual in transmutation of one's own energies—the most advanced work of the disciple. This is part of the preparatory stage of initiation. They assist the student of the Christ Mysteries in learning to re-orient the self to the life and energy of the soul. They manifest opportunities for the individual to evidence a readiness for initiation. They awaken opportunities to demonstrate increasing sensitivity. They assist in all areas of transmutation and sublimation. It is their task—as assigned by the Christ—to link the lights of form, soul, and life so that he or she may rise like a sun. During the fall season they help to reveal any lack of unity, any selfishness, or any conflict with the duality of life. They work to manifest the spiritual fighter so that a higher unity may manifest through the course of the year.

Angels of Sagittarius

In the final month of the fall season, the angelic hierarchy working through Sagittarius come into play. They work during this month in the final preparations of the individual for the awakening of the feminine forces that will occur in the following three months. It is their task to awaken the Christ aspirant to a directed and focused light. It is their task to assist the individual in becoming a beam of light that will illuminate the greater light ahead. It is through their efforts that humanity was lifted above the animal kingdom. They work to teach humanity to Christ, the mind. Dealing with the untrained and materialistic aspect of the mind may then come to the forefront during this time. They assist the individual in developing freedom in thought and single-pointedness. They specifically work in purifying lower ambitions and re-awakening an aspiration that will ultimately give birth to the feminine powers of idealism and intuition. Helping the individual to overcome self-centeredness is part of their task. Eventually, through their influence, the individual moves from an "experimental approach" to the mysteries, to a directed approach that leads one to the gates of initiation. One of the paths that may open to the true student of the mysteries is that known as the "Path of the Beneficent Magician." In this path the individual learns to work with the law of supply and to become the true "sower" in all of its esoteric significance—as found within modern Christian scripture.

ANGELIC HIERARCHY OF THE WINTER

Angels of Capricorn

The angelic hierarchy of Capricorn help inaugurate the winter season. They work to help teach humanity the true importance of the astral body and how to mold and shape its energies. They assist the individual in balancing the emotions and awakening the inner potentials. They stimulate, within the individual, introspection and insight, and they inspire a new seriousness for greater depths of meditation and realization. They assist the individual in opening the initiatory process to the Feminine Mysteries. They assist the individual in clearing a way to the "mountaintop" and to transfigure the soul. They awaken to the individual opportunity to conquer death in some form within their life—and thus open to the mysteries of new birth. Death and life go hand in hand, and this is part of the lesson of the Feminine Mysteries being awakened at this time of the year. To the undeveloped individual, everything will only have an outer, earthy significance, but to one developing, the depths of the life situations will begin to reveal themselves. It is this group of beings who work with the Christ through this sign to assist humanity in that process.

Angels of Aquarius

The second month of the winter season is one that can more directly align us with the group of celestial beings that work through the sign of Aquarius. It is this group who will oversee much of the initiation in the "Aquarian Age" which is upon us. They strongly influence the etheric body, working to make it more receptive to the higher influences. They work to stimulate higher clairvoyance, so this is an excellent time to develop and exercise one's leaning toward it. They will help those of higher initiation to fashion "The Golden Wedding Garment" of the New Testament scriptures—the soul body. Those who would meet the Christ within the etheric realms must weave this garment through fulfilling obligations, life tasks, and responsibilities. During this month they assist in transmuting superficiality and selfishness, which can block the manifestation of the Divine Feminine. To the undeveloped, the individual tries to be all things to all people, but to one who opens fully to their assistance at this time of the year, there will grow a dedication to the soul and there will be revealed a greater understanding of the mysteries of the vital functions of the body. They assist the individual during this time of the year to awaken the Christ Light that ever shines within the dark. They help open the individual to the light that heals and nourishes.

Angels of Pisces
The last of the months of the winter season is influenced by a group of the angelic hierarchy who work through the sign of Pisces. These beings hold the key to perfected humanity. They work to assist those who will attune to them the light of life itself. They open the realization of the way to end the darkness of various areas within the individual's life circumstances. It is their task to assist humanity in bringing the physical body more under the balanced control of the masculine and feminine. During this month there is a call to the depths within. It is an ideal time to arouse great exaltations. It is a time for healing—physically and spiritually. They assist the individual in transmuting a self-centered dreaming to a vision dedicated to the higher service of humanity. This in itself is reflected through the Christ Mysteries. Pisces is the Age of the Christ Mysteries. This is a time in which those of this hierarchy work to reveal the karma of one's life, its increased opportunities for balancing it and for revelation of one's destiny. They work to assist us in lifting our psychic energies into a higher, spiritual force and to initiate a process of ending the darkness of matter—for ourselves or for others. Those of this sign work to open initiation into the Feminine to those who would be receptive—or at least to reveal this path of initiation yet to be walked.

ANGELIC HIERARCHY OF THE SPRING

Angels of Aries
The beings of light working through this sign of the zodiac work to stimulate a "Call to the Great Overcoming"—the conquest of the personality by the spirit. They stimulate and awaken energies of self-sacrifice and transmutation. In the unaware or undeveloped person, the influence of them seems to only manifest undirected experiences in life. For those working toward advancement, they stimulate greater effort toward directed personality development. In the disciple, there will awaken through these angelic beings a

recognition of the "Plan of the Divine" and work with it. They assist the individual in merging self-control with wisdom. Depending upon one's development, the energy may be experienced through instinctual reaction, a higher form of desire, or directed will. They assist the individual in the search for the Light that can best be used for the expression of the divine within them.

Angelic Hierarchy of Taurus

This group of the angelic hierarchy have a dynamic purpose in the manifestation of the Christ energies during the spring season. In more ancient times, festivals for the living were often celebrated in the month of May. This is a time in which the angelic hierarchy work with the individual who will attune to them to stimulate opportunities for change and new expressions of one's abilities and desires. They assist in the overcoming of selfish desire and the awakening of higher aspiration—with opportunities to follow such aspirations. They awaken a light and love of the earth, and of all manifestations of life upon it. It is their task to assist the individual in developing control over the manifestations of their individual light. They assist the individual in developing discrimination and the removal of glamour from their own life circumstances. As the glamour is removed, they are able to penetrate into the higher spheres of illumination. They assist those of humanity who wish to do so, to more closely attune to all life within nature—animal, plant, or mineral kingdoms.

Angels of Gemini

As the spring season enters its last month, the angels of the sign of Gemini come into greater play upon the earth. Theirs is the task to begin to awaken the polarity aspect of Christianity. This is reflected within its glyph (♊). They work to unite the soul with its physical form more intimately. They work to awaken a governing of polarity—the equalizing of the masculine and feminine—so that they can be united to create new life. Before they can unite—as is reflected in the sign of Cancer (the two swirls moving together)—the polarities must first be established and balanced in equanimity (symbolized by the glyph of Gemini). This month, and the work of these celestial beings during it, provides force which produces change in consciousness in regard to all areas of life. They work to reveal the light that exists in spirit and in physical form. For those who align with them through the Christ Rituals, the evolution is traced from service to oneself to service to others and on to service to the "One Light beyond all Lights." They help the individual to develop discrimination in the art of relating—on physical and on spiritual levels.

ANGELIC HIERARCHY OF THE SUMMER

Angels of Cancer

The summer begins when the sun enters the sign of Cancer. This is the high point in the Year of the Soul. It is the time of the Mystic Marriage, the time to initiate the process of blending the masculine and the feminine—to fertilize the egg so that new life will spring forth. The mysteries of the sexual energies—applied both physically and spiritually—is in the hands of this group of celestial beings. They are the guardians of the "holy places" of the planet. They guard the Holy of Holies, the Mystery Tombs and Pastos. They teach humanity to use, rather than abuse, our most treasured possession—the holy water and the sacred seed of life. They work to assist the individual in developing the intellect into higher intuition. They work for the development of purity and chastity in esoteric manners that permit the highest transmutation of the fires and waters of life. They work to reveal to the individual who is receptive, the light within all substance—a light that is always waiting to be stimulated.

Angels of Leo

When the summer sun moves into the sign of Leo, those of its angelic hierarchy become more active. It is their task to awaken in humanity the power of life. It is their task to live the Christ precept: "Thou shalt love the Lord thy God with all thy heart, with all thy mind and all thy soul, and thy neighbor as thyself." They assist humanity in learning to apply the newly born power of love that arises from the united male and female. They help individuals to learn that all are connected, and that we are all part of the same family. They stir greater expression of individuality during this month, and a greater will to illumine and a will to rule. Theirs is the task of assisting humanity in acquiring self-knowledge and self-mastery through the balance of the male and female forces of life. To those who are receptive to their influence, they awaken the ability in the individual to reflect the divine out into the lives of others. They learn to overcome the lower self and to express the higher, to find the hidden and to reveal it for all.

Angels of Virgo

The last of the groups of the angelic hierarchy working through the summer play of the Christ energies are those associated with the sign of Virgo. Theirs is the task to awaken even further the spark of Christ consciousness so that in the Year of the Soul which begins with the following month, it will be given still greater expression. They open the individual to the true meaning and purpose of wisdom—Sophia. They open the doors of initiation through service and sacrifice. They awaken greater ability in synthesizing the essence of one's experience, so that it can be transformed into true soul wisdom. They assist the individual in synthesizing the Divine Feminine, and they manifest opportunities for change and an incentive toward discipleship. They have the ability to teach the individual how to blend the light of God with the Light of Form. In the undeveloped or unaware individual, the force simply germinates, but as one becomes more advanced and works toward unfoldment, the germinating force of the Divine Feminine in its "Mother" aspect becomes creative, and the Christ Light is no longer hidden.

RECEPTIVITY TO THE ANGELIC HIERARCHY

How then does one make oneself more receptive to the influence of this hierarchy as it operates within our lives? It is not as difficult as it seems. It is important, though, to become "ever watchful" as all the masters have cautioned their students. Pay attention to everything within your life. Remember that the occult significance of everything is "hidden" and must be searched out.

The input of the celestial beings within our lives is more available now than at other times because of the incarnation of the Christ, but there must still be a searching out. The meditations and "rites" in the next few sections will not only explain the Christ Mysteries more specifically, as they are reflected within the seasonal changes, but they will help attune the individual to those Christ energies and to those of the angelic hierarchy assisting the Christ.

Take time each month to reflect upon the season, and upon the sign of the zodiac with its corresponding group of celestial beings. Reflect upon their functions during that month. Doing this at the beginning when the sun first enters the new sign is beneficial, as is repeating it at the end of the month, when you can look back over the events of that time period and draw correlations. Remember that they play upon humanity in a pattern that can be discernible for everyone, but they also will behave in a manner specific to you, as you have your own unique energy system.

Meditate upon the Apostles associated with the sign of the zodiac for each month, as the sun enters that particular sign. These were listed in the first half. This develops a greater consciousness and perceptiveness of the Christ Mysteries, as they are revealed within your own life situation.

Create a meditation involving the Blessed Mother Mary—the Queen of Angels. Use the scripture that esoterically reflects on one level her position in the Christ Mysteries and with the angelic realms (see below). Remember at all times that the Christ Mysteries were to be a Mystery School. There are hidden within the scriptures and writings much of what was taught in other societies. They outline the path of initiation and illumination. They reveal the means to awakening the Divine Feminine and the more dynamic expression of it within all aspects of our life. Visualize, imagine, see, feel, and experience yourself as the archetypal force of the Christ Mysteries, as they play upon and through the earth evolution:

> "A great sign appeared in the sky, a woman clothed with the sun, with the moon under her feet, and on her head a crown of twelve stars."
>
> Revelation 12: 1

Chapter Seven

THE RITE OF THE AUTUMN EQUINOX

"With the beginning of autumn appears the spirit of 'strength in beauty', the while Nature hides her beauty, driving the adversary too into concealment. With such thoughts and feelings did men of ancient times keep the Festival of Michael in their hearts."

Rudolph Steiner

The autumn equinox opens the cycle of the Year of the Soul for one who wishes to attune to the true Christ Mysteries. The nature of the force poured forth upon the planet varies with the season, each manifesting subtle changes and opportunities for those who are aware. It is like planting a seed that over the following seasons and months will germinate, take root, sprout and then be harvested.

The energy of the autumn equinox is felt weeks before the actual event. When the sun enters the sign of Virgo, it is the time of the Immaculate Conception. The earth and any individual upon it can prepare themselves for a new cycle of growth within his or her life. As the sun moves into Libra, the Christ energy begins to affect the whole surface of the earth. The energies of plants, for example, are drawn inward; the energies move toward the heart, the seat of the Divine Feminine. The Christ force, now a permanent part of the Earth's energy fabric, begins to draw inside of us to cleanse the heart, so that a new birth can unfold at the time of the winter solstice. Then, within the course of the rest of the year, this birth will be brought out into greater expression.

The Christ force becomes active, in a manner that triggers opportunities for transition. Its energies create a time to determine new values and make new decisions. It is the harvesting time for what has previously passed; a time for purifying the mind and to begin the process of transmuting that which needs transmuted. It is the Archangel Michael who will assist the Christ energy in the transmuting and testing that can be triggered with this season.

This is a time of the year in which the energies available to us can assist us in the following ways:

1. In purifying and transmuting the lower.

2. In overcoming obstacles.

3. In opening the inner temples of awareness.

4. In purifying the basic life force of the sacral center.

5. In cleansing and purifying the heart chakra, the seat of much karma.

6. In aligning with the angelic kingdom.

7. In determining what still needs to be transmuted for the greatest growth in the coming year.

8. In more easily turning our attention from the outer to the inner worlds.

9. In developing harmony between the laws of love and karma.

10. In a renewed testing of the soul, necessary for higher illumination.

11. In balancing the flesh and the spirit.

12. In initiating a time of weighing, measuring, determining values, and decisions for the physical and spiritual life of the individual.

13. In awakening the testing of judgment.

14. In manifesting opportunities to reap the rewards of past sowing, and to sow seeds for the future.

15. In manifesting the contest between the lower and the higher, the right or left hand path of development.

Because of this, the three days prior to and the day of the autumn equinox are the most powerful, but every day of the fall is the time of holy preparation.

Behind all physical phenomena lie specific spiritual archetypes, which is why the physical sciences were sacred in more ancient times. The ancient wisdom of Gnosis and Sophia comprised religion, science, art and especially astronomy. The movement of the stars and the changes of the seasons all reflect specific interplays of energy between the divine and the physical.

Each month is a miniature duplication of what occurs within the course of a year. The four phases of the moon reflect the four seasons—a continual reminder to keep the sacredness of the seasons alive.

To the Western world, the mysteries of Egypt were handed down through Greece and its masters (Orpheus, Pythagoras, Plato, Aristotle, etc.). The Greeks recognized that humanity was strongly affected by two stars. These two stars are more visible at the changes of the seasons. The first, Sirius, is more active at the time of the solstices, and the second, Alcyone, is more active and visible at the time of the equinoxes.

The atomic structure of all life alters in its vibrational frequency with each change of the season. This creates opportunities for growth and expression and transition in each person's life. Communication with other beings and dimensions occurs more widely and with greater ease. Knowing the energies in play at each season is the first step to learning to direct them, so as to manifest their effects more powerfully within your own life.

The ancient Egyptians ascribed to the autumn equinox the origin of all evil. This is, of course, symbolic. In a more general sense, it can be likened to the crucifixion of the Cosmic Christ (not to be confused with the historical Christ Jesus). It is the time in which the Christ force, as the great Solar Archangel, drew near to the earth, to touch humanity more tangibly. It is the time of the sacrificing of the

Cosmic status to become an indwelling Logos of the Earth. Its force reaches its deepest point at the winter solstice—touching the very heart of the earth—and through the rest of the year begins the process of resurrecting the Christ life within all beings.

The autumn is a time of transition, a time which offers opportunities to change, purify, and transmute the conditions of one's life. Each student of the Christ Mysteries must approach the sacred festivals of the seasons from his or her own point of evolvement. In more ancient times, the autumn was a time of serious recapitulation. It was the ideal time to assess the past year's experiences and determine any changes still needed. It was the time to plant new seeds for the coming year.

To one who begins the process of aligning with the force available at this time it will serve as a catalyst; so that throughout the season on the lower consciousness it will be a testing time for the soul. For all who do align with its force, though, it brings the individual opportunities for preparation, the development of judgment, and opportunity for renunciation. For some it may bring the "test of Abraham"—a willingness to give up that which is most sacred.

Throughout this season, it is important to keep in mind that when the tests are passed, there is always spiritual compensation. There is always special assistance and spiritual guidance during this time. First, there is the hierarchy of angels working through the signs of the zodiac, but even more helpful is the dynamic assistance of the governor of this season, the Archangel Michael. He provides protection and balance to those open to alignment with the Christ Mysteries through the yearly cycle of the soul.

MICHAELMAS

The coming of the Christ was partly to invest the sacred seasons with greater impulse, so that with each yearly cycling, humanity could feel the impulse of the Christ to a greater degree. It served to imbue the seasons with even greater power and placed their effects within the reach of all. In orthodox Christianity, the Feast of St. Michael falls at the time of the autumn equinox. As we will see, this is most appropriate, for we need someone of great strength to assist us in balancing and transmuting our lives.

Michael had much to do with the Christ impulse upon the earth. Esoteric tradition teaches that it was Michael who hovered over Christ Jesus at Gethsemane, assisting him in transmuting the earth streams of hate and despair into "currents of love and healing." The work of Michael has always been for purity and transmutation; but without the Christ impulse being planted upon the earth, Michael's influence was limited mostly to the elect. Initiation is now open to all, and Michael is the Initiate-Companion of every student of the Mysteries. The Mysteries of the Holy Grail are the Mysteries of Alchemy, the Mysteries of Transmutation. Tradition speaks of how Michael oversaw the teaching and training of Arthur and the Knights of England—to perpetuate those mysteries.

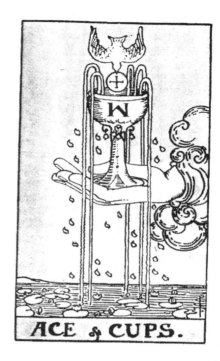

The Holy Grail is the inspiration for this tarot card, the Ace of Cups from the Waite deck.

Michael is often given the title of "Dragon Slayer." This has great significance in regard to the process of "Meeting the Dwellers upon the Threshold" discussed earlier within this work. One must remember, though, that Michael did not slay the dragon. Michael drove the dragon to the depths of hell. Dragons are not meant to be slain. They are meant to be controlled and transmuted.

This great being of light has a long occult tradition concerning his influence in the evolution of humanity. He has been a part of almost every society's scriptures and esoteric lore. He is known as the Prince of Splendor and Wisdom. He is the great protector. Legend tells us that in the days to come, he will take over the responsibilities of the Christ. He brings to all the gift of patience.

Michael works with others of the angelic hierarchies to transmit divine consciousness into the minds of humanity through greater knowledge. A group of the angelic hierarchy, working through the planet Mercury, will assist him in initiating the more advanced of humanity into the higher truths necessary for spiritual leadership in the age to come. They work to teach individuals self-mastery, and they work to teach individuals to leave and re-enter the physical body at will.

To the early Egyptians and Greeks, Mercury was considered the "captain of the planets." It is a planet that touches every sign of the zodiac in its revolution around the sun in the course of one year. It is a symbol of illumined reason—that which Michael comes to stimulate each autumn.

In some esoteric literature, Michael is associated with the planet Saturn. Saturn is the Great Mother, the Great Teacher. One tradition speaks of how Saturn is where the Spiritual Hierarchy for this solar system gathers, and it is Michael who oversees it. In many traditions and many lores, he has been known by different names, serving a variety of functions on the behalf of humanity:

1. Angelic head of the Ray of Power.

2. Guardian of the southern quarter of the earth and the element of fire.

3. Guardian and Keeper of the Flaming Sword.

4. The Chaldean worshipped him as something of a god: "Who is as God."

5. Chief of the archangels, second only to Christ.

6. Prince of Presence.

7. Chief of the Virtues.

8. Angel of repentance, righteousness, mercy and sanctification.

9. Guardian of Jacob.

10. Founder of the Mystery Schools in the time of Atlantis.

11. Conqueror of Satan.

12. Author of Psalm 85.

13. Stayed the hand of Abraham at his greatest testing.

14. Patron and protector of the Universal Church.

15. The Order of Michael/The Brotherhood of Michael guard the galaxies from lesser forces of light, except where necessary to train or test a soul.

16. In the Eastern Church of Constantinople, he was more healer than protector.

17. It was Michael who spoke to Joan of Arc.

18. The Cherubim were formed from the tears he shed over the sins of humanity.

19. In the Dead Sea Scrolls, he is called the Prince of Light in the war between the Sons of Light and the Sons of Darkness.

20. Tradition says it was Michael who gave man his first name—Adam.

21. He was known as Marduk of Babylon who slew Tiamut, Apollo who slew Pytho, and St. George who slew the dragon.

22. To the ancient Hebrews he was known as the "countenance of Jehovah."

23. He was guardian at the times of Lao Tse, Confucius, Buddha, Zoroaster, Pythagoras, Ezekiel, and Daniel.

24. He works with the transformational powers of images which can neither be created nor destroyed without his assistance.

25. He was one of the four archangels that held the guard of honor around the manger at the birth of Jesus.

The student of the Christ Mysteries would do well to spend time meditating upon Michael and his work, particularly upon the images of the Flaming Sword and the repelled Dragon. The dragon is the lower self, the untransmuted elements of the soul, and Michael aids in transmuting such. To those aligned with the full power and significance of this season, Michael assists in the great overcoming. He acts within your life to assist in purifying so that greater illumination of the intellect will occur. He works to help the individual manifest opportunities to transmute the dragons of their lives!

THE RITE OF THE AUTUMN EQUINOX

This exercise, if performed on the three days prior to and the day of the autumn equinox, will release energy into the individual's life that will manifest opportunities for purification and preparation. This time frame is one in which the veil between the physical and the spiritual is the thinnest, and it is easiest to access the Christ energies for awakening of the Mysteries throughout the rest of the season. It can also be repeated as the sun moves into the other signs of the zodiac associated with the autumn season (Scorpio and Sagittarius).

If this meditation serves as a catalyst for too many or too intense changes within your life, it can be softened through meditation and focus upon Michael—particularly upon the image of Michael extending to you the Flaming Sword of Spiritual Law and Discrimination. It is an image which will invoke extra assistance, strength and balancing. Keep in mind, though, that the more we purify and prepare through the fall, the more we will give birth to throughout the rest of the year.

This meditation will also stimulate opportunity for change and opportunity to sow new seeds. Before you participate in it, make sure that you want to trigger such within your life. There is an old saying: "Be careful what you ask for, for that is what you will receive." This is an exercise which asks and invokes the energy of the Christ Mysteries to act more dynamically within your life.

The most effective time to perform this exercise in this four day "Holy Interval" is at a time of intersection—dusk or dawn, prior to sleeping or upon awakening. On the day of the equinox itself, if you can perform it as close to the time as possible, so much the better. If you cannot do so at these times, at least find some time to do it each of the four days.

Four is the number and rhythm of a new foundation. This is a foundation of new energy that you are invoking into your life to use in the coming year to awaken and express greater potentials and creativity. Feel free to adjust the meditation to yourself. We each must approach the energies of the seasons and their Mysteries from our own point of perspective and evolution.

Preparations

Make sure you will be undisturbed.

If you choose to meditate with candles, use candles in the colors of autumn—brown, green, russet.

Ears of corn and corn husks (such as are often found in Halloween decorations), add to the energy and symbology of the meditation.

This can be an effective meditation to perform outdoors at dusk.

The images are powerfully invoking to the archetypal energies of the Christ Mysteries as they manifest through the autumn. Allow yourself to relax, and as you do, feel yourself lifting slowly and gently up toward the heavens. The stars are brilliant, filling the dark night sky with diamond sparkles. In the distance is one star which stands out among the rest. It scintillates with a brilliancy that shimmers and pours streams of light down below it.

Meditation

As you float gently through the heavens, your eyes trace the path of light from this one great star to the earth beneath. There on top of a high mountain, overlooking the earth, is a temple. The light from the star outlines the four columns that separate the inner from the outer. From your height, it appears in the shape of a cross, with one column standing in each of the four directions.

You begin to feel yourself gently descending, and ever so softly, you come to rest in the soft grass outside this grand temple. You stand before the doors. Emblazoned into the massive frame above it is a large flaming sword. As you step to the door, the sword begins to glow brighter and a sound fills the night air, making the earth and yourself tremble.

You step back from the door, and as you do, the earth on either side of it rips open and two large trees burst forth. The limbs and branches stab in every direction, twisting and entwining, until the door to the temple is barely visible and virtually impassable. The trees are growth gone astray. There is no form or shape. They twist and entangle, knotted together, preventing any further growth. They have grown wild and are beginning to suffocate the growth of each other.

The sounds soften and there is silence. You stand before the blocked doorway of the temple, unsure what the next step should be. Within that silence comes the answer. A soft light begins to form between you and the trees. It is a soft pastel red, that grows into a mighty column of light extending from the earth into the heavens. A gust of wind blows across you, and the column shimmers, shrinks and there stands before you a beautiful being of great strength and light.

The eyes are steely and strong. Dressed in robes of the colors of autumn leaves—russets and reds—he holds your attention. Within his hand is a sword which is more light than substance. Mingled with the energy of his own essence, you cannot help but feel the strength about him. You wonder how he is able to control such force, and he smiles as if reading your thoughts.

He waves his hand at his feet and a great hole within the earth opens. You can see deeply within the heart of the earth and beyond. There within the depths was a powerful and magnificent dragon of red and gold. With each breath, light and energy of primal force pour forth from it towards all life upon the earth.

Michael raises the Flaming Sword over this primal energy as it rises up and softens and surrounds him, pours through him and out from him in blessings of strength and love to all.

"We each must face our own dragons. We each must face that which we most fear. As we learn to transmute our dragons we give birth to light and love. As we learn to wield the Flaming Sword of spiritual law and discrimination within every aspect of our lives, we control the dragons rather than being controlled by them."

He waves his hand over his feet again, and the image disappears. You look at him, drawing strength from his gentle words. He steps to the side of the temple doors.

"Before all are the trees of Life and Knowledge. Before one enters into the inner temple, the trees must be pruned, trimmed. Just as a bush is pruned in the autumn so that it may grow greener and more fruitful in the spring, so must your lives be pruned. Look upon these trees and see within their tangled mess what must be pruned and trimmed from your own life for greater fruitfulness."

You gaze into the two trees, tangled and knotted. You see the people and situations, the habits, behaviors, attitudes, and knowledge that is blocking your own growth. As you look upon the two trees, you see all that you must do to untangle your life. You see yourself trimming and pruning the tree, one branch at a time. The task seems great—even overwhelming.

"We are never faced with more than we can handle."

The soft words break the reverie and fill you with encouragement.

"Now look again."

You look at the trees once more. No longer are they entangled and knotted. They are trim, full, and green. There are blossoms, hinting of the fruit they will bear in the future. The doors to the Inner Temple are no longer obstructed. Slowly they swing open, and a golden light and a chorus of song surrounds you.

You see an altar upon which rests an equal-armed cross. In the middle of the cross is a large white rose. A light shines down upon it from above, and you remember the star whose beam of light led you to this temple. Before the altar stands a magnificent being of shimmering rays of blue and gold light. He turns, acknowledging silently your presence. He slowly raises a Golden Chalice—the Grail of Life—to the heavens in silent prayer.

The door closes slowly, leaving you only with the joy of a memory that has emblazoned itself upon your heart. Michael stands before you, his look tender and loving.

"With strength, we all must prepare that we may enter the inner temples of the mysteries of the Divine. There was a time, though, when each had to accomplish it alone, but that time has passed. Today there is guidance and strength from many sources for those who will but open their hearts."

He raises his flaming sword and softly touches your breast with its point. He closes his eyes and intones a word both foreign and familiar. You feel your heart seared with the light of the Flaming Sword. You look down upon your breast, and you see within your heart center your own Sword of Truth aflame.

"When you touch the heart and when you imagine the Flaming Sword within, I will come. For as you awaken to the Christ within and learn to express it without, you become a Son or Daughter of the Flaming Sword."

His sword grows blindingly bright, encasing you in light, and then fades. As it does, you find yourself alone outside of the Temple, but you feel the warmth of the Flaming Sword alive within your own heart. You look to the sky and see the one star that led you to this moment. As you look upon it, you feel yourself lifting up gently once more into the heavens, carrying forth your experience, your memory and the energy invocation of purification and preparation for entrance into the Mysteries of the Inner Temple.

Chapter Eight

THE RITE OF THE WINTER SOLSTICE

"The Christmas Festival is the Festival of the Holy Night, celebrated in the mysteries by those who were ready for the awakening of the higher self within them, or as we should say within our time, those who have brought the Christ to birth within them."

Rudolph Steiner

The winter solstice is connected to humanity's life of feeling. When it is rightly understood, it deepens the life feeling which can be found within each of us, and it overflows into the astral energies. It is a time which can bring great peace to the soul. It is the time within the Christ Mysteries in which the energies affecting humanity are most appropriate for awakening the Divine Feminine within. The seven Feminine Mysteries of occult Christianity are linked to the winter season (see pages 71–72).

This is a season often associated with modern Christianity, but the significance of this time of the year has been celebrated in many ways throughout the world. The solstice is a time in which the sun turns northward. In the northern hemisphere, it marks the shortest day of the year—with the sun shining longer each day thereafter throughout the winter season. In Egypt and Asia, the winter solstice was a time of celebration, a festival connected to the victory of the sun over darkness—a time when light triumphs over darkness upon the earth. It is the light of the inner potential—the Divine Feminine. Hanukkah, the Hebrew Festival of Lights, and Christmas, celebrating the birth of Jesus, are two modern feasts reflecting ancient celebrations at this time. Many still enjoy the lighting of the yule log at this time of the year. This is the ancient rite of the rebirth of the Divine within the fires of the Mother Goddess.

All life is touched by the energies playing within and upon the earth at this time of the year. The astral plane is brought into alignment with the physical, facilitating the communion and ministrations of the angelic hierarchies with humanity. The inner heart, cleansed and prepared through the autumn season, can now give birth to a new expression of energies which will germinate and unfold through the rest of the year. The Christ energies amplify this dynamic play of energy, creating a quickening on an atomic level within all of humanity. Few are untouched by the energies of this time of the year. Each has the ability and the opportunity to attune to this energy more intensely and thus give greater birth to the inner feminine potentials and energies.

The winter solstice triggers a time in which the Inner Light is kindled in spite of outer darkness. It is a time to give birth to and awaken the higher self. If celebrated properly, the Christ impulse is born anew within the individual, adding light and strengthening the love principle within humanity.

Compassionate ones have always entered the earth plane at this time of the year to serve as guides to humanity. The highly evolved soul of the one we call Jesus was such a being—one who had an even more powerful purpose. The Christ Star hovered near at the time of the birth of Jesus, since he would be the means for the Christ's earthly incarnation.

This is a time of the year best suited to learning the ancient significance of the "Feast of the Interior Light." It is a time of dedication and the renouncing of the false. It is a good time to step away from outer activities—reflected in the scriptural stories of the birth of Jesus. It is a time best suited to turning inward and attuning to the mystic rhythms set in motion with the winter solstice.

Unfortunately, society has created an attitude of participation in continual gatherings and outward celebrations. This is contrary to the energy and rhythms of this season:

1. The energies playing upon humanity are such that stimulate great introspection and facilitate meditative states of awareness, and time should be given for these.

2. The energies touching all at this time of the year present opportunities to awaken the seeds of inner potentials we most desire to unfold.

3. It is a time to reflect upon the miracle of heaven and earth uniting, coupling within the dark to give birth to new life.

4. It is a time which gives each individual opportunities to light the light that shines eternally within the darkness.

During this time of the year, the entire angelic hierarchy draws close to the earth and they pour forth their spiritual force upon it. Overseen by Gabriel—the archangel of tenderness, mercy and love—this force brings expansion of consciousness beyond the confines of the physical world for those who learn to attune to it. There is awakened the opportunity to develop love as a power within our lives.

All of the souls who will incarnate within the coming year draw close to the earth at this time to share in the angelic and Christ blessings. They draw near to their prospective mothers, and those mothers who attune to this season can become aware of their presence. At this time of the year all the world is basked in flows of love, and for those who open to these touches and rhythms the Great Star Call can be felt.

For the student of the Christ Mysteries, these energies will open the doors of approach to the Angelic Hierarchy. It is a time of illumination and the beginning of the process of igniting the Star Body of the Soul. For those with a dedicated mind and heart, December should be a joyous month, one attuned to angelic bliss:

1. It is a time of dedication. If the preparatory stages through the autumn have been followed, the winter solstice will initiate a time when new life begins to be experienced. It is the beginning of the birth of the divine

within. The renunciations of the fall will bring compensation in the winter.

2. The individual will begin to realize that he or she is a true child of the Divine and will never again be without inner guidance.

3. It is a time in which spirit can begin to have dominion over the physical.

4. It can lead to the state of true Initiation and the seeing of the Christ Star shining within the heart of the earth.

5. It opens new clairvoyance, and the individual can see what must still be done to become the true Christ Initiate.

6. The etheric plane and all of its energies can become more open to the individual.

7. The single-pointed focus of discipleship comes more alive.

8. We can learn from the angelic beings of light who become more accessible.

9. The hidden significance of the Christ baptism by John can be discerned.

10. We open to spiritual sight that penetrates all of our earth experiences more deeply.

11. The individual can open to great visions of all of humanity and what must still be undergone in the times ahead and how to adjust our lives accordingly.

12. We can open to the Christed Imagination so that we can give birth to the light in all aspects of darkness!

THE OCCULT SIGNIFICANCE OF CHRISTMAS

The season of Christmas is prepared for in orthodox Christianity four weeks prior to the winter solstice. This period of time is known as Advent. In many of the Mystery traditions, the last four weeks of the autumn season—prior to the winter solstice—were times of greater and more intense purification and preparation. It involved the final efforts of purification before giving birth to the Divine Feminine. Earlier in this work we discussed the seven Feminine Mysteries of Christianity. Three of these are associated with the final preparations for the winter solstice energy. They can open reception to fresh revelations about one's spiritual development.

The Annunciation

Aligned with the first week of Advent, the focus of the spiritual disciple in the Christ Mysteries should be on cultivating purity as a power. Physical, emotional, mental, and spiritual purity will unfold the higher faculties that open one to the Divine Feminine. This purity will assist the individual in being able to consciously perceive the celestial realms and the glorious beings that inhabit them through the holy days of winter. The Annunciation was the moment when Mary became aware of the presence of Gabriel and he announced to her the role she would play in the Christ Mysteries. Developing purity as a power can open us to that same kind of revelation.

The Immaculate Conception

The second of the seven Feminine Mysteries of Christianity should be the focus during the second week of Advent. There should arise a growing realization that we all can conceive the Divine Feminine Wisdom and Love within our own lives. When we achieve the appropriate cleansing and purifying, we open to the promise of attainment. This Mystery holds the Divine promise of attainment for *all*. It involves the ultimate realization that the self is a reflection of the Divine, but it is up to us to prepare and to conceive the expression of divinity within the unique circumstances of our own lives.

The Holy Birth

The third of the Feminine Christ Mysteries should be the focus of the third and fourth weeks of Advent—the last two weeks prior to the actual winter solstice. This is the heart of the Christ Mysteries. Birth only occurs through a union of the male and the female. One without the other cannot conceive and give birth. This is the symbol of beginning the process of lifting the Holy Child within each of us from the manger of the lower self to its rightful place within our lives. On another level it is the raising of the energies along the channel of the spine to the heart and up to the head—to the third ventricle of the brain where the higher birth occurs. This is the Feminine Mystery of learning to follow the Star of one's own Higher nature!

This brings us then to the time of the Mystic Midnight Sun—the winter solstice. At this point the astral plane and the angelic hierarchy begin to open the floodgates to infuse the earth with the angelic power of the Christ. This flood of energy reaches its highest point on midnight of Christmas Eve and then remains pouring forth at that intensity upon the earth for thirteen days, through January 6, the time of Epiphany. In the more traditional mystery systems, the Epiphany was a time of baptism into new life and initiation. During this time the sweetness of the song of the angels awakens in all life upon the planet the feminine energies.

In the Egyptian and the Persian Mysteries, at the hour of midnight (of what we call Christmas Eve), the priests would gather around them their truest disciples and the teachers of their people, and would speak of the great mystery of the victory of the sun over darkness. They would teach them the Mystery of the immortal soul becoming victorious over the animal forces of nature and the reawakening of the consciousness. It was a celebration of confidence, trust, and hope. This was known as "seeing the sun at midnight."

The energies associated with and manifesting upon the earth are triggered with the beginning of the winter solstice, and they then open to their fullest intensity by midnight of December 24. Interestingly enough, this is a day in traditional Christendom dedicated to Adam and Eve. Again we find the importance of the Mystery of Polarity within the Christ teachings. As mentioned, they then pour forth at that intensity for thirteen days, at which time the flow is ceased, but the energy remains throughout the rest of the season.

There are special meditations that can be used during those days to open one to a true vision of the Christ energy within one's own life. If worked with during this time, by the last day, the Christed Imagination will begin to awaken and an awareness of what must still be done will reveal itself. During this time the soul may pass through deep—even cathartic—experiences, and close attention to dreams will provide insight.

The vision that comes from the concentrated work through this holy time can open one to an awareness of what humanity still must endure in its evolution. Often this comes through the stimulated imagination. The individual can open to what he or she personally must do to bring the Light out into the individual life circumstances.

The Twelve Days of Christmas

Each of those holy days has an apostle who works to influence humanity, along with a group of the angelic hierarchy of one of the signs of the zodiac. Thus each day from Christmas to the Epiphany is a day in which the angelic hierarchy of each sign of the zodiac will manifest and pour forth great energy:

December 26 – The angelic hierarchy working through Aries intensify their energy play upon the earth with the assistance of James, the brother of John. This is a day to focus upon becoming a spiritual pioneer and to move toward new levels of discipleship. Meditating on the following phrase will help attune you to that energy on this day: "Behold, I make all things new." (Revelation 21:5)

December 27 – The angelic hierarchy working through the sign of Taurus intensify their energies upon the earth on this day with the assistance of the Apostle Andrew. It is a day to focus on the development of the quality of humility. Meditating upon the following phrase will help attune you to the celestial energies of this day: "He that dwelleth in love dwelleth in God." (John 4:16)

December 28 – The angelic hierarchy working through the sign of Gemini intensify their energies on this day with the help of the Apostle Thomas. This is a day to focus on transcending doubt to manifest true Christ power. Meditating upon the following phrase will assist in attuning to the celestial energies of this day: "Be still and know that I am God." (Psalm 46:10)

December 29 – The angelic hierarchy working through the sign of Cancer intensify their energies on this day with the assistance of the Apostle Nathaniel. This is a day to focus on developing mysticism without any sense of deception. Meditation upon the following will assist you in attuning to the celestial energies of this day: "But if we walk in the light, as He is in the light, we have fellowship one with another." (John 1:7)

December 30 – The angelic hierarchy working through the sign of Leo intensify their energies on this day with the assistance of the Apostle Judas and/or Matthias. This is a day to focus upon the transforming power of love. Meditating upon the following phrase will assist you in attuning to the celestial energies of this day: "Love is the fulfilling of the law." (Romans 13:10)

December 31 – Those of the angelic hierarchy working through the sign of Virgo intensify their energies with the help of the Apostle James the Just. This is a day to focus upon purity of character and selflessness. Meditation on the following will assist you in attuning to the celestial energies of this day: "But he that is greatest among you shall be your servant." (Matthew 23:11)

January 1 – Those of the angelic hierarchy working through the sign of Libra intensify their energies with the help of the Apostle Jude. It is a day to focus upon the beauty that lies within all souls and all individuals, regardless of outer appearance. Meditating upon the following will assist in attuning to the celestial energies of this day : "You shall know the truth and the truth shall set you free." (John 8:32)

January 2 – Those of the angelic hierarchy working through the sign of Scorpio intensify their energies on this day with the help of the Apostle John the Beloved. This is a day to focus upon the energies of transmutation. Meditation upon the following will help you to attune to the celestial energies of this day: "Blessed are the pure in heart for they shall see God." (Matthew 5:8)

January 3 – Those of the angelic hierarchy working through the sign of Sagittarius intensify their energies on this day

The twelve Apostles and Mary, the mother of Jesus.
Engraving by Gustav Doré

with the assistance of the Apostle Philip. This is a day to focus upon developing the higher mental capabilities of the Christed mind. Meditating upon the following will assist in attuning to the celestial energies of this day: "You are the light of the world." (Matthew 5:14)

January 4 – Those of the angelic hierarchy of the sign of Capricorn intensify their energies on this day with the assistance of the Apostle Simon (brother of James and Jude). This is a day to focus upon awakening the energy that will turn reluctance into complete dedication. Meditating upon the following will assist you in attuning to the celestial energies of this day: "Let the Christ be formed in you." (Galatians 4:19)

January 5 – Those of the angelic hierarchy working through the sign of Aquarius intensify their energies on this day with the assistance of the Apostle Matthew. It is a day to awaken the energies that will assist you in renouncing the physical world for spiritual illumination. Meditation upon the following will assist you in attuning to the celestial energies of this day: "You are my friends." (John 15:4).

January 6 – Those of the angelic hierarchy working through the sign of Pisces intensify their energies on this day with the help of the Apostle Peter. This is a time to invoke a strength that will allow the newly awakened feminine energies to become a foundation of rock within your life. Meditation upon the following will assist in attuning to the celestial energies of this day: "So God created man and woman in his own image." (Genesis 1:27).

As you work through each of these twelve holy days, following the Feast of the Christ Mass, there will awaken then throughout the rest of the winter season a growing vision and awareness of the inner potentials capable of being manifested within your life by you. This is the time of new birth!

OTHER OCCULT SYMBOLS
WITHIN THE WINTER MYSTERIES

Within the Christmas scriptures are many hidden significances. These are important to understand if one is to increase awareness of the true Christ Mysteries.

The Cave (grotto or stable)

This is the lower self, wherein the soul dwells. We must first give expression to the lower before the higher can be achieved. It is also an ancient symbol of the womb and thus the feminine energies.

The Manger

The solar plexus was often referred to as the "manger." It is the point of lower birth or the physical birth. The higher manger is the point between the pituitary and the pineal. We only give birth to the higher by raising our energies up. We must learn to leave the manger of our lower senses for a new manger formed from the Mystic Marriage of the Masculine and Feminine.

The Star in the East

The East is traditionally a symbol of the rising sun—the Christ Light rising in prominence upon the earth. It also reflects the aspect that we all must follow—our own star—to our higher soul. The inner Light guides us body, mind, and soul. It also reflects the Christ overlooking the one through whom he would be able to incarnate and walk the earth plane.

The Magi

On one level the Magi represent the three-fold dedication of body, mind, and spirit to the spiritual quest. Three is significant also in that it is the number of polarity, and the birth that arises from true polarity. On another level, according to Rudolph Steiner, the three Magi reflect the seeds of the three major Root Races of humanity that would be harmonized and united in all of humanity through the Christ—the new expression of the ancient mysteries for all of humanity:

Caspar – the representative of the seeds of the Lemurian age
   of humanity.

Balthazar – the representative of the seeds of the Atlantean Age of humanity.

Melchior – the representative of the seeds of the beginning of the Aryan Age of humanity.

The Gifts of the Magi

Frankincense – purifying and illuminating, it represents the cosmic ether in which spirit lives and which influences our union with the divine.

Myrrh – symbol of victory of life over death, the higher over the lower.

Gold – the symbol of the alchemical process and the outer, wisdom-filled being.

THE MINISTRATIONS OF GABRIEL IN THE CHRIST MYSTERIES

Gabriel is the archangel of love and hope. He is the governor of the winter season, working with the Christ in angelic influence upon the planet during this season. It is the task of Gabriel to assist in the purifying, elevating, and spiritualizing of humanity. He is the initiator of the mysteries of Love—primal creative Love.

To the neophyte, he brings experiences of love consciousness through the lower emotions—beyond the confines, though, of friends, family, and benefactors. At this time of the year he works to stimulate a greater appreciation of the Divine Essence within all. He works to develop the power of Love within the life of the individual—a power which has no emotional or sensory thrill. It is the power of Love that is offered as an attribute to be attained.

To those who work to attune to the rhythms of the winter season, Gabriel helps reveal the significance of the "Nativity Mysteries" as a step toward initiation. On the supreme mystery night of the year, he works to open the tender sweetness of the angel song, and he activates the feminine element in all beings upon the planet, as he has charge of all nurturing throughout nature.

Gabriel is the guardian of the sacred waters of life—the seed and the egg in the male and female. He is also overseer of the sign of Cancer—the direct opposite of the sign of Capricorn, which inaugurates the winter season.

The lily is the symbol, and it is also associated with Mary. Sometimes the white rose is substituted for it—as they are often interchangeable. Mary is the way-shower for all mothers and fathers—for the linking of the male and female in a manner that gives birth to the Holy Child within. It is the task of Gabriel to assist in this process.

The lily is a symbol of purity and self-control, the norm for any true disciple of any mystery tradition. It is a symbol which invokes angelic influence—particularly that of Gabriel during this season. It stimulates the energy of the throat chakra and all of the centers of the head, so that the creative power of the "Word" can be unfolded and expressed within each person's life.

A wonderful exercise is visualizing the lily forming within the body. Its step extends up the spine, and at the point of the throat, the flower unfolds, encompassing the head. This activates the Light Body or what could be called the "Lily of Light" within one's life. This will gradually awaken the true significance of the Immaculate Conception, a key to the ending of illness and the other limitations of birth. This exercise activates the ability to conceive with Love as a force.

THE RITE OF THE WINTER SOLSTICE

This exercise should be done from the night of the winter solstice through the Night of the Mystic Midnight Sun. It has a powerfully healing effect upon the individual, and it will plant seeds that will sprout within one's life by spring. These seeds are seeds of abundance, prosperity, love, and illumination.

This exercise uses a symbology that will assist the individual to align with the dynamic rhythms of this season and to be more receptive to the angelic and Christ ministrations throughout it. It can have a significant effect upon one's dreams, and thus you should pay close attention to them throughout the season. It will also open a new vibrancy to the meditative experience, and it will manifest opportunities over the following months to give greater expression to the Feminine energies of Love, Illumination, and Intuition. It will manifest opportunities to bring your own light out in the coming months. It will, of course, be up to you to take advantage of such opportunities.

Preparations

Make sure you will be undisturbed.

Use candles of a color appropriate to this season. Red and green are traditional, but black and white are powerful also for winter solstice celebrations.

Have a single white taper candle that you can hold in your hands—for the beginning of the meditation.

Have a rose (preferably white, although the red rose is an outer symbol of the inner white rose) that you can place upon your lap throughout the meditation.

If possible, also have a Christmas lily. You may interchange it with the rose.

Meditation

Light the single white, taper candle. As its light begins to shine within the darkness of your meditation area, focus upon the flame. Then close your eyes, and remember how the flame looked. Imagine that flame coming to life within the heart/solar plexus area of the body. When you can feel and see that flame of light within you, softly extinguish the candle. Be aware now of the small flame of light that shines within the darkness. As you do you hear the gentle words: "At last, my child, come up higher."

You focus upon this inner flame, and allow yourself to float upward into the night sky. See and feel it. The sky is black except for one lone distant star that shimmers in the distance. You feel yourself floating toward it, and as you draw closer, you see that the star hovers over a large temple, set high upon a mountain, looking over the earth. You follow its trail of light down until you come to rest before it.

The entire temple is bathed in soft light, and although you were here at the celebration of the autumn equinox, it appears so much different now. The two trees are trimmed, and you can see that the temple is great in size, more so than you remember. It has twelve sides, and the star above it makes it shine a luminous white. Raised above the temple is an equal-armed cross against a five-pointed star.

The door is closed, but through the window you can see that the inner temple is filled with a shimmering white mist. In the center stands an altar, and above the altar is a spotless white cross. Where the poles of the cross intersect is a single white rose. Around the outside of the altar are circular tiers of seats. They are filled with those dedicated to service. These are the "Compassionate Ones"—and they are both familiar and unfamiliar.

They are uniting their spiritual forces and directing them toward the unfoldment of that single white rose. Their voices rise in waves of harmony that fill the temple and carry to the outer world. As their song touches the rose, it unfolds petal by petal, giving off a golden hue. The light from this rose pours forth through the twelve windows of the temple, suffusing the landscape.

The light surrounds and fills you. You are enfolded within its light. You feel yourself being cleansed of selfish desire and your mind fills with a clearness and the brilliance of a diamond. You close your eyes and feel the energy as it heals and nurtures.

As you open your eyes, there is standing before you a beautiful being of great light and gentleness. The light is a soft emerald that touches your soul. Within his hand is a lily of great luster, and you know that this is the one called Gabriel.

The door behind is open, revealing the workings of the Inner Temple more clearly. Gabriel reaches forward and touches the crown of your head in blessing. You are filled with a love that goes beyond comprehension. You feel it pouring down through you, overflowing into your heart. You look down and you see the inner flame that brought you here shimmering. It dances and shifts and forms itself into a soft white rose. Gabriel then takes you by the hand and leads you into the doorway of the Inner Temple.

"You have opened your heart to the ministrations of the Servants of the Light. Hour by hour they will pour forth their energies. You are being shown so that you will remember and someday lead others to this point."

The voice speaks softly within your mind and it touches your heart. Your eyes fill with love for this magnificent being and the inner cross and rose grows even more lustrous, pouring forth greater energy out of the temple and down the mountainside to the world below.

"With each expression of love, the entire world is touched. At this time of the year the great beings of light shall ascend and descend, surrounding the earth and pouring forth energies to touch and awaken the hearts of all upon the earth."

Your eyes are drawn to the ceiling. It is open to the night sky and to the Great Star above. From the star to the temple, streams of light ascended and descended, the angelic hierarchy working to suffuse the earth with streams of love.

"These streams will touch all parts of the earth. Some are directed to the foulest areas of the earth. Some are released to the battlefields. Some become the benedictions at hospitals. Many are balms for hearts laden with sorrow. Some serve to help new souls re-enter the earth life stream, and others to assist those newly released from the body through the transition you call death. These are the labors of love for the world."

Gabriel turns toward you, and he touches your heart.

"Look within the inner white rose of light and see the love that is your divine heritage." You look into your own heart at the rose. Petal by petal it unfolds, and as it does, you see what you must do to become the true child of the Divine. You see the vision of the Christ within you.

As you lift your eyes from this vision, the temple is gone. Gabriel is gone. At your feet lays a red rose, a gift and an outer reminder of that which lives forever within the heart. You raise your eyes to the night sky, feeling yourself being drawn up to that distant star. The music of the inner temple sounds softly within your mind, and your heart is filled with the song of the angels: "Glory to God in the highest, and on earth peace—good will to all!"

Chapter Nine

THE RITE OF THE VERNAL EQUINOX

"Behold, I make all things new!"
Revelation 21:5

The Ancient Mysteries call forth a return to Nature's rhythms on an intuitive level. Spirit and Nature in Harmony! The earth seasons are designed to promote specific evolutionary needs. The autumn is the seed planting time; the winter is the gestation of the seed and the taking root. The spring is the bursting forth of those new seeds to release new aspiring life to be harvested in the summer. These are also reflected in the true Christ Mysteries.

The spring equinox opens the veil between the physical and the spiritual so that a resurrection in our lives can be inaugurated. The keynote of this season is creation. It is the drive to move our lives upward, like a seed pushing forth out of the earth into the air. The spring is the time when the creative powers we have been nurturing through the winter can be expressed to initiate a new world of opportunities for ourselves.

It is at this time of the year that the sun leaves the water sign of Pisces and enters into Aries, the creative fire sign. Fire was always regarded as something holy and mysterious. Many traditions speak of how fire first belonged to the gods. Plentiful are the myths of the ancient firestealers and the creation of humanity. It is an element which consumes and changes—it is both destructive and creative.

Aries is the fire sign of new beginnings, and much esoteric significance is attributed to this time of the year. The ancient Hebrew tradition speaks of how God fashioned the world at this time and that Moses led the Israelites out of Egypt in the spring. Resurrection myths, associated with the spring season abound: from Christ Jesus to Osiris of Egypt, Adonis of Babylon, and Tammuz of Sumeria. In the Roman Mysteries the death and resurrection of Attis was celebrated at this time of the year.

This is the time for the fires of the new. The spring is the beginning of the alchemical process of the seasonal changes. Because humanity had lost the sensitivity to attune to the seasons, it became necessary for the Christ energy to play upon humanity in the cyclic manner.

For the student of the Christ Mysteries it is important to recognize that each season, each day, and even each hour has its own peculiar quality. We must learn to attune to them to take advantage of them. We are being exposed to a universal cycle of influence.

While the winter season is the time of the Feminine Mysteries (the water element) in Occult Christianity, the spring season is the time for the Masculine Mysteries (the fire element). The time of the equinox is the time of the alchemical and magical blending of water and fire. The living waters within us (the awakened Feminine energies) are flooded with a new radiance (the fire of the Masculine energies) so that they can be expressed more fully within our life circumstances. This is the time which releases energies that manifest opportunity to understand the mystery of polarity the balancing of the masculine and feminine so they can eventually be blended to create new life. Spiritually and physically this is a time of great creative power.

In the Western hemisphere, the creative forces begin to grow. There is a fresh outburst of exuberant life and it holds many opportunities for those who align with its rhythms and forces:

1. It is an excellent time to initiate a new order within one's life.

2. It is an ideal time for the burning out of the old—the burning of the dross—so that the new seeds have room to sprout and be given new expression. Thus one of the hidden significances in the Christ teaching: "Do not put new wine into old skins."

3. It is also a time in which the veil between the physical and the spiritual is thinned, easing opportunities to access and invoke dynamic spiritual energy into one's life.

4. Its energy can be used to accelerate one's own initiation or to open new patterns for it throughout the rest of the spring.

5. It is an excellent time to invoke energy that will assist you in making things new within all areas of your life.

6. It is easier to release the fiery spark of the divine.

7. The inner temples are more accessible so that the secrets of life can be more deeply attuned to.

8. It is a powerful time for releasing fiery healing energies.

9. For the advanced disciple it is an ideal time to fashion the soul body so that the individual can function consciously in the spiritual world.

10. It is a time for awakening new teachers upon the earth plane.

For the true student of the Christ Mysteries, it is during the spring that the energy is available that facilitates the undergoing of discipleship. The individual must learn to roll away the stones of personal and sense limitation and come forth—bring the inner light out into the external world. At this time of the year the individual can open to the path of probation and learn to access the vibrant force of the planet to heal the self and others. This is the ideal time to open to new understanding of the dynamic process of healing—so much of which was outlined through the life of Christ Jesus. A study of the healings performed by Christ Jesus can assist the individual in understanding the intricate play of energy within humanity's life.

This is a time to focus upon conscious transmutation. This is the ideal time to assert the will force over the personality. It is the time to balance the polarities. This balance is necessary to fully comprehend the significance of the greatest symbol of the Christ Mysteries—one that is associated with this season. That is the symbol of the Holy Grail. The Mystery of the Grail is intricate and has many levels. For most, who are involved with the Christ Mysteries, initially it is the blessing of both the male and the female.

THE OCCULT SIGNIFICANCE OF EASTERTIDE

As we have discussed, the Christ Mysteries—the Christ Path of Initiation—was acted out within the course of the life of the individual of Christ Jesus. This becomes even more evident as we explore the culmination of the historical events associated with this being at this time of the year.

The entire initiatory path of the Christ Mysteries is outlined during Eastertide. Easter is still the one holy day determined by the stars. It falls always on the first Sunday following the first full moon of spring—after the vernal equinox. Esoteric tradition tells us that only the highest initiates are able to participate in the Mysteries and energies that occur at the equinox itself. For the general masses and students and even disciples, the celestial energies of the equinox are celebrated in a "reflected" manner at the time of the full moon. (Students of astrology will recognize that the moon reflects the light of the sun, and thus has significance to the time at which Easter is celebrated.)

We have an ideal opportunity during Eastertide to access energies to transfigure our lives. It is a time supervised by the Archangel Raphael—the Keeper of the Holy Grail. It is his task at this time of the year to help open the senses so that the soul can truly see and know what must be done by the individual in this path.

This is a celebration that can assist us in our ever upward spiral. It is a time of great angelic celebration, a time when we can connect more fully with the angelic messengers so as to resurrect our own lives. It is a time in which new teachers are often awakened to their tasks and purpose. It is a time in which the esoteric power of music and flowers can be discerned by those who have such a leaning.

The initiatory path of the Christ Mysteries is outlined through the events that we know of as Easter week. Every event in the life of Christ Jesus reflects events in the life of every human who seeks to unfold Christ consciousness. They were enacted within the physical to make us more cognizant of them, but they must not be taken literally. There is that "hidden significance." This is a time of great celebration, and not of mourning!

HOLY WEEK

Wednesday
This is the time of the betrayal and self destruction of Judas. Meditation should be upon the killing off of lower desires and clearing the way for greater light.

Thursday (The Last Supper)
This involves the Mystery of the Eucharist—the highest teaching about the alchemical process. It is a time for meditating upon transmuting the male and female energies for higher expression.

Thursday (Garden of Gethsemane)
This is the time to work and focus upon "Meeting the Dwellers on the Threshold", a process often repeated in the life of a true student of the Mysteries.

Friday (Crucifixion)
The most joyous time of the season, it represents the last stage of initiation. Here we learn to carry our own crosses, that we alone are responsible for our lives. We give up the lower for the higher.

Saturday
In more traditional mystery systems, this was a day for Baptism, an act that loosened and illuminated the fabric of energy of the individuals that brought full conscious sight to the inner spiritual planes of Nature. The veils between the living and the dead, the physical and the spiritual are permanently rent.

Sunday (Resurrection)
The most exalted ceremony, a time of angelic celebration over one who has risen above the lower self and given full expression to

the true Christ energy. It is the time of full and true communion with the angelic hierarchy.

The energy of the Christ upon the earth at Easter makes demands upon our understanding. It requires insight into the esoteric aspects of the Christ Mysteries for this to be seen as a time of great joy. For those who align with it, it has the potential of carrying the faculty of understanding to new heights.

PREPARATION FOR THE CHRIST FIRE MYSTERIES

Just as the teachings and steps of unfoldment around the Feminine Mysteries of Christmas and the winter solstice had a time of preparation (season of Advent), so do the teachings of the masculine energies of Fire within the Christ Mysteries. This is the season of Lent.

The Lenten season enables each individual to begin a preparatory process to experience the lessons and energies of the events outlined at Eastertide. Each individual, attuning to the Christ Mysteries and their rhythms, will experience them in his or her own unique manner. The seven masculine mysteries are often experienced by everyone during the spring season, in some form or another.

The Lenten season is a time to be spent in deep meditation upon the upcoming mysteries associated with the expression of the inner fires and their conscious transmutation. The amount of preparation will determine to what degree the individual will meet the trials and tests in order to accomplish the full awakening and expression of the inner fires. This was always a time of great soul preparation in the Mystery temples, prior to the influx of energies triggered upon the planet by the vernal equinox. It has many significances, mystical and otherwise:

1. It occurs forty days prior to Easter. Forty days was a symbolic duration, signifying a period of extensive preparations. After the Baptism of Christ Jesus, he went into mountains for forty days. The Baptism was the last of the Feminine Mysteries, and it would be followed by the expression of the Christ energy in the outer world.

2. It is a time to prepare for high spiritual endeavor so as to release energies which will manifest an opportunity to learn and to be initiated.

3. What is accomplished and manifested within one's life is dependent upon the efforts of the individual—it could take forty days, forty years, or forty lifetimes.

4. It was a time of probation in the ancient Mystery Temples:
   a time of deep soul searching
   a time of great soul assessment
   a time of extreme inner self-examination

5. The ceremony of Ash Wednesday is symbolic of our dedication and the selflessness necessary to begin the deeper Mysteries of Golgotha. The ashes symbolize the failures to live true to the ideals that were awakened on Palm Sunday in the past year.

6. Palm Sunday of the Lenten season was a time to open to new ideals for the coming year and the celebration of those who wish us well with our spiritual endeavors.

7. In the Hebraic traditions, the Biblical Books of Job and Jonah were used as manuals of initiation and preparation during this time.

Depending upon the degree of preparation, the individual of the Christ Mysteries can expect to experience the energies on one of three levels. These are of course not cut and dried, and there is some overlap. An individual may expect to experience aspects of several of them. These three degrees of energy set in motion through alignment with this season are those of *Purification, Illumination* and/or *Mastership*:

Purification (The Student of Gethsemane)
   For the individual who is opening to the Christ energies in their cyclic play upon humanity, the work and efforts at this time of year may trigger a narrowing of their spiritual path. The individual may have situations arise that will test the ability to utilize faith,

love, purity, and strength in various areas of his or her life. The individual may be guided to a path that leads to even greater dedication to service, and opportunities to serve others in a variety of ways. If pursued consciously, it will ultimately lead to conscious freedom from the physical body—at will. It may stimulate greater calls for purity and selflessness.

Symbolized by the rite in the garden, the energy of purification may manifest opportunities to learn to transmute one's conditions. It will create opportunities to cleanse the lower nature, and it will open a wider vision of the future. As part of the spiritual compensation of the efforts and trials of this time, it will also make it possible to develop techniques for first-hand knowledge of the facts of other planes of life beyond physical cognition.

Illumination (Student of the Trial)

At this level of the Christ Mysteries, the individual may possess an energy that will move him or her further along, but it will also manifest subtler tests of discrimination and balance. The further developed we become, the more subtle, powerful, and penetrating are our daily trials. The individual will develop through alignment with the energies at this season opportunities which bring home the importance of selflessness in training. One must learn to walk the straight and narrow. The spiritual compensation at this level is that of true, awakened clairvoyance and clairaudience. The training and work at this level involves consciously awakening the energy centers, and thus there begins to develop an awareness that we can open to the spiritual in full, normal, waking consciousness.

Mastership (The Student of the Crucifixion)

One who has aligned to the Christ Mysteries of the spring season and is more highly developed in areas, may encounter the learnings associated with the crucifixion. At this degree, with the intensity at which it manifests within the life of the individual, many turn back. The strength developed to this point may not be enough, and more work may be necessary on other levels. The subtle testing will continue to manifest. The scourging of this event is the symbol of the individual learning to awaken and control the inner serpent fire. Many may actually manifest situations that reflect being nailed to the cross, but they will not be able to endure it being raised. The spiritual compensation at this level of attunement is the awakened ability to pass at will from the physical to the spiritual and back at will. The personality is joined with the spirit.

It is good to be introspective at times throughout the spring season, so that you can identify how your attunement with the seasonal rhythms is manifesting situations on the path of the Christ Mysteries. Occasionally taking account of one's life circumstances and placing them into one of the three categories helps one to determine work needed and to understand the hidden significance of the life circumstances. Initiation, although enacted out in scripture, will occur through the normal circumstances of life—with the people with whom we are most involved. It does not occur in artificially contrived situations. This was important to impress upon humanity through a life enactment of the Higher Mysteries.

SEVEN MASCULINE MYSTERIES
OF OCCULT CHRISTIANITY

The original seven steps of the ancient mystery initiation process were expanded and re-expressed into the fourteen steps of the Christ Mysteries. These in turn are divided into seven Feminine Mysteries and seven Masculine Mysteries, each of which is associated with the energies activated with specific seasonal changes upon the earth.

The Feminine Mysteries (element of water) are linked to the winter solstice and the winter season. In these the work is centered in the heart and solar plexus, the centers for birth. They are the tender Mysteries that give birth within the individual to the Divine Feminine potential that resides within each of us. In the historical events of the life of Christ Jesus, they are associated with the experience of the Annunciation, and end with the Baptism.

The masculine Mysteries (the element of fire) are tied to the vernal equinox and the spring season. In these the work is difficult and involves the development of self-discipline. It requires giving expression to the inner potentials within the outer world—living the life that you are trying to give birth to. The individual must learn to unveil the creative forces given birth to in the previous season. The individual must learn to walk alone, expressing those creative fires with developed and concentrated Will.

Transfiguration

This is the event that bridges the Feminine Mysteries with the Masculine within Occult Christianity. It links the Christmas Mysteries with those of Easter—the male with the female as equal but separate poles of energy within the individual. It is the stage of development where the individual must learn to express both aspects with equal polarity. On the highest level, it can awaken the pituitary (seat of the brow chakra and the feminine energies) and the pineal (the crown chakra and the seat of the masculine energies). When this is accomplished, it brings conscious contact with the great spiritual masters, regardless of time or space. In the Christ Mysteries, this was the time when Christ Jesus appeared in his Archangelic essence to those three disciples capable of raising their consciousness enough to behold it.

Triumphal Entry

This is that part of the path that represents the joys one finds along the way. Jerusalem was the heart center where the Christ came to life (born in the time we associate with the Feminine Mysteries). The processional is symbolic of the path of the candidate who is victorious in transfiguring his or her life. It represents the outer recognition that does come to those who unfold and express the higher, inner potentials. This event has outer and inner significance. It is an opportunity for those who have benefited from the ministry to show homage and gratitude, and it is indicative of the approach of even greater work—the Entrance into the Temple of Light. This is the event of acclamation of those who also achieved and attained this degree of unfoldment and expression of the creative force. The Ass is symbolic of the soul wisdom, and the palms are symbols of victorious attainment.

Feast in the Upper Room

This is the time of the "Last Supper" in the scriptures. It is symbolic of the Feast of the Eucharist or the feast of Polarity which had been passed down from Melchizedek to Abraham, and from the Christ to all of humanity. This practice was a part of all the ancient mystery traditions. This is the final and ultimate teaching of the alchemical process. Only those who attained a certain degree of unfoldment sat at the table and shared in this mystery which demonstrates how to conserve the life essence so as to produce a

The Transfiguration
Engraving by Gustave Doré

vital force which would radiate from the body and could be drawn upon at will. This is the mystery of the blending of opposites—the equality and equilibrium of the male and female in all relationships. Esoteric tradition teaches that Mary held a similar Feast in an adjoining chamber for the twelve female initiates. The actual ceremony includes both men and women, and those who participated were taught how to demonstrate powers of mastership in healing and spiritual enlightenment. The bread is the ancient symbol of the Divine Feminine (water mystery) and the Wine is the ancient symbol of the Masculine Energy, or fire element. Bread and wine, bread and salt, cakes and ale, manna, the Last Supper—they are all part of the same ancient tradition.

Garden of Gethsemane

This was the teaching of the highest power of the transmutation of energies to the three apostles most capable Peter, James, and John. They could not stay awake to assist the Christ Jesus, thus they still were not capable of the task. Learning to access the balanced power of the "Upper Room" demands in the life of the spiritual disciple that the power be used to transmute lower conditions. The Christ had no lower self to transmute, and thus chose to transmute the accumulated negative energy of humanity. At this event the Christ would slow his own vibrations down to come into complete attunement and resonance with the vibratory rhythms of the earth. This was necessary so as to conform with the energy conditions of the entire planet. At the "giving up of the ghost," then, the Christ could become an indwelling Logos of the Earth, a permanent part of the energy fabric of the earth itself, to stimulate a greater impulse toward the higher in all. The three apostles were to assist, but they could not handle the task. The keynote of this Masculine Mystery is selflessness and sacrifice. True spiritual surrender must imprint itself upon the soul at some point. With most spiritual students, it happens periodically within the unfoldment process. We all experience our "Gardens of Gethsemane"—our feelings of aloneness, feeling the weight of the world and all of its responsibilities upon our shoulders. We must face the responsibilities and ultimately be able to proclaim: "Not my will, but Thine be done."

The Trial

The "trial" represents a very critical point upon the path of the spiritual student. By this time, a certain degree of knowledge and power has been gained by the individual—beyond that of the ordinary individual. This always results in temptations. The individual must choose between the long-range effects and the immediate—and the immediate may be anything within the present incarnation. There can arise temptations to misuse the energy or to flaunt it for self-aggrandizement. The temptations that arise are usually one of three kinds, and they may come in varying intensities:

The temptations of the mortal mind and its lower desires (represented by Christ Jesus being brought before Annas).

The temptation of worldly ambition (represented by Christ Jesus sent before Caiphas).

The weakness and vacillation of the mind when taking a stand for one's life and one's truths, even when it may endanger your personal position (represented by Christ Jesus before Pilate).

The scourging and the discomfort is the symbolic pain of the spiritual fires of new birth and the fully awakened centers of the body touched by the serpent fire of wisdom as it rises to the head. The crown of thorns is also a symbol of the effects of the awakened serpent fire as we refuse to give in to the temptation to misuse or expend our energies and abilities unnecessarily. As the serpent fire (kundalini) touches the pineal and the pituitary, it also touches the frontal sinus and cranial nerves, opening the mind to full spiritual realization.

The three falls of the "trial" period are symbolic of the moral failures to which humanity can succumb upon the path to higher enlightenment:

The first is the weight of matter that veils the spiritual.

Second is the falling because of earthbent desires.

Third is falling because of uncontrolled fancy and glamor to which the undisciplined spiritual mind will give way.

Crucifixion

At this point in the unfoldment of the inner divine potentials, the path becomes narrower. Many turn back at this point, not having the strength. They either find that the shortcuts have not properly prepared them, or that it will involve more than what can be given at this time. Many have allowed themselves to "be nailed to the cross," but they could not bear the pain of having it elevated. At this level, the individual must bring out the innermost aspects into the light and transmute them.

There is subtle testing always, and many tests will involve choices of the spiritual over the physical and personal. The individual must learn to meet all misunderstandings, ridicule, and persecutions in an unflinching manner—even from those nearest. It may demand a willingness to give up fortune and fame.

Mary walked every step with the Christ Jesus, and thus she had also achieved this level of initiation being acted out for humanity. Upon the cross, Christ Jesus would be surrounded by three women, symbolic of the feminine aspects which make the achievement possible. At this level, the individual can come to pass at will from the physical to the spiritual realms. The individual learns the lesson of conscious immortality.

Resurrection

The last of the seven Masculine Mysteries of Occult Christianity is celebrated on Easter—the resurrection of the Christ. Death is the last enemy and fear to be overcome. This event indicates the teaching of conscious immortality—one who can operate in both the physical and the spiritual realms in full consciousness. It is sometimes called the "Glory degree of Initiation."

On many levels we experience many deaths and many resurrections. These are reflected within the continual cycle of the seasons and the changes in Nature. We always die to one aspect of ourself as we are born to another. For many people change is difficult and painful, but only as long as we remain emotionally attached to what is no longer beneficial. Part of the task of the spiritual student is to see each day as a resurrection.

At its highest level, esoteric tradition teaches that you may still experience more lives upon the earth as a teacher, but you will never again know the interruption of consciousness between the inner and outer planes of life, between life and death.

"... and there was a darkness over all the earth ..."
Engraving by Gustave Doré

THE MINISTRATIONS OF RAPHAEL

Raphael is the overseer of the season of spring. He is sometimes symbolized by the sun or the returning sun. He is the angel of brightness, beauty, healing, and life. The name literally means "God has Healed." He instructs in the art of healing and thus the caduceus is often his symbol as well. He works to help humans link the heart and the mind in the healing process.

Information about Raphael originally came out of the Chaldean tradition, but he is also one of three great angels named in post-Biblical lore. In the Biblical Book of Tobit, he is companion and guide to Tobias, the son of Tobit. At the end of their journey together, he reveals that he is one of the "seven holy angels" that attend the throne of God.

In the *Zohar*, Raphael is charged to heal earth and "through him . . . . the earth furnishes an abode for man, whom he also heals of maladies." He is also the angel of science and knowledge, and he was the preceptor of Isaac. One legend tells how Solomon prayed to God for help in the building of the Temple. God answered with the gift of a magic ring brought to the Hebrew kin personally by Raphael. The ring, engraved with the five-pointed star had the ability to subdue all demons, and it was this "slave labor" of demons that enabled Solomon to complete the Temple.

Raphael is the keeper and guardian of the most sacred symbol of the Christian Mysteries—the Holy Grail—throughout the Piscean Age. He works to awaken the Great Quest—the quest for our true spiritual essence and how best to manifest it within this life.

He bestows valor and grace upon humanity, and with a group of beings of light known as the Malachim, he is the chief besower and bringer of miracles, coloring our lives with wonder. It is from his influence and this group known as the Malachim that our individual Holy Guardian Angel comes, to teach us and guide us as we begin to take more conscious control of our evolution.

THE RITE OF THE VERNAL EQUINOX

This is a meditation that has a dynamic impact upon the life of the individual when performed at or around the time of the vernal equinox. It releases energy into your life that manifests opportunities for change and movement. It stimulates choices and decisions that help us to grow. The opportunities will arise; whether or not you act upon them is free will.

This meditation opens you to a play of energy that will allow you to begin to express, in the outer life, circumstances that you have been nurturing and developing through the winter season. It awakens new insight and stronger intuition, and it may also call for a testing of your inner goals and desires. Are they really what you wish to have manifest within your life, or are you just dabbling for the fun of it? The energy of this season, activated through this meditation, will bring you face to face with this question. It is important to follow your heart. Do what you know in your heart is right for you—that which you have been nurturing through the winter.

This meditation in the spring opens contact with new people and opportunities to extend yourself in all areas of your life. You will only be limited by your own attitudes and perspectives. This releases the energy of initiation—initiating new activities, new people, new learning, and new spiritual growth and unfoldment. It initiates a new realization and expression of the inner potential you knew you had all along. All that is necessary is the faith and the courage to follow through upon them. It has been said that we are never given a hope, wish, or dream, without also being given opportunities to make them a reality. The only thing that can shatter that possibility is compromise. This is not a time to compromise, but rather to go forward with what you have already sown!

Preparations

Make sure you will be undisturbed.

This is most effective to perform during the three days prior to and the day of the vernal equinox.

Repeat the meditation again at the time of the full moon that follows the vernal equinox.

Repeat again on Good Friday, the Saturday before Easter, and especially in a sunrise meditation on Easter Sunday. (You may wish to also repeat it at other times during the Holy Interval between the vernal equinox and Easter.) Meditating with fresh flowers at this time enhances its effect.

Pay close attention to the events in your life that occur—day-by-day and week-by-week throughout the spring season. This will help you to understand the seasonal power of the spring as it manifests energy within your own unique life situation.

Meditation

As you begin to relax, the awareness of your present setting fades. A cloak of darkness surrounds you, and you feel strangely safe. As you look within the darkness, it begins to lift. You see yourself upon the breast of a small hill that overlooks a still river. Its waters are black and deep. The sky above is filled with dark gray, swirling clouds. The trees and bushes are bare and gray. Across the river sits an ancient temple—in ruin. It is dusk, and the sun is going down behind you, taking the last of the daylight with it.

You are standing upon a path that leads down to the dark river below. It is lined with people on both sides who are painted and dressed for mourning. You walk silently between them, unsure how to respond to their sadness or even if you should.

At the river's edge is a small barge, and raised up on it is an altar, draped in black. It reminds you of an open sarcophagus, and the thought does not comfort you. Next to the walkway stands a tall figure dressed in black. Upon his breast is the symbol of a golden chalice, encircled in a field of blue. On the barge itself, next to the open sarcophagus, stand three hooded figures—silent and stoic. You step onto the barge, searching their shielded faces for some indication of the events to follow. Silently they assist you in stretching out upon the altar, and you are draped up to the chin in black silk cloth. Embroidered into it is the figure of a giant phoenix rising from the fires and ashes.

The barge is shoved off from the shore, and at a nod from the guide with the chalice emblem, one of the other three draws from beneath his cloak a white rose, and the second brings forth a great sword. The sword is touched to the rose, and it turns a fiery red. It is then dropped into the water beside the barge. The water bursts into flame, igniting the entire river. The flames surround the barge—water and fire together, neither extinguishing the other. When your guides are sure that you are fully aware of the fires, the black cloth is pulled up and draped over your head.

Again the darkness. You are alone. You can see and hear nothing. You know the fire is burning in the water, but you do not know how it will affect the barge. Will it consume the barge? Will it consume you? You force yourself to breathe deeply and relax. Somehow you know you may stop if you wish, but you also know the trip must be made sometime. As always, the choice is up to you.

Within your own mind you hear the words "Thy will be done," and the decision is made. All is silent. You are left to your own thoughts—on the sacredness of your own life. Your mind begins to look back upon the events of your life. You look back at all the people and events you have encountered. All the changes you have been through within your life float before your eyes, showing you how you have become who you are at present. You see those whom you have hurt and those who have hurt you. You see and feel the love you have given and the love you have lost. You see your life intertwined with the lives of so many, each one adding to the essence of creativity that you now are.

You remember all of the unfinished tasks and all the things you promised yourself that you would do. You see all the illusions of life that you have encountered, and all the blessings you have received. You remember the abilities you have manifested in the past and can give birth to once more. You see the dreams and hopes and wishes you have yet to fulfill, and there arises within you a realization that the opportunities for such are never past. They are ever at hand!

There is a slight bump, as the barge touches a shore. It draws you from your reverie. You arch your back, feeling the stiffness that has settled. It lets you know that a great length of time has passed. Slowly, you draw the black cloth off your face. The waters of the river are no longer on fire. It is pre-dawn, the sun has not yet risen. And your guides are gone.

You see that you are on the distant shore from whence you began. Up the slope, you can see the outline of the ancient temple. You raise yourself from the altar and step off the barge onto the earth.

You climb the slope toward the distant temple. As you reach the crest, you see that magnificent temple standing in luminous glory. No longer is it in ruins. The two trees bordering the door are full and green, and you look about you. All of the earth is green again. The trees and bushes are budding with new life.

It is then that the first rays of the sun streak the horizon to the East. With that the temple door opens wide, inviting you in. At the altar in the center are your four guides, but no longer are they dressed in black. Theirs are the color of the great beings of light, for your guides are the archangels of the seasons—Michael with his flaming sword, Gabriel with the white rose, Auriel in luminous white, and Raphael in the middle, holding high above his head the Great Chalice of Life.

The temple swells with the music of harmony and life. All who had mourned are dressed in brilliant shades of rainbow light, and as they sing forth their song, the sun rises over the horizon. Its light fills the temple, breathing new fire and life into all. It touches and fills the Holy Grail, radiating and reflecting out upon the earth.

You look back toward the river and you see the golden sunlight reflecting and filling the waters with new radiance and a fire of light, not flame. As you turn back to the altar, Raphael turns to you, holding aloft the Golden Chalice. He raises his eyes to the heavens and the light pours forth over you. It spirals in and through you, and you are renewed. You are born afresh. Your aura is ignited with new radiance and you can see it in its true glory. It is infused with a cross of radiant light that shines out from you like a great star in the heavens that will shine upon all within your life.

You close your eyes in gratitude and prayer, lifting your thoughts and your heart to the divine through the song of the Inner Temple. As you open your eyes, the temple lifts from around you, but you feel its impress within you still alive. Its energies will grow like the rising sun, and your life will be fused with the creative fires of the Christ.

Chapter Ten

THE RITE OF THE
SUMMER SOLSTICE

"The most beautiful thing we can experience is the mysterious. It is the source of all true art and science. He to whom this emotion is a stranger, who can no longer pause to wonder and stand arapt in awe, is as good as dead; his eyes are closed . . ."

Albert Einstein

The summer solstice is the high point of the Year of the Soul. It is that point in the year in which the energies of Nature reach their culmination, and it is the time in which the Christ energies touch the body, mind, and soul of all living things. This is the time of the Mystic Marriage, the uniting of the male and female to give birth to the Holy Child within us.

This is the time of the year to establish a relationship between our Will and the Christ force within and upon the earth, and all of those who have aligned with it. It is the time to awaken to spiritual ecstasy. It is the time in which contact with the angelic hierarchies can occur most easily and most intimately. Greater concentration is required, as there is often more outer world activity which can distract, but it is a time in which the alignment of the more subtle planes of life with the physical provides great access.

The highest and most esoteric teachings of the Christ Mysteries are infused within the Sermon on the Mount, as previously discussed. Esoteric tradition teaches that it was at this time of the year that it occurred.

This is also the time of the year associated with the Ascension in the Christ Mysteries. The Ascension, though, is not an ascension of the Christ into the heavens away from the earth. It is the extension and activation of the full etheric energy of the Christ to enable all of those upon the earth to bridge to the spiritual realms. The occult significance of the Ascension is the impulse of freedom that fills the entire energy system of the individual who attunes and aligns with it. This breaks down bonds of dependency, and a uniting on new spiritual heights occurs. From the time of the Ascension, the Christ energy filled the earth and extended to the spiritual realms, making them accessible to humanity for eternity. Thus the significance of the phrase: "I am in the Father, and He in me and I in You."

Magnetically, the physical, etheric, astral, mental, and spiritual planes are drawn into alignment on the three days prior to and the day of the summer solstice. The physical and subtle bodies of humanity are also aligned at this time. For one who works with these energies, a new and more stable alignment can be established, which will open for even greater growth as the next Year of the Soul is unfolded.

For those who align with the rhythms of the seasons and the Christ Mysteries the summer solstice can trigger a time in which much can be accomplished:

1. It awakens great spiritual inspiration and can stimulate the development of conscious etheric vision of the inner planes.

2. There is an awakening of greater strength to transmute the lower.

3. There arises greater opportunity to link with others who are involved in the Christ Mysteries.

4. There will manifest opportunities to create harmony and unity in various areas of our lives.

The Ascension
Engraving by Gustave Doré

5. There can arise a revelation of the path that will lead to a higher "ascension" of your own abilities in the year ahead.

6. There increases greater opportunity to work and commune with the Nature Kingdom and those beings that work with humanity through it. On Midsummer Night (the solstice), the year's work of the Nature Spirits is completed. This is a time in which the "Fairy realm" is opened for those prepared to see.

7. This time releases energies that manifest opportunities for confidence, strength, and hope.

8. It provides opportunities to balance all the elements of the earth and the physical body.

9. The Holy Interval (three days before and the day of the summer solstice) is a powerful time of purification and alignment. It can be used to cleanse the etheric of negative habits and thoughtforms, so that you do not repeat the same mistakes.

10. There occurs a general expansion of the faculties and intuitive energies.

11. There can arise opportunity to invoke greater energy into our own chakra centers and employ them in a more directed manner.

12. It is the ideal time to renew the mind and attune to the highest realms through a merging of the brow and crown chakras—the male and female forces. This will ultimately awaken the opportunity to become a channel of Light.

This season is governed by Auriel. Auriel is sometimes considered the tallest of the archangels, with eyes that can see across eternity. Sometimes called the Son of the Star, this has ties to a name by which early Christ Initiates were known. Auriel brings with the summer season beauty and an awakening of vision. One who opens to the ministrations of Auriel during this season can behold the streams of life that are infusing the entire planet.

THE OCCULT ASTROLOGY OF THE SUMMER

Cancer is the mother sign of the zodiac. It is the sign for manifesting the new waters of life. It is the sign for giving birth to a new polarity and expression of that polarity. The two swirls that comprise the glyph for this astrological sign reflect the blending of the male and female into new expression.

Easter and the vernal equinox bring with them the lessons of death and rebirth. The cross—the predominant symbol of the spring season—is an indication of the juxtaposition of the poles of the masculine and feminine energies within us all. As we learn to realign and balance those poles, they become parallel columns, creating a doorway by which we may enter into the inner mysteries of new birth and new expression. Gemini, the sign that ends the spring season, has as its glyph the twin columns standing parallel rather than juxtaposed. Once balanced, then, the process of blending can begin—as reflected within the sign of Cancer which follows Gemini.

As the sun enters the sign of Cancer, there is a stimulation of varying intensities of a new expression of the Divine Feminine. This stimulation affects people differently, according to the sensitivities developed. This varying intensity is reflected through the three planets that are associated with Cancer in esoteric astrology. These three planets influence all of us in unique ways, giving impulse to new processes of energy manifestation within our lives. These processes are those of generation and regeneration. These three planets also reflect the three levels upon which the influence of the summer solstice can affect us, in accordance with how attuned we become to the energies of this seasonal change. These three levels can be on a physical level, a soul level, or on a spiritual level.

The moon, which rules Cancer, affects everyone on a physical level at this time of the year. Most people respond to this lunar influence, involving themselves in new physical activities, etc. The moon is a symbol of the physical energy of generation.

The planet Jupiter and its affect upon us is also stimulated when the sun enters into the sign of Cancer. How it specifically affects us can be determined by its placement within our astrological chart, but during this time of the year its influence will be felt on a more subtle level. Anyone engaged or wishing to engage in a creative or artistic endeavor can open themselves to great inspiration by attunement to the energies of this time of the year. This is the primary affect of Jupiter upon individuals as the sun enters this sign. Jupiter has ties to that aspect of soul awareness within us that helps us to bridge the physical with the spiritual. It increases and expands the energies of the etheric body, thereby opening the individual to greater vision and inspiration. The more we attune ourselves to these rhythms, the greater the effect upon us.

The esoteric ruler of the sign of Cancer is Neptune. Neptune is the planet of initiation, and when the sun enters this sign the influence of Neptune and the energies of initiation can be attuned to and invoked within one's life. The influence of Neptune is felt by all, although it is not usually consciously recognized. Neptune is the planet of regeneration, and those who are capable of undergoing a new birth will feel the pull of initiation. Neptune is a planet associated with the sea, and much of the Christ teachings occurred around the Sea of Galilee. The fish, a symbol for Neptune, was a symbol of the Christ Mysteries as well. The influence of these three planets and the angelic hierarchy that works through them has been described in extant literature and scripture. Even the Biblical scriptures reveal this hidden influence:

"Except a man be born again, he cannot see the kingdom of God . . . except a man be born of water (moon in Cancer) and of the spirit (the Jupiter influence on humanity through Cancer), he cannot enter the kingdom of Heaven (the Neptune influence on humanity through Cancer)." (John 3:5)

The archangels associated with the planets of this sign also provide insight. Gabriel is the archangel of the moon. He is also the ruler of the season that begins in the sign opposite Cancer—Capricorn. Auriel is the governor of the summer season, but Auriel also is known to work through the influence of the planet Jupiter to awaken the soul qualities of inspiration within humanity. It is the Christ who is most commonly associated with the esoteric ruler of Cancer—Neptune. Working through the influence of Neptune, the Christ works to stimulate the feminine into greater and purer expression in all people.

Cancer is the sign of the Madonna, the woman with the moon under her feet and with a crown of twelve stars. It is also the sign of the prodigal son, the return to new birth and to new expressions of the divine feminine. Cancer is the sign of birth and the principle feminine sign of the zodiac.

The Cherubim are the angelic beings associated with this sign. They are considered the guardians to the sacred places upon the planet and to all the sacred waters of life. These sacred places are termed: "The Holy of Holies," "The Ark of the Covenant," "the Holy Grail," etc. They guard the sacred secrets to the sexual force. These sacred places we must learn to build within ourselves and within all expressions of our energies by becoming one of the "pure in heart." It is this task which is most accessible to us at this time of the year. (The Sermon on the Mount was given to teach humanity how to become pure, so that greater inspiration could unfold within one's life.)

As the sun moves through the rest of the summer, it is the task of the students of the Christ Mysteries to maintain the equality of polarity within themselves. This is accomplished through self-authority and self-triumph. This is the season—through the great beings that come into play within our lives during it—that enables us to prepare for the Rite of Mystic Marriage within the inner temple of the soul.

THE MINISTRATIONS OF AURIEL

Auriel is the governor of the summer season, working to help the Christ energies be diffused throughout the earth. Auriel is known as the angel of beauty and vision. Auriel is also considered the tallest of the angels, with eyes so clear that they can see across eternity. The name Auriel means "God is Light."

The colors associated with this great being vary according to tradition. When contacted through work with the nature spirits and beings, the traditional colors are yellow and black. At the highest vibrational aspect, the color of this being's raiment is a combination of crystalline white and ethereal blue, filled with the silvery stars of the Madonna. During the summer months these colors veil the earth, especially at the time of the summer solstice.

Contact with Auriel opens one to the "fairy" kingdom and to fairy vision. This vision usually begins with the appearance of glimmering lights and then subtle forms. From here the vision of the figures of the angelic hierarchy begins to open. Through work with Auriel, one can open to true etheric vision—on a fully conscious level.

One tradition speaks of Auriel being the teacher of the prophet Esdras. Auriel awoke within him the gift of spiritual vision whereby he was able to see the Christ face-to-face and prophecy.

Like Michael, Auriel is often associated with the Flaming Sword. Invoking Auriel was a means by which individuals could manifest the appearance of this Flaming Sword. This is the sword of discrimination and comprehension of spiritual law. In the ancient grail legends and scriptures, this sword was also interchangeable with the lance or spear which shed the blood of Christ Jesus while upon the cross. Through work with Auriel during the summer, the spiritual force symbolized by the sword is awakened in those aspiring to lead a life of initiation. It is a symbol of the divine force which animates all creation, and it represents the power that the ego has acquired through its many incarnations. When awakened through work and attunement with the seasonal cycles of the Christ energy, it can be used to heal and to bless, but only as long as there is a true willingness never to inflict wounds even if it means that you will receive the wounding yourself. What one hurts, one must heal, and what one kills, one must bring back to life.

Auriel was once known as the "Fire of God" and some ancient works ascribe the process of alchemy to this being. Anyone who works with nature, nature spirits, and the alchemical processes of life could do no worse than to meditate upon and invoke the aid of this great being.

Auriel rules the summer season, the point at which the energies of nature reach their peak and also begin their decline toward a new cycle. This is the process of alchemy: birth, death, and rebirth. It is the assistance of Auriel that enables us to see these laws operating within our own unique life circumstances, so that we may truly transform ourselves in the manner that is best for ourselves.

THE RITE OF THE SUMMER SOLSTICE

This powerful meditation has great potential for setting in motion a harvesting within one's life that creates new birth on many levels. It manifests an energy that opens a probing of how you came to be. It may manifest a testing of your ability to place

Divine Will first. There will begin to unfold increasingly through the summer months an understanding that there must truly be a reason for who you are and where you are—even if you don't know the specifics.

This is an exercise which will increase the intuitional faculties. You will become aware over the following months of the effects you have on other people. Others often comment about something "different" about you, even though they cannot put their finger on it. It has to do with the new energy being born within your auric field.

The qualities of idealism, devotion, and the following of a higher calling become more important. There may manifest a testing or confronting of hypocrisy. There will occur a release of pressure in your day-to-day events.

Intuition, inspiration, fertility, compassion, and an expanded vision will awaken and grow through the summer. There will unfold a greater connectedness to others, and it is not unusual to have individuals from your past step back into your life as a way of proving to yourself how much you have changed.

Dream activity becomes vibrant. This dream activity can often reveal past life information important to where you are going. There will begin to unfold through the dreams glimpses of what the higher can bring.

Preparations

Make sure you will be undisturbed.

Perform this meditation three days prior to and on the night of the summer solstice. It can be repeated periodically throughout the summer.

Have cake and ale, bread and wine, or one of the Eucharistic combinations available—a physical participation and grounding of the spiritual energies you invoke through this exercise.

This is a powerful exercise to do in a group situation, or it is powerful also if done with a partner of the opposite sex. (Make sure the individual is one with whom you have a good connection.)

Keep an air of celebration about this. You are participating in the celebration of new life—a new birth.

It is powerfully effective if performed outdoors, as the summer solstice is the high point of the forces of Nature in their yearly cycle. There is almost always a full or new moon at or around the time of the solstice. Make sure you perform this exercise then for maximum results.

Meditation

Relax and breathe deeply the fresh summer night air. As you relax, allow your eyes to close. Feel the warm embrace of summer soothe and nurture you. Feel and imagine yourself being lifted into that summer night sky and being carried gently to the top of the high mountain that is now becoming familiar. As you allow yourself to be gently lowered before the beautiful Temple, imagine yourself as coming home. It is like a reunion or a wedding which draws all together.

As you stand outside the temple doors, you notice the trees on either side are still full and green. Over the past year there has been growth, and you can already see where there may need to be future trimming. These thoughts pass quickly as you look up into the night sky. It is filled with shades of deep blues and purples.

There is but one constellation visible, and one star among it shines brightly. Although you do not recognize the constellation, somehow you know that this is the star called Sirius. The Egyptians named it for the union of Isis and Osiris.

The door to the Inner Temple opens, and you bring your attention to the event at hand. You step through the doorway, and you find the temple seems much larger than you ever remembered. You are surprised to find yourself wearing a robe of white with images of emerald ivy and rich grapevines embroidered along its edge. The robe is tied at the waist with a silver cord, with a buckle inscribed with the symbol for the sign of Cancer.

A magnificent being of fire and light steps forward, its eyes embrace you, and it calls you by name. You recognize Auriel and are humbled. Auriel steps behind you and places upon your shoulders a cape of deep blue silk.

You step further into the Temple and look about you. The ceiling has a window in the shape of an equal-armed cross that opens the Temple to the heavens. In the distance you can see that one star shining down through it. The light casts its gleam in the shape of that cross upon the floor of the temple.

Around the temple, in tiers, sit men and women, alternating from all ages and all races upon the planet. These are the masters of the ancient wisdoms. Behind them sit all of those who, like you, are on the path to self-knowledge. Auriel steps forward and with a motion shows you your seat.

Once seated, you turn your attention toward the altar in the center. There in front stands the High Priest. He is dressed simply in robes of deep blue, and there are silver streaks in his hair. You hear your name spoken softly, and you see that the High Priest has fixed his eyes upon you—acknowledging you as he has with all who are present. His eyes hold your attention. They are older than time, and they are filled with a mixture of pride, pain, love, and despair. This is Melchizedek, the Prince of Peace.

He turns to the altar and he raises the Golden Chalice from it and lifts it high over his head. He sings out a word that is foreign and yet which touches your heart. In the four directions appear great columns of light. In the East a column of blue and gold rises and then forms the figure of the Archangel Raphael. In the West, a column of emerald green rises and then shimmers into the figure of the Archangel Gabriel. To the South, a column of brilliant red fire rises and then forms the figure of the Archangel Michael. And then to the North a column of crystalline white brilliance shimmers and before you is the Archangel Auriel.

A sound begins to fill the temple. A light streams forth down from the star above, blessing the chalice. A wind blows through the temple, and you have never felt more alive than at this moment. You never knew that the heavens had a song, but it is that song that fills you now. The temple fills with the force of this sound, and you surrender to it, are drawn within it and recreated by it.

And then there is silence. As you become aware of the temple ceremony once more, you see yourself in ethereal form, standing before the High Priest. Then from out of you steps the other half. For every male, there is the female, and for every female there is the male. They live within us all.

Auriel steps forward, and Melchizedek stands aside. You watch as Auriel takes the hand of the Female you and places it within the hand of the Male you. Auriel holds the two hands together and then breathes upon them, binding them together for eternity. You watch as your male half and your female half turn to each other and embrace. The two forms seem to melt into each other—blending, changing, swirling—until there stands a single figure with the essence of both. In the light around them you see faintly the sign of Cancer. You shiver and you feel the blended essence of both once more within you.

Melchizedek steps forward and pours wine into the Golden Chalice, and he breaks the bread upon the altar into pieces for all in attendance. As the bread is passed around, with its taste comes the awareness that you will never again lack for loving guidance. And as the wine is blessed and passed around, its taste fills your mind with the thought that in love there is no division of faith!

These are part of the High Mysteries that as yet you have only seen through a veil. You feel a gentle touch upon your shoulder. It is time to leave. The rest you are not ready for. Auriel leads you to the door and the twin columns formed by the trees. You are filled with a sense of peace.

Auriel steps forward, embraces you, and kisses you gently upon the head. With the kiss comes a feeling of exquisite joy. Gently you reach out with your heart and your mind, daring to touch this magnificent being, aware of a new power within you. For a moment the intensity is too much to endure, but for a few brief seconds you find yourself at one with this great being of light and you know your life will never be the same. The door to the Inner Temple closes, but you know it will never seal you out. You know it will be a part of all aspects of your life forever, as you bring it alive within your life!

Afterword

THE CHOICE OF THE MODERN CHRISTIAN GNOSTIC

"I love those who love me; and those who seek me shall find me."

Book of Psalms

In medieval times, it was not uncommon to find Christian Gnostics being labeled heretics, and then being imprisoned or even killed. No unusual view of theological Christianity was acceptable by the Church or even the common people. Humanity has changed since then, and although there still exist those who would hold to the literal interpretation of the scriptures, many find their knowledge of the Divine interaction within the world limiting.

The Christ Jesus taught personal responsibility and personal action in the unfoldment and manifestation of the Divine within the individual's life. Blind faith has its place, but only when it has developed into a true force, and not just a concept that anchors the individual to a belief that is impartial, at best. Modern Christian Gnosticism should teach us the personal experience and knowledge of the Divine within our lives.

188 - The Occult Christ

Humanity faces many choices. How and what we choose determines our growth and the environment and experience that we will encounter. It is part of our "free will" and to ignore it is to ignore the divine energies of the world. Each must make his or her own choices, according to his or her own needs. It is how we learn. It is how we grow. It is how we evolve.

Christianity was meant to be a mystery system. In the ancient traditions, the initiation process underwent seven specific stages. These can be expressed in "Christian" terminology:

1. *Birth*—the awakening of the heart center; control of the ego and the physical body.

2. *Baptism*—the awakening and flowering of the throat chakra, the development of creative will and control of the astral body.

3. *Transfiguration*—the entire body and all of its energy centers are awakened and flooded with new light; the head centers open to new spiritual sight and awareness.

4. *The Great Renunciation*—(Suffering, Crucifixion, and the Resurrection)—our suffering and overcoming of karma.

5. *Ascension*—the initiate becomes an adept and opens to full consciousness of all planes at all times.

6. *Lord*—one who oversees large groups of people in their spiritual studies; involved with more of a planetary occultism.

7. *Christed Initiation*—able to understand and wield the laws of a solar system; the becoming of a "sun" god (in the ancient myths the stories of the sun gods are the same as those of the sons of god).

These seven steps were being misused, and thus the Christ Jesus broke them down into the 14 initiatory steps previously discussed. Those which previously had been just the initiations of "Birth" and "Baptism" were elaborated, developed, and enacted so that the Feminine would be restored to balance. Without the full development of the Feminine, the higher initiations could never be taken.

Of the seven listed above, the first two are associated with the Feminine Mysteries. (In the Christ Mystery system they were broken down into seven steps to assist humanity in understanding their importance and their function.) The second two are associated with the Masculine Mysteries. (In the Christ Mystery system, they are further broken down into seven steps to facilitate humanity in understanding and achieving them.)

The fifth is the Ascension. The Ascension is the blending of the male and the female. As we learn to do this a higher step ensues. It is interesting to the occultist that the fifth involves the blending. Five is the number of the microcosm, of a humanity that reflects all of the divine forces of the universe. We only become the true microcosm of the universe when we can balance and blend the masculine and feminine forces within.

It is always safer to not use the choices available to us. It is easier to allow another to tell us the significance of a teaching. We must have guidance, but there also is a point at which we must put forth our own efforts and draw upon the well of truth that lies within. We must seek out our own personal experience of the divine.

The Christ Mysteries were acted out in a historical setting to imprint upon humanity the path of initiation for those who would be willing to put forth the energy. It is not an escape from the reality of life, but an intensifying of our own participation within it. Tradition teaches that there are seven fields of service in which a person can participate within the world and not compromise the Mysteries to which they open:

1. *Politics*—Although often seen as a most "unspiritual" work, it involves the effort to bring a vision of planetary life, a more cosmic realization of life, into actualization.

2. *Education*—The process of understanding oneself and assisting others in understanding themselves; the learning of new ways through which inner enlightenment can be reached.

3. *Philosophy and Communication*—This is the following of the urge to discover the wisdom hidden within all

phenomena and to find ways of relaying that wisdom to others.

4. *Art*—This is the process of learning to create sounds, colors, and other harmonies as a means of opening and bridging the physical senses with the intuitive aspect of our essence.

5. *Science*—This is the life process of searching out the laws and principles behind physical phenomena and manifestations and the process of striving to create conditions in life that will facilitate the advancement and evolution of the individual.

6. *Religion*—This is the life process of learning to relate to the Divine Life around us and to establish greater and more creative contacts with it.

7. *Economics and Finance*—Another of the activities that few feel is spiritual, it actually is the process of sharing and organizing the right distribution of energy and matter. Money is a manifestation of energy.

A child uses many books to progress through school. All are important. The Christian Gnostic recognizes that all aspects of life are significant. Everything has its "hidden" side—even our orthodox religions and the way we choose to live our lives. All reflect much about our own spiritual growth. It is often said that one never truly knows where he or she is upon the spiritual path until complete dedication to the spiritual is achieved. The level of discipleship is revealed.

We must learn to begin where we are. We have a choice as to whether to accept things at face value or to recognize that there may be underlying significance. All teachings, all experiences have value. Some are easier to discern than others, but all serve a purpose. Truth is truth whether found in the Koran or in the Bible or within the experiences of one's own life. There is no such thing as Christian truth or Hindu truth or Jewish truth. Truth comes through personal soul knowledge and experience. It touches all lives. When humanity limits perceptions to the superficial, we close off the Divine aspect of our selves. This the Christian Gnostic recognizes and seeks to overcome through his or her science: "Occultism is more than a science to be pursued objectively; it also provides a philosophy of life derived from experience, and it is this philosophical, or even religious, aspect, that attracts most of those who devote their lives to it . . . [the seeker] is no longer dependent upon [blind] faith. He has had personal experience and out of that experience, he tends to formulate a religious belief in which he himself aspires to share in the work usually assigned to saints and angels as the ministers and messengers of God."[17]

Life is not life that restricts. A god is not a god that segregates. Truth can be found everywhere. It is the Divine's gift to humanity to have the freedom with which to seek it out. It is this seeking that brings the light. This is the goal of the gnostic. This is the goal of the Occultist—to be less hidden. To reveal the truth and the light in any form—and with love—is a noble endeavor. To become the Occult Christian is to lead the noble life.

---

[17] Fortune, p. 11.

Appendix A

READINGS AND SOURCES FOR THE HISTORICITY OF SCRIPTURES

The following writers, contemporary of the gospels and post contemporary provide much information concerning the validitiy of the gospels from an historical perspective.

Ignatius of Antioch

Iranaeus *(Proof of Apostolic Teaching* and *Against Heretics)*

Clement of Alexandria

Hippolytus

Origen

Justin Martyr *(Dialogue with Trypho* and *The Defense of the Christians)*

Flavius Josephus *(Jewish Wars* and *Antiquities of the Jews)*

Talmud Texts (100–150 A.D.)

Pliny the Younger *(Letter to Emperor Trajan Regarding Christians)*

Cornelius Tacitus *(Annals)*

Seutonius *(Lives of the Caesars)*

Tertullian

Marcion

Basilides (all either heretic or pagan writers)

Lucian

Celsus

The Dead Sea Scrolls

Muratorian Fragment (writings of the Church in last half of the second century)

Appendix B

READINGS AND SOURCES FOR THE MYSTICISM OF THE COSMIC CHRIST

The Cosmic Christ has been referred to by mystics and scriptural writings. Most refer to the Christ as the Love-Wisdom aspect of the Divine, but they are one and the same. There are many connotations of the Cosmic Christ within Biblical scripture, references that imply a cosmology of mysticism that often goes undetected or ignored today. All angel tales and references in the Bible imply a cosmology to the universe beyond the historical theology of the scriptures. The Bible is one of the greatest works of angelogy available to humanity, but references to them and phrases such as "glory," "clouds," "Lord," "devil" also imply a grander, and yet hidden, mystical cosmology within Christianity. The following are references in the scriptures themselves that reflect the concept of the Cosmic Christ, as the epitome of the Divine Love-Wisdom Force of the universe:

Job 28:12	Phillipians 2:1–24
Proverbs 1: 20–33	2 Peter 1:4
The Book of Wisdom	Romans 8: 14–39
Sirach 24	Ephesians 1: 3–14
Jeremiah 23: 23–24	John 1: 1–18
Isaiah 11	Revelation
1 Corinthians 1:30	Colossians 1: 15–20

"Wisdom is glorious and never fadeth away: Yes she is easily seen of them that love her."

(Book of Solomon 4:12)

The following are a list of Christian mystics and gnostics and other writers who over the years have referred in their writings to a greater cosmology and significance to the scriptural events of orthodox Christian theology:

Justin Martyr (especially in his *Apology*)
Clement of Alexandria
Philo
Pliny the Younger
Flavius Jsephus
Basis of Caesarea
Gregory of Nyssa
Athanasius
Hildegard of Bingen
Jacob Boehme
Francis of Assissi
Thomas Aquinas
Meister Eckhart
Teilhard de Chardin
St. John the Divine

Bibliography

Bailey, Alice. *Esoteric Astrology*. New York: Lucis Publishing, 1975.

Besant, Annie. *Esoteric Christianity*. Illinois: Theosophical Publishing, 1966.

_____. *Path of Discipleship*. India: Theosophical Publishing, 1980.

Bolen, Jean Shinoda. *Goddesses in Every Woman: A New Psychology of Women*. California: Harper and Row, 1984.

Burman, Edward. *The Templars: Knights of God*. United Kingdom: Thorsens Publishing, 1986.

Burt, Kathleen. *Archetypes of the Zodiac*. St. Paul: Llewellyn Publications, 1988.

Campbell, Joseph, and Bill Moyers. *The Power of Myth*. New York: Doubleday, 1988.

_____. *Myths, Dreams, and Religion*. Texas: Spring Publishing, 1970.

Canon Law Society. *Code of Canon Law*. England: Collins Publishing, 1983.

Cooper, J. C. *Symbolism*. Northamptonshire: Aquarian Press, 1982.

Cox, Michael. *Handbook of Christian Mysticism*. Great Britain: Crucible Publishing, 1983.

Dart, John. *The Jesus of Heresy and History*. California: Harper and Row, 1988.

de Coppens, Peter Roche. *The Nature and Use of Ritual*. St. Paul: Llewellyn Publications, 1985.

Delaforge, Gaetan. *The Templar Tradition in the Age of Aquarius.* Vermont: Threshold Books, 1987.

Fortune, Dion. *Sane Occultism.* Northamptonshire: Aquarian Press, 1979.

_____. *Aspects of Occultism.* New York: Weiser Publications, 1979.

_____. *Practical Occultism in Daily Life.* Northamptonshire: Aquarian Press, 1981.

_____. *The Training and Work of an Initiate.* Northamptonshire: Aquarian Press, 1981.

Fox, Emmet. *The Sermon on the Mount.* New York: Harper Brothers, 1938.

Fox, Matthew. *The Coming of the Cosmic Christ.* California: Harper and Row, 1988.

Foy, Felician. *1984 Catholic Almanac.* Indiana: Sunday Visitor, Inc., 1984.

Frazer, James G. *Folklore in the Old Testament.* New York: Avenel Books, 1988.

Furst, Jeffrey. *The Story of Jesus.* New York: Berkeley Books, 1971.

Graham, Lloyd. *Deceptions and Myths of the Bible.* New York: Bell Publishing, 1979.

Graves, Kersey. *The World's Sixteen Crucified Saviors.* New York: Truth Seeker Company, 1960.

Hall, Manly P. *The Mystical Christ.* Los Angeles: Philosophical Research Society, 1951.

_____. *The Twelve World Teachers.* Los Angeles: Philosophical Research Society, 1965.

_____. *Man—Grand Symbol of the Mysteries.* Los Angeles: Philosophical Research Society, 1972.

_____. *The Secret Teachings of All Ages.* Los Angeles: Philosophical Research Society, 1977.

_____. *Lectures on Ancient Philosophy.* Los Angeles: Philosophical Research Society, 1984.

Harding, M. Esther. *The Woman's Mysteries*. California: Harper and Row, 1971.

Hartley, Christine. *The Western Mystery Tradition*. Northampton-shire: Aquarian press, 1986.

Heindel, Max. *The Rosicrucian Cosmo-Conception: Mystic Christianity*. California: Rosicrucian Fellowship, 1973.

_____. *Ancient and Modern Initiation*. California: Rosicrucian Fellowship, 1986.

Heline, Corinne. *New Age Bible Interpretation, Vol. IV–VII*. California: New Age press, 1961.

_____. *Mythology and the Bible*. California: New Age Press, 1972.

_____. *Questions and Answers on the Bible*. California: New Age Press.

_____. *The Blessed Virgin Mary: Her Life and Mission*. California: New Age Press, 1986.

Heline, Theodore. *The Dead Sea Scrolls*. California: New Age Press, 1980.

Hick, John. *Philosophy of Religion*. New Jersey: Prentice-Hall, 1973.

Hodson, Geoffrey. *The Hidden Wisdom of the Bible, Vol. 1–4*. Theosophical Research, 1980.

Hoeller, Stephen. *The Gnostic Jung*. Illinois: Quest Books, 1982.

Jeffers, Joseph. *Yahweh—Yesterday, Today and Tomorrow*. New York: Vantage Press, 1974.

Jombart, Emille. *Catechism of the Vows*. New York: Benziger Brothers, 1945.

Jung, Carl. *Psychology and Alchemy*. New York: Princeton University Press, 1953.

_____. "Transformational Symbolism in the Mass" from *The Psychology of Religion—West and East*. New York: Princeton University press.

Kittler, Glenn. *Edgar Cayce on the Dead Sea Scrolls*. New York: Warner books, 1971.

Knight, Gareth. *The Rose Cross and the Goddess*. New York: Destiny Books, 1985.

_____. *Experience of the Inner Worlds*. London: Helios Books, 1975.

Lamsa, George M., ed. *The Holy Bible From Ancient Eastern Manuscripts*. Tennessee: Holman Bible Publishing, 1981.

_____. *Idioms in the Bible Explained and a Key to the Original Gospels*. California: Harper and Row, 1985.

Leadbeater, C.W. *Science of the Sacraments*. India: Theosophical Publishing, 1980.

_____. *Ancient Mystic Rites*. Illinois: Theosophical Publishing, 1986.

Levi. *The Aquarian Gospel of Jesus the Christ*. California: DeVorss Publishing, 1964.

Lewis, H. Spencer. *The Mystical Life of Jesus*. California: Rosicrucian Fellowship, 1929.

_____. *The Secret Doctrines of Jesus*. California: Rosicrucian Fellowship, 1937.

Lofthus, Myrna. *A Spiritual Approach to Astrology: A Complete Textbook of Astrology*. Nevada: CRCS Publishing, 1983.

McCafferty, Ellen Conroy. *The Astrological Key to Bibilical Symbolism*. New York: Weiser Publications, 1975.

McDermott, Robert A. *The Essential Rudolph Steiner*. New York: Harper and Row, 1984.

Meyer, Marvin, ed. *The Ancient Mysteries: A Sourcebook*. California: Harper and Row, 1987.

Moltmann-Wendel, Elisabeth. *The Women Around Jesus*. New York: Crossroads Press, 1986.

Moran, Gabriel. *The Theology of Revelation*. New York: Herder and Herder, 1966.

Oken, Alan. *Complete Astrology*. New York: Bantam Books, 1980.

Parrinder, Geoffrey. *World Religions*. New York: Facts on File Publishing, 1971.

Pine-Coffin, R. S. *Confessions of St. Augustin*. New York: Dorset Press, 1961.

Platt, Rutherford H., ed. *The Lost Books of the Bible*. New York: Bell Publishing, 1979.

_____. *Forgotten Books of Eden*. New York: Bell Publishing, 1980.

Prophet, Elizabeth Clare. *The Lost Years of Jesus*. California: Summit Press, 1984.

Schure, Edouard. *The Great Initiates*. California: Harper and Row, 1961.

_____. *From the Sphinx of the Christ*. California: Harper and Row, 1970.

Steiner, Rudolph. *The Festivals and the Meanings*. London: Steiner press, 1981.

_____. *The Four Seasons and the Archangels*. London: Steiner press, 1984.

_____. *Cosmic Memory*. California: Harper and Row, 1959.

_____. *The Appearance of the Christ in the Etheric*. New York: Anthroposophical Press, 1983.

_____. *The Spiritual Hierarchies & Their Reflection in the Physical World*. New York: Anthroposophical Press, 1983.

Stewart, R. J. *The Underworld Initiation*. Northamptonshire: Aquarian Press, 1985.

Stone, Merlin. *Ancient Mirrors of Womanhood*. Boston: Beacon Press, 1979.

Szekely, Edmond. *The Essene Gospel of Peace*. International Biogenic Society, 1981.

Taylor, Thomas. *Iamblichus on the Mysteries*. San Diego: Wizard's Bookshelf, 1984.

Waite, A. E. *The Holy Kaballah*. New Jersey: Citadel Press, 1976.

On the following pages you will find listed, with their current prices, some of the books now available on related subjects. Your book dealer stocks most of these and will stock new titles in the Llewellyn series as they become available. We urge your patronage.

TO GET A FREE CATALOG

You are invited to write for our bi-monthly news magazine/catalog, *Llewellyn's New Worlds of Mind and Spirit*. A sample copy is free, and it will continue coming to you at no cost as long as you are an active mail customer. Or you may subscribe for just $10 in the United States and Canada ($20 overseas, first class mail). Many bookstores also have *New Worlds* available to their customers. Ask for it.

In *New Worlds* you will find news and features about new books, tapes and services; announcements of meetings and seminars; helpful articles; author interviews and much more. Write to:

Llewellyn's New Worlds of Mind and Spirit
P.O. Box 64383-019, St. Paul, MN 55164-0383, U.S.A.

TO ORDER BOOKS AND TAPES

If your book store does not carry the titles described on the following pages, you may order them directly from Llewellyn by sending the full price in U.S. funds, plus postage and handling (see below).

Credit card orders: VISA, MasterCard, American Express are accepted. Call toll-free in the United States and Canada at 1-800-THE-MOON.

Special Group Discount: Because there is a great deal of interest in group discussion and study of the subject matter of this book, we offer a 20% quantity discount to group leaders or agents. Our Special Quantity Price for a minimum order of five copies of *Occult Christ* is $51.80 cash-with-order. Include postage and handling charges noted below.

Postage and Handling: Include $4 postage and handling for orders $15 and under; $5 for orders *over* $15. There are no postage and handling charges for orders over $100. Postage and handling rates are subject to change. We ship UPS whenever possible within the continental United States; delivery is guaranteed. Please provide your street address as UPS does not deliver to P.O. boxes. Orders shipped to Alaska, Hawaii, Canada, Mexico and Puerto Rico will be sent via first class mail. Allow 4-6 weeks for delivery. **International orders:** Airmail – add retail price of each book and $5 for each non-book item (audiotapes, etc.); Surface mail – add $1 per item.

Minnesota residents please add 7% sales tax.

Mail orders to:
Llewellyn Worldwide, P.O. Box 64383-019, St. Paul, MN 55164-0383, U.S.A.

For customer service, call (612) 291-1970.

THE BOOK OF GODDESSES & HEROINES
by Patricia Monaghan

The Book of Goddesses & Heroines is an historical landmark, a must for everyone interested in Goddesses and Goddess worship. It is not an effort to trivialize the beliefs of matriarchal cultures. It is not a collection of Goddess descriptions penned by biased male historians throughout the ages. It is the complete, non-biased account of Goddesses of every cultural and geographic area, including African, Egyptian, Japanese, Korean, Persian, Australian, Pacific, Latin American, British, Irish, Scottish, Welsh, Chinese, Greek, Icelandic, Italian, Finnish, German, Scandinavian, Indian, Tibetan, Mesopotamian, North American, Semitic and Slavic Goddesses!

Unlike some of the male historians before her, Patricia Monaghan eliminates as much bias as possible from her Goddess stories. Envisioning herself as a woman who might have revered each of these Goddesses, she has done away with language that referred to the deities in relation to their male counterparts, as well as with culturally relative terms such as "married" or "fertility cult." The beliefs of the cultures and the attributes of the Goddesses have been left intact.

Plus, this book has a new, complete index. If you are more concerned about finding a Goddess of war than you are a Goddess of a given country, this index will lead you to the right page. This is especially useful for anyone seeking to do Goddess rituals. Your work will be twice as efficient and effective with this detailed and easy-to-use book.

0-87542-573-9, 456 pgs., 6 x 9, photos, softcover $17.95

HOW TO MEET & WORK WITH SPIRIT GUIDES
by Ted Andrews

We often experience spirit contact in our lives but fail to recognize it for what it is. Now you can learn to access and attune to beings such as guardian angels, nature spirits and elementals, spirit totems, archangels, gods and goddesses—as well as family and friends after their physical death.

Contact with higher soul energies strengthens the will and enlightens the mind. Through a series of simple exercises, you can safely and gradually increase your awareness of spirits and your ability to identify them. You will learn to develop an intentional and directed contact with any number of spirit beings. Discover meditations to open up your subconscious. Learn which acupressure points effectively stimulate your intuitive faculties. Find out how to form a group for spirit work, use crystal balls, perform automatic writing, attune your aura for spirit contact, use sigils to contact the great archangels and much more! Read *How to Meet and Work with Spirit Guides* and take your first steps through the corridors of life beyond the physical.

0-87542-008-7, 192 pgs., mass market, illus. $3.95

IMAGICK
Qabalistic Pathworking for Imaginative Magicians
by Ted Andrews

The Qabala, or "Tree of Life," is a productive and safe system of evolvement—one of the most effective means for tapping the energies of the universe. But it is not enough to study the Qabala; intellectual studies of the correspondences will not generate any magickal changes nor will a mere arousal of the energies. In order to achieve your hopes, dreams and wishes, you must also bring the Qabála into your day-to-day life. You must practice "Imagick."

Imagick is a process of using the Qabala with visualization, meditation and imaging—in conjunction with physical movement—to stimulate electrical responses in the brain that help bridge normal consciousness with spiritual consciousness. The *Imagick* techniques, and especially the pathworking techniques described throughout this book, are powerfully effective. Their repeated use will build roadways between the outer and inner worlds, creating a flow that augments your energies, abilities and potentials.

There is a great mystique associated with the occult practice of pathworking. Pathworking shows you your blockages and brings them out so that you must deal with them. You open up the channels that create transition—cleaning out the debris you have accumulated. The pathworking techniques in this book help you search out hidden fears, overcome them and open yourself to higher and stronger knowledge and experience. Dance the Tree of Life and open the inner temples of your soul with Imagick.

0-87542-016-8, 312 pgs., 6 x 9, softcover   **$12.95**

THE HEALER'S MANUAL
A Beginner's Guide to Vibrational Therapies
Ted Andrews

Did you know that a certain Mozart symphony can ease digestion problems ... that swelling often indicates being stuck in outworn patterns ... that breathing pink is good for skin conditions and loneliness? Most disease stems from a metaphysical base. While we are constantly being exposed to viruses and bacteria, it is our unbalanced or blocked emotions, attitudes and thoughts that deplete our natural physical energies and make us more susceptible to "catching a cold" or manifesting some other physical problem.

Healing, as approached in The Healer's Manual, involves locating and removing energy blockages wherever they occur—physical or otherwise. This book is an easy guide to simple vibrational healing therapies that anyone can learn to apply to restore homeostasis to their body's energy system. By employing sound, color, fragrance, etheric touch and flower/gem elixers, you can participate actively within the healing of your body and the opening of higher perceptions. You will discover that you can heal more aspects of your life than you ever thought possible.

0-87542-007-9, 256 pgs., 6 x 9, illus., softcover   **$10.00**

IN SEARCH OF THE PRIMORDIAL TRADITION & THE COSMIC CHRIST
by Father John Rossner, Ph.D.

This is a new book on the identity of Jesus—the occult Jesus overlooked by conventional New Testament scholars. It is a must for those interested in the Western Esoteric Tradition and its relevance to the contemporary crisis in religion, science, and human culture.

Fr. Rossner finds ample evidence for the existence of an "ancient gnosis," or tradition of arcane wisdom spanning the centuries from Egypt to India, Persia, Greece and Rome. He traces the entry of this gnosis into pre-Christian Jewish mystical traditions, and from there into the fabric of the canonical gospels, New Testament epistles, and the church's creeds and sacramental rites.

He also argues that only those who are familiar with the transformative effects of live psychic and spirit phenomena can fully appreciate the original Biblical experience. He calls for an entirely new approach to the study of religion and spiritual insight in the West, one that will bring a "Second Copernican Revolution" and a greater understanding of the inner dynamics and capabilities of the human psyche and spirit.
0-87542-685-9, 320 pgs., 6 x 9, illus., softcover   **$12.95**

SACRED SOUNDS
Transformation through Music & Word
by Ted Andrews

Sound has always been considered a direct link between humanity and the divine. The ancient mystery schools all taught their students the use of sound as a creative and healing force that bridged the different worlds of life and consciousness.

Now, *Sacred Sounds* reveals to today's seekers how to tap into the magical and healing aspects of voice, resonance and music. On a physical level, these techniques have been used to alleviate aches and pains, lower blood pressure and balance hyperactivity in children. On a metaphysical level, they have been used to induce altered states of consciousness, open new levels of awareness, stimulate intuition and increase creativity.

In this book, Ted Andrews reveals the tones and instruments that affect the chakras, the use of kinesiology and "muscle testing" in relation to sound responses, the healing aspects of vocal tones, the uses of mystical words of power, the art of magical storytelling, how to write magical sonnets, how to form healing groups and utilize group toning for healing and enlightenment, and much, much more.
0-87542-018-4, 240 pgs., 5 1/4 x 8, illus., softcover   **$7.95**

ARCHETYPES OF THE ZODIAC
by Kathleen Burt
The horoscope is probably the most unique tool for personal growth you can ever have. This book is intended to help you understand how the energies within your horoscope manifest. Once you are aware of how your chart operates on an instinctual level, you can then work consciously with it to remove any obstacles to your growth.

The technique offered in this book is based upon the incorporation of the esoteric rulers of the signs and the integration of their polar opposites. This technique has been very successful in helping the client or reader modify existing negative energies in a horoscope so as to improve the quality of his or her life and the understanding of his or her psyche.

There is special focus in this huge comprehensive volume on the myths for each sign. Some signs may have as many as four different myths coming from all parts of the world. All are discussed by the author. There is also emphasis on the Jungian Archetypes involved with each sign.

This book has a depth often surprising to the readers of popular astrology books. It has a clarity of expression seldom found in books of the esoteric tradition. It is very easy to understand, even if you know nothing of Jungian philosophy or of mythology. It is intriguing, exciting and very helpful for all levels of astrologers.

0-87542-088-5, 576 pgs., 6 x 9, illus., softcover $14.95

EVOKING THE PRIMAL GODDESS
Discovery of the Eternal Feminine Within
by William G. Gray
In our continuing struggle to attain a higher level of spiritual awareness, one thing has become clear: we need to cultivate and restore the matriarchal principle to its proper and equal place in our conceptions of Deity. Human history and destiny are determined by our Deity concepts, whatever they may be, and for too long the results of a predominantly masculine God in war, brutality and violence have been obvious.

In *Evoking the Primal Goddess,* renowned occultist William G. Gray takes you on a fascinating, insightful journey into the history and significance of the Goddess in religion. For the first time anywhere, he shows that the search for the Holy Grail was actually a movement within the Christian church to bring back the feminine element into the concept of Deity. He also shows how you can evoke your own personal image of the Mother ideal through practical rituals and prayer.

It has been said that whatever happens in spiritual levels of life will manifest itself on physical ones as well. By following Gray's techniques, you can rebalance both your male and your female polarities into a single spiritual individuality of practical Power!

0-87542-271-3, 192 pgs., 5 1/4 x 8, photos, softcover $9.95

Prices subject to change without notice.

APOCALYPSE NOW
The Challenges of Our Times
by Peter Roche de Coppens
During the last two decades of the 20th century, humanity is being given, collectively and individually, a very major "test" in the School of Life—true and lived initiation. Many prophecies have been made, in symbolic form, to tell us what to expect at this time, named at different times the Apocalypse, Armageddon, the Great War between the Forces of Light and Darkness, or the Coming of the Antichrist.

Most people have interpreted these prophecies and visions as pertaining to the physical world, implying the destruction of civilization and even the end of mankind and of the world itself. While it is true that our outer physical world (and culture) will be greatly affected and transformed, it is the inner world of man—consciousness—that is directly affected by this great test.

The Apocalypse really refers to an inner process of purification and transformation, not to an outer one. The battle between God-consciousness and the antichrist, our dark, unregenerated self, takes place within. How, then, do we prepare ourselves for this great change? That is the purpose of *Apocalypse Now*. It offers a program for not only understanding the challenges of our times, but also for personal transformation and spiritual growth to fulfill the opportunity and potential of this New Age, now!

0-87542-677-8, 288 pgs., 5 1/4 x 8, softcover $9.95

EVOKING THE PRIMAL GODDESS
Discovery of the Eternal Feminine Within
by William G. Gray
In our continuing struggle to attain a higher level of spiritual awareness, one thing has become clear: we need to cultivate and restore the matriarchal principle to its proper and equal place in our conceptions of Deity. Human history and destiny are determined by our Deity concepts, whatever they may be, and for too long the results of a predominantly masculine God in war, brutality and violence have been obvious.

In *Evoking the Primal Goddess,* renowned occultist William G. Gray takes you on a fascinating, insightful journey into the history and significance of the Goddess in religion. For the first time anywhere, he shows that the search for the Holy Grail was actually a movement within the Christian church to bring back the feminine element into the concept of Deity. He also shows how you can evoke your own personal image of the Mother ideal through practical rituals and prayer.

It has been said that whatever happens in spiritual levels of life will manifest itself on physical ones as well. By following Gray's techniques, you can rebalance both your male and your female polarities into a single spiritual individuality of practical Power!

0-87542-271-3, 192 pgs., 5 1/4 x 8, photos, softcover $9.95